Also by JAN COFFEY

SILENT WATERS
FIVE IN A ROW
FOURTH VICTIM
TRIPLE THREAT
TWICE BURNED
TRUST ME ONCE

JAN COFFEY

THE
PROJECT

MIRA®

ISBN-13: 978-0-7783-2406-5
ISBN-10: 0-7783-2406-0

THE PROJECT

Copyright © 2007 by Nikoo K. and James A. McGoldrick.

All rights reserved. Except for use in any review, the reproduction or utilization of this work in whole or in part in any form by any electronic, mechanical or other means, now known or hereafter invented, including xerography, photocopying and recording, or in any information storage or retrieval system, is forbidden without the written permission of the publisher, MIRA Books, 225 Duncan Mill Road, Don Mills, Ontario, Canada M3B 3K9.

All characters in this book have no existence outside the imagination of the author and have no relation whatsoever to anyone bearing the same name or names. They are not even distantly inspired by any individual known or unknown to the author, and all incidents are pure invention.

MIRA and the Star Colophon are trademarks used under license and registered in Australia, New Zealand, Philippines, United States Patent and Trademark Office and in other countries.

www.MIRABooks.com

Printed in U.S.A.

To our Hashemi sisters—
Shabnam, Sepideh and Nassim
and
Arianne and Dori
Family transcends blood...

Prologue

Freezing rain, razor-sharp on the skin, continued to fall. Across the five boroughs of the city and into the suburbs, traffic moved at a crawling pace on every expressway. The Cross County was the usual parking lot, and the Henry Hudson was down to one lane. But the worst was the Cross Bronx, completely shut down because of a horrendous accident.

The driver of the limo leaned over and switched off the radio, apparently abandoning all hope of finding a reasonably clear route out of the city. Now they would simply inch along, one car in a line of the thousands of other commuter vehicles going north on the FDR Drive.

In the backseat, the passenger pushed aside the work he'd brought and glanced at his watch. He was going to be late for dinner. His daughter and her husband and three children were in from the West Coast until Sunday. Christmas week had been spent with his daughter's in-laws in New Hampshire, and this week the gang had been with them in Connecticut. He'd have liked to have it the other way around. He'd been home most of last week. This week, though, with the exception of New Year's Day, his schedule was booked.

His wife phoned him at the office to tell him their daughter was now considering staying for another couple of weeks with the kids in Connecticut. He looked again at the electronic scheduler and shook his head as he paged through it. There wouldn't be any relief now until the end of the month. Not until the company's big deadline. He wouldn't be able to spend any time with them.

He reached for his cell phone to call his wife. He had an eight-thirty breakfast meeting in the city tomorrow morning, and he contemplated telling the driver to turn around and take him to his apartment in Midtown instead. He could do without this commute tonight.

The cell phone rang before he could make the call home. He looked at the display and felt his spine stiffen. A bitter taste edged into his mouth, and he considered not answering the call. He wished that were an option, but it wasn't. He knew he'd be answering.

He even knew what the call was about. His old partner had phoned him daily this past month. Old skeletons were peeking out of the closet. This wasn't the first time; over the years, the episodes had come in waves. But this one was worse than anything they'd faced before. There was no getting around it. Still, they just had to put up with situations like this until the test samples were all gone. The last time he'd counted, there were only seven left.

Seven.

He pressed the button on the console and waited until the window between him and the driver slid shut before answering the call.

"Hello, Mitch," he said, looking out at the blackness enshrouding the East River.

"Have you been watching the news this afternoon?" his partner asked without a greeting. The agitation in his voice was clear.

"No." He reached for the TV remote and turned it on.

"There's been another shooting, this time in San Francisco."

He switched the channel to CNN and muted the sound. In a moment, the closed captions began to scroll across the bottom of the screen. "Was he one of ours?"

"Yes," Mitch said, his voice rising.

"Did he live?"

"No."

Six left, the passenger thought grimly.

"Then we don't worry about it." He glanced at his watch again. "I've got to go."

"Wait," his partner snapped before he could end the call. "This is different from anything we've seen before. The violence is worse."

"That's not because of us," he said calmly. "All the

test cases have been the same. The ones that remain are the earliest specimens. They're older now than the others were. Adolescent hormonal shifts are complicating the equation. That can result in more damage."

"Curtis, they're flipping every couple of days," his partner said, obviously trying to keep his voice down. "How could you be so relaxed about it?"

Unlike his old friend, who'd turned his back on industry and was quickly becoming fossilized teaching biology to imbeciles in the California state university system, he was having a late-career resurgence. Over the course of this past year, all the doors were again opening. Money was pouring in. His name was the talk of the business. For a change, everything was going right.

It was hard to imagine that the two of them had, at one time, worked so closely. They had always been like night and day in terms of composure, in their goals, in their hunger for results, in their willingness to take risks to succeed.

"Listen to me, Mitch. I'm not relaxed about any of this." This was exactly what the other man needed to hear. "But there's nothing we can do about it, just as there was nothing we could do about it three years ago when we lost a large sample size, or fourteen years ago when we found out everything was going wrong and we had to shut the project down."

"You're not hearing me," the other man said, his voice now bordering on hysteria. "There are others who are getting dragged into this. Innocent people." He spat out each word slowly. "And there *is* something we can do about this. We can identify them, pull them out of…"

"Do you really want to tell the world what we did? It's not only your neck and mine that we're talking about. How about our investors? Do you want to expose them? And do you really think they would put up with it? Do you really believe that coming out into the open would solve all the problems?"

The pause on the other end of the line gave him some reassurance. His partner was still as timid as he'd always been. He needed to keep Mitch from panicking, but fear was good.

"I want you to stop watching the news."

"I…I can't."

"You can," he said forcefully. "There are only six left, Mitch, and they're taking care of themselves. Time is on our side. All we have to do is sit tight, and everything will go away."

There was another pause at the other end. He couldn't understand why his old partner couldn't quite fathom the probable consequences of this "coming out." So many careers would be ruined. More than a few corporations and major hospitals would be rattled to the foundations, possibly irreparably. Some would go down. Politicians would lose their seats. Some of them would end up in jail. The Merck fiasco with Vioxx wouldn't hold a candle to what they'd be facing. There'd be criminal charges in this case. He didn't want to go there.

"Are you still on the line?" he asked.

"I'm here," Mitch said heavily. "There's one thing that I can't shake loose."

"What is it?"

"What happens if one of them *does* make it through after an episode of violence? What happens if one of them survives?"

There would be more detailed tests, interviews, close scrutiny. The intellectual and psychological conditions of the object would become unstable. And then there was the possibility of early memory triggered. There would be no end to their problems.

"You leave that to me. I've taken care of those kinds of details before. I'll take care of them again when I need to."

One

Monday January 14, 11:56 a.m.
Wickfield, Connecticut

During the night, a thick crust of ice had formed on top of the six inches of snow that had fallen over the weekend. The pale disk of a sun had done nothing to soften it this morning. The street and the two driveways at the end of the cul-de-sac had been plowed, but the large pair of boots punching through the snow between the two houses carved its own path.

His head hurt. The pounding was louder. Voices, faces, places, numbers, all writhed in his pulsing brain.

He ripped a branch off a young oak tree that snatched at his jacket. Icicles showered down on him in retribution. He threw the branch fiercely to the side, and it bounced and skittered across the unbroken glaze of snow. He blinked through the gray haze that seemed to cover everything. Sky, snow, houses, everything was gray, and yet his eyes still stung from the light and the pain in his head.

He barely noticed the cold, but it was a labor to breathe. Somewhere, in a dark corner of his mind, the idea pulled at him that he wanted to lie down on the snow and just go to sleep. But he couldn't. His feet kept stomping ahead of him toward his neighbors' back porch.

The pounding voices in his head wouldn't go away. He knew where he had to go, what he had to do, how to end it all.

He didn't bother to knock on the door. Neither car was in the driveway. He turned the knob and pushed open the kitchen door. Wickfield was safe. Nobody locked their doors.

He'd been in the house many times. He knew they were in the basement. The cat appeared in the doorway leading to the living room and stared at him with distrust for a moment before disappearing. The pulsing flashes of light and the voices were getting louder. He had to stop them.

He stumbled across the kitchen, his boots leaving clumps of gray snow on the tiled floor. He yanked open the basement door with such force that it rebounded off the wall and smashed him hard in the shoulder. He didn't feel it, not at all, and went down the wooden steps without bothering to flip on the light switch.

The cabinet was against the wall on the far side of the chimney. The four rifles seemed to call to him through the glass display front. The barrels, long and blue-gray, looked cool and smooth. The wooden stocks gleamed with a warmth that seemed unnatural. He pulled the knob. It was locked. He looked around him and saw the old fireplace tools against the basement wall. His fingers wrapped around the poker.

A phone started ringing upstairs. He didn't pause. He didn't care. His head hurt; that was all he knew. He took one big swing at the cabinet. Glass flew around him, blanketing the floor with glittering shards. He reached inside and touched the barrel of one of the guns. It was cool and smooth, just as they said it would be.

It would all work out now.

Finally, he could end the pain. Silence the noise.

Two

The large lobby in the guidance office at Wickfield High School was packed with teachers, and the meeting was already in progress by the time Kevin Gordon walked in. The band room and the cafeteria were still victims of the school renovation project, and this was the next best space. It wasn't too good.

The principal, Scott Peterson, paused midsentence and looked around the room for an empty seat. There were none. Kevin shook his head at him and leaned a shoulder against the door, taking the weight off his bad knee.

"Are you sure you're okay?" the principal asked.

Kevin nodded again. He'd survive. He was going in for knee surgery over the spring break. Everyone knew it, and Peterson's question prompted two teachers who had their backs to him to start to get off their chairs. He placed a hand on both of their shoulders.

"Stay where you are," he said quietly. "I'm okay."

The e-mail had said a fifteen-minute meeting. Thanks to the justifiably nervous mother of one of his flunking juniors, Kevin was five minutes late. She'd been waiting for him at the office when classes ended. Ten minutes on the old knee wasn't too bad.

"Since we have everyone we need here," Peterson told the group, "let's go back to the agenda item we skipped and finalize the award recipients for the end-of-term assembly on Friday."

The room was filled with the sound of notes being shuffled. Kevin didn't need to look at his. He knew who had his votes.

"The academic awards are straightforward," Peterson said for the sake of saving time. "You have the names. No surprises there."

Everyone in the room was in general agreement. The one interesting new variable was the "effort" grade that they were now assigning.

"Okay, let's go over this semester's citizenship award. I have everyone's submissions." Peterson leafed through a folder before him. "We've got some passionate recommendations on this one."

Kevin pulled on his invisible boxing gloves. He was ready to go to battle. Before the fur began to fly, though, he shot a quick look across the room at Sally Michelson. She was in charge of guidance, and she nodded to him. Sally was on his side in this. She'd only come into the discussion later, though.

"To bring everyone quickly up to date on this," Peterson said, addressing the three first-year teachers. "The citizenship award is given twice a year, at the end of each semester, to the student who has shown through their words and actions that they possess the qualities and characteristics we hope to instill in all our students."

"And the award has *always* been given to a senior," one of the music teachers interjected.

"That's correct," Peterson agreed. "That has been the tradition."

"And because of that, I don't think we should be thumbing our noses at this graduating class." Ed Torangeau, a history teacher, was Kevin's biggest opponent in this. "The recognition should go to an upperclassman. This is a moment in the sun for one of these kids."

"But not their only opportunity," Kevin corrected. "These students have plenty more chances to win all kinds of awards before they graduate. And last night I went through the awards we've given. Every senior worth his or her salt has gotten numerous awards, and next month we sit down to decide on the graduation prizes."

"What's your point, Kevin?" the music teacher cut in.

"Well, by giving the citizenship award to a deserving sophomore—like Juan Bradley—we're sending the message that recognition for effort and accomplishment is not simply tied to the fact that you're graduating. It reinforces the importance of making significant contributions to the school and the larger community *throughout* the four years a kid is here. This will send the message that being prepared for class and getting good grades isn't the whole picture for underclassmen."

"I'll settle for just having them stay awake in class," a young woman, who was teaching two sections of general math, said under her breath.

A few laughed, and others looked empathetically in her direction.

Sally stepped in. "I agree with Kevin. We should look for and reward good citizenship with the same diligence that we correct mistakes. Giving a citizenship award to Juan Bradley will definitely hammer a point home."

"Make up another award," Torangeau suggested. "Give him a ribbon or something."

"That's not the same thing," Kevin argued. "There's recognition that already goes along with the citizenship award. Students talk about it. The name of the winner goes on the plaque by the office next to all the past winners. Every day, kids go by and are reminded why those students' names are there. There's status and he deserves it."

A few started talking at the same time. Sally had warned Kevin that the old guard wouldn't go along with his suggestion without a little kicking and screaming.

Another teacher took Torangeau's side. "We need consistency here. There's nothing to indicate that Juan won't keep up the good work he's doing and earn it by the time he's a senior. He should wait for his turn."

"If we give the award to Juan now, what's going to stop him from winning it two or three times more before he graduates?" someone else suggested.

"And why would that be a bad thing?" Sally responded before the principal could speak. Her expression clearly conveyed what she thought of the last question. "If he's 'walking the walk,' why not give it to him? We need to get away from thinking that seniors are the only ones who should be rewarded and given a pat on the back. Let's start early…even let freshmen win that award if they deserve it."

Kevin jumped in where Sally left off. He didn't want to let the group get distracted with small talk.

"If we could just take a minute, let's go over Juan's qualifications," he said. "First thing, his grades. He's always been at the top of his class. Extracurricular activities…he plays two varsity sports in addition to being a section member in the school orchestra. Consider his achievement in civics and government courses, his performance in civics and government-related extracurricular activities. He's a member or an officer of a half-dozen clubs. His community service is exemplary. I've lost count on how many places in and out of school that he volunteers."

The room went silent for a moment. Faculty discussions didn't usually get this animated.

"All I'm asking," Kevin said, taking it down a notch, "is that we judge his qualifications against the seniors who applied and see where he stands."

Kevin Gordon wouldn't admit it to anyone in that

room, but this campaign was personal. He'd been the one who'd brought this up at the parent-teacher conferences in November and encouraged Juan to write the qualifying essay for the award. Kevin had asked the principal's opinion on it back then. Peterson had been open to the idea.

When it came right down to it, though, Juan Bradley was a very special human being. His gifts transcended his intelligence. He didn't only shine as a student, he brightened the existence of everyone in the classroom and everyone, it seemed, who knew him. He extended himself to help others...whoever, whenever.

Kevin was driven to reward the fifteen-year-old. And as an English teacher who taught mostly honors courses, he'd had most, if not all, of the seniors who were possible nominees for this award. None of them came close to Juan.

Kevin Gordon surveyed the room for those teachers who'd already had Juan in a class.

The geometry teacher quickly took the hint. "I think that's only fair," she said. "Give Juan a chance to get compared against seniors. Frankly, I believe he holds his own."

"His essay was very impressive," another member of the English department announced. He'd had Juan second semester last year and had also been one of the judges for the writing. "I've read all the personal essays, and his was the best by far. A lot of the seniors simply rehashed their college admissions essays."

The senior member of the faculty, an older teacher

who had Juan for Algebra II, stirred. "Juan was absent today."

Sally brushed off the comment as irrelevant. "It's the time of the year. Kids get sick, and Dr. Bradley was on the phone before 7:00 a.m. this morning. His attendance is not a problem."

Ed Torangeau shrugged his shoulders. "I think we should put it up for a vote."

Kevin looked at Scott Peterson. He'd hoped that the principal would say a few words on Juan's behalf. The boy was a good friend to Scott's son, Jake, though. Perhaps Scott didn't want his actions to be construed as a conflict of interest. Whatever.

"As someone who feels no pull one way or the other," a science teacher said. "I'd like to know who the top three or four students are before I vote. We all agree that Juan is one. Who are the other candidates?"

"That's what I want to vote on," Torangeau said. "We need to decide whether or not an underclassman should be a finalist."

"We can do that, Ed," the principal said before responding to the science teacher. "Kay, a finalist list was put in everyone's mailbox last Friday."

"I didn't get one," someone else mumbled.

"I must have misplaced mine," she said. "Do you have an extra one?"

"We're clearly not ready to vote on anything yet," another teacher commented.

Everyone was talking at the same time, complaining, others questioning the finalist list. Kevin shook his head and leaned more heavily against the door. The knee was killing him. He looked at Sally. She was clearly annoyed. They weren't getting anywhere today.

Suddenly, he realized that the noise level outside had grown louder than the argument in the room. Nobody else seemed to notice it, though. Kevin opened the door slightly and peeked out into the hall.

When he'd come in, the usual athletes and after-school crowd were milling about. Now a dozen students were running full speed down the corridor. One girl was screaming and the sound of more screams came from the library, across the hall.

There was no fire alarm. No sirens.

"What's going on out there?" he heard the principal say over his shoulder.

Kevin stepped into the hall.

"Don't do it," a woman cried. "Please don't."

He crossed quickly to the doorway of the library. Inside, Sue, the librarian, was standing chalk-faced behind the counter that separated her work area from the rest of the library. Her hands were extended in front of her, and Kevin could see them shaking.

"Put that down, right now. Please." She spoke tensely.

Three girls were huddled on the floor by the wall of books, crying hysterically. There were other students under the tables and hiding behind the library shelves.

Without thinking, Kevin stepped in.

"Put the gun down," Sue said more authoritatively. "Now!"

He should have walked out and sounded the alarms,

called for help, but Kevin Gordon made the mistake of turning toward the assailant first.

"Juan!" he blurted, staring in horror at the fifteen-year-old. "What are you doing?"

The boy seemed to be stoned. No recognition registered in his pale face. The glassy eyes stared straight ahead.

"Juan, put that gun down," he ordered.

As if it were happening in slow motion, Kevin watched the barrel of the rifle swing in an arc away from the girls on the floor. In a moment, it was pointing at him.

Kevin was looking directly into Juan's emotionless brown eyes when the boy started firing.

Three

The nightmare was back.

Bryan Atwood had spent three years of his life working on these kinds of cases. He'd spent another five years seeing a shrink, trying to get over it. And here they were dragging him into the middle of it again. He couldn't fucking believe it.

"December 11. Ten people, including a teenage suspect, dead in this small town south of Chicago." Don Geary, the FBI special agent in charge who was heading the investigation, pointed to a thumbtack on the large United States map spread on one wall. "A quiet suburb of Pittsburgh. Five students and a teacher gunned down at a school dance on December 14. The female suspect…yes, female…kills herself on the scene."

Bryan glanced at his old partner. Hank was looking at him and gave him a discreet shake of the head. He couldn't believe it, either. With everything they had on their plates…with everything they'd been through in the past…it was incredible that they would drag both of them back to this.

Geary stabbed a fat finger at the next location on the map. "Four days later in Eugene, Oregon, a freshman opens fire with a semiautomatic rifle in a high school cafeteria, killing two students and wounding twenty-two others. He also kills himself on the scene."

Bryan watched the news. He knew all of this. It was the worst outbreak of school violence the country had ever witnessed. The most widespread. It was a horrible tragedy. He flexed his neck and his jaw. The pain in his head was threatening to split it open. Bryan had gotten it the moment he received the message from his director about being put on a new assignment, starting immediately. No details. Just turn over the work he had to the others in his office. He'd be helping the FBI until further notice.

Bryan's suspicions about the assignment had been confirmed the moment he'd walked inside this packed conference room.

"Two days later, on the day before the Christmas school vacation in Las Vegas, Nevada, a fifteen-year-old student kills two classmates and wounds another thirteen people during a shooting spree before taking his own life." Geary was relentless.

Nearly ten years ago Bryan Atwood, a senior agent

with the United States Secret Service, and Hank Gardner, a forensic psychologist, were assigned the task of conducting an inquiry into a series of high school shootings spanning fifteen years.

As part of this investigation, the two agents had worked with CDC, the Center for Disease Control and Prevention, as well as the Federal Department of Education and the National School Safety Center to identify common features of school-related violent deaths. They'd investigated and analyzed a total of thirty-seven incidents involving forty-one student attackers. The study involved the extensive review of police records, school records, court documents and other source materials, and included interviews with ten school shooters who were serving various sentences in jail. The focus of the study had been to develop information about the school shooters' preattack behaviors and communications. The goal was to provide information to educators about characteristics that may be identifiable or noticeable before the violent act occurs, to inform those at risk just how to prevent school attacks.

The Secret Service Safe School Initiative had been the study published by the group. There'd been a lot of press coverage afterward, and a few politicians had patted them on the back. But they obviously didn't have all the answers, for a decade later violence in schools was back with more intensity and frequency than ever before.

Geary moved to the other side of the map. "January

3. San Francisco, California. A fifteen-year-old guns down eight students as they walk to school from the bus. The crossing guard is shot dead. The suspect kills himself on the sidewalk by the front door of the high school," the SAC continued with the same intensity.

Bryan saw Hank sink lower in the chair. He had a good idea that his friend hadn't been given any say, either, on whether or not he wanted to work on this case.

They both had said *never again.* The prison visits, interviewing the kids, parents of the victims and accusers, the grief that surrounded everyone associated with these tragedies had been overwhelming, even for reasonably tough guys like them. Because of what was going on in his life, Bryan had taken the hit harder than Hank. It had been more than just feeling low. It had messed with his head.

And on top of it all, they hadn't been able to solve anything. It was back.

"Wickfield, Connecticut. Yesterday, another fifteen-year-old male opens fire on a teacher and fellow students in the school library. Seven injuries, two critical. Miraculously, no deaths. More amazing, the suspect is alive but in critical condition." The FBI special agent stopped and looked around the room.

This was his chance, Bryan thought. His seniority should count for something. After twenty-three years in the service, he was practically ancient. He could say screw it and walk out. He'd been here, done this. Bryan wasn't the right person for this case. He could cite medical reasons if they tried to force him. Hank would support him. So would the department shrink, who'd spent months observing him and talking to him. Outside doctors would attest to it, too. His department had kept him away from these kinds of cases since the study was published. Why was he back in now?

"Everyone has already met Secret Service Agents Atwood and Gardner," the SAC continued.

There were nods across the room. Most of them were half his age, Bryan thought. Green and tough. They would bounce back…most of them. A case like this was a young person's game.

"Last week, we were going over the reports you wrote on this topic," a female FBI agent announced, sounding impressed. "The process you outlined for threat assessment in schools is still the benchmark."

She didn't look much older than his eldest daughter. How old was Andrea? Seventeen. Bryan ran a tired hand through his hair.

"Years ago, I sat in on one of the talks you gave to discuss your research," Geary said to Bryan directly, as if knowing he was the more resistant of the two. "I recall the results being very well received."

Bryan nodded. "I think I can speak for Agent Gardner when I say that you've seen, read or heard everything Hank and I have to offer on a project like this," Bryan said. "I really don't know why we're here."

"Reports can never replace firsthand expertise," Geary said.

"True, but we weren't really involved in the initial investigative stage of those cases," Hank put in. "We were the Monday morning quarterbacks. Paperwork shufflers. We analyzed data and wrote the reports."

That was a lie, but Bryan wasn't going to correct his old partner. He understood what Hank was trying to do. It was the same thing that he would do himself. Neither of them wanted to be involved with this.

"You're too modest, Agent Gardner," Geary said in the smooth tone befitting of a true paper-shuffler. "But your reputation precedes you. This is a very high-visibility case. Everyone, going up as far as the president, is sensitive and anxious about results. People all over the country are nervous about sending their kids to school. There have been six shootings, all within a month. It's as if these kids are like time bombs, ticking away, and they're going off too close to one another."

For ten days of that period, most school districts across the country had been shut down for the Christmas holidays. What other acts of violence had been committed by kids in the same age group—acts that didn't occur on a school property and as a result weren't on that map?

Bryan realized what he was doing. He was already thinking about it.

"Frankly, there hasn't been enough time for us to go over all the background on what you two accomplished in working up that report. We doubt we're asking the right questions. We all know what the post-9/11 shakeups have done to our organizations. Terrorism has been the priority. Now we need expertise on this." Geary turned directly to Bryan. "And your names are the ones that have come up over and over again. The latest call I had came from the White House."

Geary was lathering it on thick. He was one of the new generation of post-9/11 SACs. Some of these guys spent as much time learning to be politicians as they did learning law enforcement. Of course, there was also the fact that their asses were being held over a bonfire with these shootings.

"Similar to the panel you worked on before, we need group intelligence to crack the case," Geary explained.

"I keep hearing you repeat the word *case*. There have been six shootings. Are you saying that you've already established a tie between all of them?" Bryan asked.

"I think we may have, but we're not sure," Geary said, motioning to an agent to his left to pass two thick files to them. The younger agent had straight shoulder-length black hair, pierced ears and an untucked shirt over blue jeans. He'd been introduced to Bryan as Nick Luna when they'd first arrived. Christ, things were changing.

"They were all honor students," the younger agent explained. "And by that, we don't mean the top ten percent, but absolutely the very top of their class. The top one percent of the national population IQ rate."

As father of two very bright students himself, Bryan knew about the battle gifted kids faced. The school systems didn't want to hear it. The taxpayers remained deaf to it. But at the time of cuts, gifted programs topped the lists. They didn't understand that they had to keep these kids active, challenged, busy, or they got bored and robbed your houses or became ax-murderers.

"They were all the work of fifteen-year-olds," Nick continued.

"Tough age for kids, especially for boys," Hank commented. "Their brain capacity makes them so smart that they become stupid. What else?"

"There's more to the age thing," Geary broke in. "They all turned fifteen within this past month."

"These teenagers have different toys to play with today than what was available ten years ago," Hank said. "Internet, chat groups, instant messenger, cell phones, Xbox 360, all kinds of shooter-type video games. We were told the shootings were widespread across the country, but were these kids in contact with one another in any way? Could it be a cyber-gang of some sort, tied to their birthdays? Maybe the violence is even part of a ritual?"

A few of the agents started scribbling down notes furiously. A couple of others leafed through the folders before them.

"Another thing, has anyone compiled a list of the prescription drugs these teenagers were taking?" Hank continued.

Bryan leaned back against his seat. Hank was in. But it wasn't like they had any options.

"Put up what we have on the board," Geary said to Nick Luna. He looked like he'd just eaten the canary. "We're ready to go to work."

Bryan wished that was true. He hoped it would be

easy to zip shut the bag of worms he could feel wriggling deep inside of him.

Whatever happened, he had to stay strong enough to make it through this investigation without losing it.

Four

Her son needed help, but Lexi was helpless. Her feet were planted in soft, wet cement. She tried to scream, but no sound came out of her throat. They were taking him away, and no one saw her. There was no one to help her go after him. Darkness was closing in around her, and Juan was being swallowed by it.

Her leg jumped uncontrollably and Lexi's eyes opened wide. She'd fallen asleep. It was only a dream, a mishmash of every nightmare that had ever haunted her sleep.

The cold vinyl seat was stuck to the back of her sweatshirt. Her neck was sore, her bones ached. She looked around. The sterile hallways of the hospital stared back. The smell of disinfectant was familiar and instantly sobering. Reality was much scarier than the nightmare she'd just had. She didn't know what had become of Juan. An invisible hand was thrusting itself into her chest, grabbing her heart and squeezing so hard that she couldn't breathe. Tears rushed to her eyes as the events of the past two days played before her eyes.

She'd arrived here on Monday. She'd left a patient on the examining table, and two more in the waiting room, and had walked out with the police officer who'd arrived at her practice, bringing the horrific news. Her denial had been instant. The son she'd raised was incapable of violence. They had the wrong boy. This couldn't be happening to Juan…not to her son. This whole thing had to be one massive mistake.

Leaning her head back against the wall, Lexi tried for the zillionth time to make some sense out of all of this. Two days later, she still had no answers. The shock of hearing that Juan had shot his teacher and classmates had been more devastating than anything she'd faced in her entire life.

Not her child. He couldn't be capable of such an act. They'd told her he'd collapsed after the shooting, passing out and slipping into a coma. Two days later, he was still the same.

Lexi rubbed her pounding temple. She wanted to know exactly what tests they'd run on him so far. She wanted to see the results. As a doctor, she knew too much. She'd been contemplating too many scenarios, all of them scary. But the officials gave her no answers. Her background didn't matter a bit to these investigators. Being Juan's mother seemed to matter even less. He was the assailant. Period. And they were in this alone.

Lexi's brother, Allan, had arrived yesterday and stayed overnight. He had to go back to New Jersey tonight, though. His wife, Donna, was having her second chemotherapy treatment for breast cancer tomorrow. His family needed him.

Bad luck came in waves. The past couple of months had been surreal, worse than a nightmare. Donna was fighting for her life. And now Juan and the shooting. Lexi felt like her life had become entrapped inside a snowball rolling down a steep hill. The farther down she went, the faster and more out of control everything became.

She reached deep inside the front pocket of her slacks and found the business card she'd stuffed there this afternoon. An attorney. A stranger that Allan had found for her. Judith McGrath's specialty was juveniles. Her brother had called the attorney for Lexi, even met with her this morning. Judy, he'd called her. She was coming over to the hospital tomorrow to see Lexi. By then, maybe Juan's condition would have improved, too. Maybe he'd be awake.

But then what? She knew the end of Juan's coma was only the beginning. Panic started to close her throat again. Her son's medical recovery would be the last of these people's concerns. There would be a trial. Lexi wondered if they'd move Juan to a prison. He'd be scared. Tears rushed in again. She wiped them away. She couldn't let her mind go there. Not yet.

"I'm going down to the cafeteria, Dr. Bradley. Can I get you something to eat?"

Lexi recognized the voice. One of the third-shift nurses. Her name was Linda. She'd been here last night, too, and had asked the same question of her and Allan. She wiped her face with the bunched tissue in her hand and looked up at the softly wrinkled black face. She'd been so kind from the very start. No judgments at all. "You don't have to call me Dr. Bradley. No one else around here does."

"Those cops have forgotten their manners. And the nurses will know better from now on. I gave every one of them the whole scoop on you."

Lexi rubbed her stiff neck. "And where did you get the scoop on me?"

"I have my sources."

Lexi shared an internal medicine practice with three other doctors. There were half a dozen nurses and physicians' assistants who worked with them. But she also worked with both Waterbury and St. Mary's hospitals. The state of Connecticut was too small for people to not know one another. "How bad was the scoop?"

"I'm mentioning no names, but the word out there is that this shouldn't be happening to you and your son." Linda patted Lexi gently on the shoulder. "Everyone is really worried about you."

Lexi choked up. For the most part in the past couple of days, she'd kept a tight rein on her emotions in front of other people, but kindness got to her.

"So how about some food?" Linda said, repeating her original question.

"Can I see my son?" Lexi asked instead.

"I'm sorry, Doc, but that's not my call," the nurse said in a hushed voice and pointed with her head in the direction of two uniformed officers stationed outside Juan's door. "And I wouldn't ask that bunch over there, either. They don't make any decisions on their own. You'll have to wait for one of the detectives in charge to come in."

Juan had been wheeled out of that room on a gurney once today. Unlike Monday, when she'd been forced to stay in the waiting area of the emergency room, or yesterday, when the hospital staff had kept her an arm's length away, Lexi had been allowed to hold his hand and walk next to him when he went to MRI. He'd slept through it all, only waking up for the first time momentarily when he'd been inside the machine. But there had been no recognition. He'd only touched his head and said, "It hurts," before going back to sleep.

Yesterday, when they told her he was in a coma, she had also learned that all his vitals were excellent. Then, Lexi had been able to coax one of the residents last night to show her Juan's charts. Everything she'd seen looked normal.

Today, no one explained whether or not anything was different. But the fact that he'd opened his eyes and spoken a couple of words, even though it was only for a moment, meant something. A few possibilities had been running through Lexi's mind. Juan could have had a stroke. Or perhaps he had a brain tumor—a sudden, dramatic change of attitude was one of the symptoms, as were seizures. As scary as the prospect of a tumor was, it made it easier for her to rationalize his actions on Monday.

Over the past couple of weeks, he'd been complaining of headaches. She hadn't done anything about it, blaming it on his allergies and a respiratory virus that was making its way around school.

She'd been blind to whatever it was that Juan had been fighting. It was right in front of her, and she'd not pursued it. Guilt was a constant companion to all other emotions raging inside of her.

"Has he shown any more alertness?" Lexi asked, knowing she had to make good use of any direct information she could get from the hospital staff.

"I don't think so, but I'll double check with other nurses when I go back."

"Are any doctors going to see him again tonight?" Lexi persisted.

"One of the residents will make the rounds of the floor in another hour."

"Do you know who's on call tonight?" Lexi asked, hoping that the same doctor as last night would be on staff.

"I'm not sure. But I can check on that, too."

"Whoever is on," she added quickly, "will you ask them to talk to me? Just to answer a couple of questions?"

She hadn't heard anything about Juan's imaging tests. By now they had to have some results. Lexi

knew she wasn't anywhere near the top of the list to
get answers.

Allan had relayed Attorney McGrath's explana-
tions. Because of the shooting and his arrest, Juan was
now in the custody of the state, and Lexi had practically no say in anything when it came to her son's care
and condition. She was at the mercy of whatever government agent or detective happened to be in charge
at the hospital.

"I'll try to do whatever I can, Dr. Bradley." Linda
patted Lexi's hand gently. "How about some food? You
haven't left the hospital for two days now. Your brother
was very concerned about you when he left. How about
a nice sandwich or at least a salad?"

"No, thanks. No food. I can't eat," Lexi whispered,
planting her elbows on her knees and sinking her face
into her hands. She wasn't hungry. She wasn't going
to go home and take a nap, or have a shower. Her
clothes were wrinkled. So what? She smelled like the
antiseptic soap in the bathroom, but she didn't care.

She wouldn't call any friends and pour out her grief,
either. She couldn't ask for anyone's help in this community. Her practice would run on its own. Her partners would take care of things. She had a couple of
phone messages on her cell phone from the people at
the office. They'd said the same thing, told her to not
worry about things there. She couldn't bring herself to
call them back. Everyone was somehow affected by
the shooting. Wickfield was a very small town. Everyone knew one another. They all knew those who were

injured at the high school. Lexi wondered what would become of their future…Juan's future *and* hers.

"You can't be much help to your son if you let yourself get run down like this," Linda said softly.

Lexi had no answer. She was at a loss for what to do, where to go, whom to contact. This was totally unlike her. She was a person always in charge.

She heard Linda's footsteps move down the hall, and unexpected tears wet the palms of her hands. Lexi didn't know she had any left. Helpless, weak, confused, scared. She wished she could fight it. But there was nothing left in her. All she felt was empty and alone.

Five

"So much for not being involved in the first stage of the investigation," Hank Gardner complained.

He and Bryan sat in the black SUV on the second level of the parking garage. A dim spotlight at the far end of the row shone on the cars and illuminated wisps of steam escaping the building ductwork next door. The air outside was crisp. All day, the radio stations had been threatening significant snowfall for tonight.

Neither of the agents was ready to leave the car.

"One good thing," Bryan said. "We have a survivor to talk to."

"Yeah," Hank said, not trying to keep the sarcasm out of his tone. "That's great."

"Look, Juan Bradley is the only shooter who has survived the recent rash of incidents," Bryan said. "His testimony could shed light on whether there are any connections with the others or not."

"That is, if he comes through alive."

"Have you gotten any straight answers about his condition?"

Hank shook his head. "One report said it was a stroke."

"Is that possible for a fifteen-year-old?"

"It is, but they didn't send me any test results. Nothing to support it." Hank looked out at the brick-and-cement wall of the hospital building next door. Yale–New Haven Hospital, together with its medical school, had to cover about ten city blocks. "So we're here."

"We're here."

Hank glanced over at his friend seated behind the wheel of the SUV. The two of them were close to the same age. They had around the same number of years with the agency. But they'd never met until they'd been assigned to the school violence program back in the nineties.

Perhaps it was the fact that they both had their own children. Or maybe it was the tragedy that surrounded those school shootings. But the two men had become good friends, and it was a friendship that had lasted through a lot of ups and downs, a couple of moves and some personal tragedies. Bryan was a company man, higher ranking than Hank. The six-foot-four, square-built agent had given *plenty* in the service of his country. There used to be a time when Bryan never refused assignments. But that had changed over the past decade. This case was a sad exception and, for his friend's sake, Hank wished he'd refused it.

"Did you get a hold of your wife?" Bryan asked.

Hank nodded. Cathy was speaking at a seminar in

Florida. He hadn't been able to get hold of her until very late last night. "She's getting back to Boston tonight." He glanced down at his watch. "Actually, she's probably landed. The girls are picking her up at the airport."

"She must have had a few things to say about what we're working on again."

Hank smiled. "She has a very colorful mouth for a psychologist turned academic." Being in the same profession as him, Cathy never kept her opinions to herself. During the years of Bryan's struggle, Cathy had been right there, helping and interfering as she saw fit. "Yeah, she called me a few names for letting you get back into this."

Bryan shook his head and smiled. "I hope you took it like a man and shouldered the blame."

"Of course." Hank looked around the quiet garage before turning to his friend again. "In all seriousness, are you going to be okay with it?"

"No problem."

"I can find a way out of this for us. We could argue that these cases are nothing like the ones we worked on before."

"How is that?" Bryan asked.

"I spent the afternoon reading over the interviews with the witnesses and school officials," Hank explained. "Unlike what we saw before, none of these teenagers appear to have planned out the attacks. None told their friends about it beforehand. They weren't loners, or Goth rebels trying to kill conceited jocks.

Every one of them seemed to just snap. If everyone is telling the truth, then that's a very serious pattern…and very different from the profile we worked up."

"Geary's group didn't mention that," Bryan said.

"That's right. Because if he admitted to it, the cases would be out of our realm of expertise. The kind of adolescent killers we worked with before didn't snap. They planned. They acquired weapons. They told their friends. They had Web sites."

"That's true. If Juan Bradley lives, his lawyer will have a clear insanity defense."

"So you see," Hank replied, nodding. "There's still time to drive away."

Bryan rubbed his neck. "What's difficult to get a handle on is the frequency of these shootings. There could be more."

"That's true."

"So, the fact is, they need us. Even though the profile is different, we could possibly do something to prevent more killing."

"That's possible," Hank agreed.

He watched his friend frown and take a deep breath.

"Then let's go." Bryan pushed open his door. "Before I change my mind."

Six

Some of the wounded had been flown to Hartford Hospital. Two of the students and the teacher, Kevin Gordon, were here at Yale–New Haven. Lexi wanted to go and visit them, but she didn't know how to deal with the anger that the parents of those teenagers and Kevin Gordon's family must be feeling. She would be lost as far as what to say to them. Swearing to Juan's innocence wasn't what they'd be after. But she believed in it. He couldn't consciously hurt anyone. Not her Juan.

She closed her eyes and pinched the bridge of her nose as more tears threatened to fall. She'd been pacing these hallways for the past two days, keeping her chin up. But tonight she was exhausted. The fatigue was pulling her under. She was losing control and she couldn't stand it.

The elevator door to her left opened. Heavy footsteps came out of it. She already recognized the sound. Cops, detectives, federal agents. Heavy-footed marchers, sending you the message that they were in charge. She rubbed the back of her neck, looking down at the shoes as two people went by her toward Juan's room.

She searched in her pocket for a tissue to wipe her face. She'd face them with a clear voice. She'd already figured they wouldn't have anything to do with her if she were upset or angry or if she displayed any emotions. Monday night had been a loss. The same thing yesterday. She'd been too upset, and everyone had simply pretended that she didn't exist. She'd been able to accompany Juan to his tests this morning only because she'd approached Jeremy Simpson, a Wickfield police detective she knew from around town and from his work with teenagers in the area. She was also Jeremy's fiancée's doctor. She'd forced herself to be calm and had approached him as a professional. As *Dr.* Bradley.

Whatever it took, Lexi told herself. She'd use every connection.

She wiped her face with the tissue. Her contacts seemed to be permanently glued to her eyes. A thick film covered them from two days of neglect and tears, making her vision a haze.

She looked at the two men who'd just arrived. They were talking with the uniformed officers by Juan's door. One was an FBI agent she'd met here the first night. He'd spent more than three hours asking Lexi all kinds of questions, right after one of the state police detectives had finished asking her the very same questions. She couldn't remember either of their names off the top of her head, but she'd written them in her Black-

Berry. Good advice that Allan had brought back from Attorney McGrath, writing everything down. Lexi had been trying to make herself do that.

More advice Allan had brought back was that Lexi didn't have to talk to anyone or answer any questions unless her attorney was present. But Lexi had nothing to hide. Everything she'd said could only be seen as defense of her son's character.

She wondered if Juan was awake and that was why the agents were back. Lexi looked at the nurses' station. The three nurses behind the divider were busy doing their thing. He couldn't be awake, she decided.

The other newcomer had his back to Lexi. He was very tall, with square shoulders. The body of an athlete. He was wearing a black suit, or maybe it was dark gray. She couldn't tell. His hair was curly and lightly sprinkled with gray at the sideburns. He needed a haircut. She hadn't seen him before. He seemed to be asking all the questions.

Lexi saw one of the uniformed officers motion toward her. The tall man half turned and looked right at her.

She held her breath. There was judgment in that look, hardness that made her think he'd decided on her character long before getting here. Her son was a criminal, and she was an unfit mother. Her insides tightened in protest. Blood rushed to her head, pounding at her temples. So far, everyone had been civilized, even the FBI agent during the hours of questioning. But this was a different person and a new battle. He had better be civilized or she knew she'd start swinging.

The tall man said something to the others and started toward her. Lexi straightened up and pressed her back against the chair. Earlier, she'd tucked one foot under her. Now she took it out. Her leg was asleep. She should never have sat down. It was so much easier to face the world on her two feet. She didn't trust herself to stand up now, though.

She wished her brother were here. Maybe she should have accepted the offer of food from Linda. She felt weak, out of sorts. She dug her hand into her pocket again and touched the lawyer's card. Maybe this was the time to refuse their questions.

He had a way of dominating the space. The lines and angles of his face were chiseled, like a movie actor from the thirties. He could have been considered handsome, she supposed, but his features seemed frozen in a deep frown, making him look even more intimidating. She forced herself not to look away. From where she was sitting, his head seemed to brush the ceiling. Her neck hurt to look up at him.

"Hello, ma'am. I'm Agent Atwood." He flashed a badge under her nose. "I need to ask you a few questions."

United States Secret Service. She was able to read that much before he whisked his badge away. She felt small and insignificant sitting there, especially since his voice had conveyed as much of a reprimand as his glare.

"Dr. Bradley," she said formally. She had to reach deep and use everything in her arsenal. Her leg was still asleep. There was no use trying to stand up yet. She extended her hand out to him.

He stared at it for a couple of seconds as if it were a loaded weapon before reluctantly shaking it.

Her fingers were swallowed up by the agent's large hand. She was quick to pull her hand back and tuck it under her leg. It annoyed her that he continued to stand up, towering over her, instead of taking the seat next to her.

"I've answered every possible question, at least twice. And I know those answers have been recorded and documented in their files." She motioned with her head toward the FBI agent and the uniformed officer. "You can save yourself plenty of time and listen to the tapes."

"Three times is always the charm."

She shrugged, rubbing the back of her neck. "Have a seat. Ask away. I promise, my answers will be the same."

"I don't want to disturb any of the patients or the staff. I'm told there's a room down the hall that we could use. It would be a lot more private."

"I don't make scenes or disturb the peace," Lexi said tensely. "I'm a pretty levelheaded individual, Agent... Officer...Detective...whatever you guys call yourself."

"Atwood. You can call me Agent Atwood."

"Agent Atwood," she said in a matter-of-fact manner.

The nurses at the station were watching. She felt everyone else's eyes in the hallway were on her, too. Not that it mattered to her. She would go through the exercise a dozen times if it could make a difference. Maybe this one would have more pull in getting them to let her see Juan, to be involved with his care. Lexi looked around and collected her pocketbook and overcoat. She'd kicked her shoes off, but they were right by the leg of the chair. She pulled them on. "Lead the way."

"After you."

Her joints cracked in protest, but Lexi pushed herself to stand. The moment she did, she knew it was a mistake. The room tilted, and she saw small suns exploding in front of her eyes. It was a miracle when she landed back on the seat again.

"Got up too fast?"

"I must have. Give me a couple of seconds," she whispered under her breath, clutching the edge of the seat, looking at the line of the tiles on the floor. Her vision continued to play games with her. She was lightheaded from sitting for too long. The agent continued to stand there, probably glaring down. She was sure that he thought she was faking it, trying to work on his sympathy. Maybe she should. She wished she were a better actor.

Lexi moved her bag and coat to one arm and stood up again. "Which way?" she asked.

He motioned with his hand past the elevator door to their left.

She turned, took a step and went down flat on her face.

Seven

There was no bona fide profile for an adolescent killer.

From his last time investigating these cases, Hank Gardner knew that the teenagers who'd committed the crimes came from many different kinds of families. Most had close friends. Few had disciplinary records. Some were honor students; others were failing.

Almost ten years later, Hank made no pretense of having any answers. The publication they'd put together, with its checklists of warning signs, was a guide, but in most cases it was useless. Over the years, he'd come to accept that the lists created a risk of overidentification. The great majority of students who fit those profiles didn't pose any risk of violence. Each child was different. Each case was a puzzle.

The only solid conclusion that Hank had from all of this was that each one of these kids, over a period of time, had cried out for help. They needed someone to listen to them.

The only physician on the floor tonight who could update Hank on the teenager's condition couldn't see him until he was done with his rounds. When Bryan went upstairs to grill Juan's mother, Hank poked his head into one of the victim's rooms. Based on the report he'd received, the English teacher, Kevin Gordon, was in stable condition and accepting visitors.

Luck was on Hank's side when he found out that the tall brunette sitting in Gordon's room was the high school guidance counselor, a woman named Sally Michelson. Curiously enough, she was very familiar with Juan Bradley's file and eager to share her thoughts with the forensic psychologist.

"I've been involved in this line of work for fifteen years, twelve of them in the New York City public school system, prior to coming to Wickfield," Sally explained. "I've dealt with students who had daily grievances and who openly bragged to their friends about what violent act they were going to commit. Some of them were pretty specific about whom they were going to shoot. Those students had easy access to weapons and ammunition. With that in mind, you should know that Juan would have been the last person I'd ever suspect of doing this."

Hank kept quiet, jotting down notes. This was exactly what he'd read this afternoon in the files of the other recent teen shooters. But he tried to stay objective. He wasn't going to make any hasty assumptions.

"I agree," Gordon put in from his hospital bed. His leg was in a full-length cast and suspended in a sling. "In fact, if I hadn't had a bullet dug out of my knee on account of this kid, I'd argue that someone else…a look-alike…was responsible for the shooting. I still have a hard time believing that Juan was the one holding that rifle. I mean, I looked right into his face. It didn't even look like him. There were no emotions there. I don't know…there was something very strange about the whole thing."

Hank took down some more notes.

"I've read a lot of articles and books on violence in schools," the guidance counselor continued. "I read the report that the Secret Service put out a few years ago, cover to cover."

Hank always felt embarrassed mentioning that he was one of the authors of the report. She obviously didn't know. He let it be.

"I've attended more workshops than I can count that dealt specifically with how to handle adolescent boys," Sally went on. "About the importance of listening to them, on how to read them. I've read studies that conclude that the way we bring up boys in America predisposes them to loneliness, alienation and sadness, and that makes them more prone to violence. As the single mother of two boys myself, I've been more than aware of this. Knowing Juan and knowing his home life, I can tell you that his relationship with his mother, his attitude, his openness in expressing his feelings and communicating with her has been exemplary. That boy has no deep-seated problems, no pent-up anger, no…"

"How is it that you're so familiar with Juan?" Hank asked casually.

"I know his family. And at the very time he entered the school, we happened to be in a faculty meeting, talking about giving him a citizenship award."

"That's pretty ironic."

"Incredibly ironic," the English teacher said, moving gingerly. "I was the one who nominated him for the award."

"So you agree with Ms. Michelson."

"He's a great kid," Gordon said, nodding his head. "I just don't understand it. There was no sign of latent hostility or violence in the creative writing he's done for my English class. None of it in his daily journals that students had to keep. Nothing."

It was curious that, despite being witness to the violence and even being a victim of it, both of these people were such fans of the teenager and continued to defend his character. Gordon's kneecap had been shattered by the bullet. But that didn't seem to make any difference.

"Does he have many friends?" Hank asked.

"He's very popular," Michelson commented. "Not a loner, if that's what you mean."

"I'd say he's probably the most respected member of his class," Gordon asserted.

"I think the local police have already interviewed quite a number of his friends from school," she added. "Between that and the information that the crisis counselors are no doubt getting, you should get a good idea of how shocking this is to everyone."

Despite the reports from the six recent school shootings, from past research Hank knew that attacks such as the one in Wickfield were rarely spontaneous or impulsive. In almost all cases, the attacker developed the idea well in advance. Most planned it out carefully and talked to their friends about it.

"Can you give me any names of classmates who were especially close to Juan? Anyone he hung out with regularly, especially over the past couple of weeks?"

"I can't come up with a name off the top of my head," Kevin Gordon said, looking at the guidance counselor.

She shook her head. "I think he regularly ate lunch with the principal's son, Jake Peterson, and Conor Doyle, another top student at the high school. I don't know if those two would be considered his best friends or not. I do know that both of them were interviewed by other investigators."

"I'm no expert," Gordon said, starting to sound like Juan's defense lawyer, "but isn't it true that teenagers who get into this kind of situation don't generally do sports or participate in so many clubs?"

"Juan has set a school standard with his high level of civic activities," Michelson added.

When the English teacher started reciting Juan's qualifications for the citizenship award that he'd nominated the kid for, Hank knew he was wasting his time. He was looking for specifics that detailed Juan Bradley's planning, communication and possible motives for the outburst of violence. These two were working up closing arguments for the defense. He was an investigator, not a judge.

A nurse poked his head in and told Hank that the doctor wanted to see him before going upstairs to check on Juan.

The psychologist escaped the room just as the two faculty members moved to possible causes of the teenager's behavior. Use of pesticides on the soccer fields at the high school was the last thing Hank heard before bowing out.

Eight

Bryan felt more than a touch of regret. The egg-size bruise on Lexi Bradley's forehead was growing by the second, and the cut just above her left eyebrow continued to seep blood. If he'd paid closer attention, he might have been able to catch her, or at least he would have noticed that when getting up a second time she was still unsteady on her feet. He'd missed the signs.

"When was the last time you had a tetanus shot, Dr. Bradley?" asked the nurse who'd stepped out of the elevator the moment Lexi had gone down on her face. Her name was Linda and the two seemed to know each other.

"It was recent enough…maybe a couple of years."

"The cut appears clean, but it looks like you may need a couple of stitches."

"No," Lexi said under her breath.

"The cut is too deep," the nurse persisted. "Don't

be stubborn. An attractive woman like you doesn't need a scar."

"It doesn't matter," Lexi shrugged.

The nurse glanced at Bryan and nodded toward the adjoining bathroom. "Take one of those cups there and get some water for her."

He went in and returned to see Lexi holding her head high so the nurse could dab and work on the cut. Her eyes stayed closed.

Back in the hallway, this nurse had been the first one to check Lexi after the fall. She'd taken charge and had told Bryan to move Dr. Bradley into this room across the hall. Lexi, though, had fought being carried and demanded to walk on her own feet. He'd held on to her arm despite her objections. Inside the room, she'd refused to lie on the bed to be examined and sat down on a chair closest to the door. There was definitely a stubborn streak in her that perhaps had something to do with being used to giving care, not receiving it.

A couple of nurses had joined them there right away, but Linda was in charge and sent the others to their station.

It would have been courteous for Bryan to leave the room and postpone the questions. But he'd decided to stay and had found a spot by the window, out of the way.

"Keep sipping that water. I still have to get one of the doctors to check you out. You were knocked out," the nurse told her, pressing an ice pack to Lexi's forehead.

"I never lost consciousness. I also have no headache,

no dizziness, no difficulty remembering things. I don't feel foggy or distracted, which means I have no concussion," she told Linda. "Unless this is the same doctor who'll be seeing Juan tonight, I don't need someone else to tell me what I already know."

The nurse sent her patient a narrow glare. "No, it'll probably be one of the interns from the emergency room or one of the physicians' assistants."

"Then I don't need one," Lexi said in a tone of finality.

"You can talk tough all you want, Dr. Bradley, but you're not fine," the nurse said brusquely. "You look as pale as a ghost and I'm not letting—"

"Please, Linda." Lexi grasped the nurse's hand in her own. Her voice turned lower, still determined. "There's only one thing I need right now to make me feel better, and that's convincing the doctor who's visiting Juan to answer some of my questions. But I figure I can't do that until Agent Atwood here is done with me. So please…"

Bryan turned from the window and looked at her. Lexi's eyes were pleading with Linda. The vulnerability in her voice and look was impossible to miss even from across the room.

"After he's done with you, you eat," the older woman said stubbornly.

"I'll eat…after I talk to the doctor."

"No. You don't know when and if that's going to happen. No more missing meals, Dr. Bradley. I'm not putting up with it."

The two looked at each other for a long moment,

stubborn wills butting heads. Finally, Lexi gave in and nodded.

"Hold this on the cut," the nurse ordered Lexi before turning to Bryan. "Don't let her get up."

She scurried out of the room but was back in a moment with a handful of bandages and an ice pack. She quickly applied several butterfly sutures over the cut on her patient's forehead and then put on a square bandage.

"You know the drill," the nurse said to the doctor. "Keep the ice on it."

"Please tell me when the doctor arrives to see Juan."

The nurse nodded. Bryan didn't miss the threatening glare she sent him before walking out. She acted as if he'd shoved the woman down himself. He was clearly not to be trusted in the nurse's eyes.

Lexi Bradley slipped her shoes off and tucked one foot under her. She laid the ice pack and the half-empty cup of water aside and sat back in the chair, staring at him.

Whatever frame of mind he'd been in when he first approached her in the hallway was gone now. The hard questions that he'd been ready to ask faded into the background. There was something incredibly fragile about her at this moment, and Bryan didn't think she could handle being pushed any closer to the edge.

He walked away from the window. Her red-rimmed blue eyes watched his every step. She wasn't afraid to make eye contact. Her face was truly ashen. Her blond hair, pulled back into a tight ponytail, was stained at the temple with blood from her cut. She had delicate features, smooth skin, a small nose, high cheekbones. He guessed she was quite beautiful under better conditions. Right now, she was clinging to a hard business edge no doubt honed through her years practicing medicine. There was real intelligence in her look, too. Around the eyes, he could see the traces of exhaustion. With her cuts and bruises, Bryan thought, she looked battered.

The nurse had left the door partially open. He reached over and closed it before turning back to her.

"How long have you been here?" he asked.

"Since Monday," she told him, tucking her hands under her legs.

"Haven't left at all?"

She shook her head. "I can't. I won't. I don't believe any parent in my situation would. Not even for a few minutes." She looked up at his face. "Do you have any children, Agent Atwood?"

The question took him by surprise. His job was to ask the questions, not answer them.

There was a lot that he already knew about Juan Bradley's family, about Lexi. Before coming here, he'd read the reports of the other two interviews she'd had with the FBI and a local detective. Still, she didn't need to know that.

"Where's your husband?"

"You wouldn't understand why I have to stay here. You're not a parent," she said instead, turning away.

"I have two daughters," Bryan replied, surprising himself by answering.

The lines in her face visibly relaxed as she looked

back at him. "I'm a single parent. No husband. Juan was adopted. I have no idea who his biological parents are. The two of us are all we have."

He stood by the foot of the hospital bed. "How old was he when you adopted him?"

"Two years and five months," she said, looking up at him. She rubbed the back of her neck. "I should stand up, but I don't want to fall on my face again. I'd appreciate it if you would sit down. You're too tall, and I have this pounding headache, so if you don't mind…"

He picked up a chair from the far wall and put it a couple of feet in front of her. He sat down.

"Didn't I hear you tell the nurse that you don't have a headache?"

"I didn't then. I do now. The headache has nothing to do with getting a concussion. It has everything to do with stress and lack of sleep," she told him. "Thank you for sitting down. This is much better."

The bandage on her head was getting stained with blood. Maybe it was the dim light in the room, but she didn't look too healthy to him. Bryan wasn't absolutely sure she wasn't going to pass out on him again, even sitting down. He slid his chair closer to her.

"I know the drill. You want me to talk about Juan."

He nodded.

"Where would you like me to start?" she asked. "Juan's childhood? His upbringing? His academic successes? Sports? Music? The gentle way he treated other people? His record as a volunteer? He's a boy any mother would be proud of. I can go on for hours telling you about things that he's done…about the truly good person that he is."

Was, maybe, Bryan thought. He could see and hear the tension building in the woman's voice and body. But in spite of the mother's defense, Juan Bradley was no angel. He'd changed all that this past Monday afternoon. The teenager had been taken into custody at the high school. Although unconscious at the time, there was no question that this individual had been the one firing the weapon at his teacher and his fellow students. Bryan didn't think Lexi Bradley was really up for a lecture on the truth right now, however.

"Before this incident, did your son ever break any laws?"

"I'm sure the local Wickfield police have told you he hasn't. He respects the law. In fact, one of his volunteer activities was with an organization that Detective Simpson of the Wickfield Police Department is involved with, as well."

"How about rules? Rules that you'd set up at home? Did he ever break them? Feel trapped by them?"

"No," she replied. "Those who know us will tell you that our home isn't very old-fashioned. I've never had to set a lot of rules. Juan has always been mature beyond his age. I have a great deal of respect for him and the same goes the other way around. We both talk and have a clear understanding of what is best for each of us, for our family. He tells me his concerns, I tell him mine. That's how we come up with guidelines, but they've never been cut-and-dried rules. We just haven't needed them."

To Bryan's thinking, this was totally unrealistic for most adolescents, but it was definitely intelligent parenting...if it were true.

"Was your son ever bullied?"

"No, never. He gets along with everybody."

"Has there been any major change in his life recently? Did he have to make any new adjustments recently? A girlfriend dumping him? Maybe a new boyfriend for you? Anything?"

She shook her head repeatedly. "No to all of the above. We've been the same for some time. No changes whatsoever. No trouble. Nothing."

This was consistent with everything she'd told the other investigators before—and consistent with what everyone else on file had said about Juan Bradley.

"Let's talk about the gun."

She nodded, the delicate line of her jaw hardening, the medical professional trying to regain possession of the mother's face.

"Your neighbors claim that as far as they know, Juan had never been in their basement. He'd never seen the gun. How did he know to go there?"

"I don't know if my son went there to get the gun," she said stubbornly. "I haven't spoken to him since the accident."

"He went there and left plenty of evidence. The tracks in the snow led directly from your house. And the gun recovered at the high school has already been identified as the one missing from your neighbor's basement."

She crossed her arms over her chest.

"Juan watched the cat for my neighbors whenever they went away for any length of time," she told him. "That wouldn't necessarily take him to their basement. But everybody in the entire neighborhood knew about Mr. Myers's gun collection. Anytime there was a raccoon or a fox spotted within a five-mile radius, he'd joke with the neighbors about getting out the arsenal and going after it."

"Did Juan ever express any interest in guns?"

She shook her head. "Unlike the rest of his friends who were into all kinds of shoot-'em-up video games and paintball and laser tag, Juan has never shown any interest in them."

"That you know of, you mean. Parents are sometimes the last ones to know."

"No," she said defensively. "I told you before, Agent Atwood. We don't have the kind of relationship where he has to hide things from me. There's no need for it. We trust each other."

He'd hit a nerve with her. Bryan watched her struggle to keep her emotions intact.

"And Juan isn't a fighter. You can ask anyone. He's the peacekeeper. He's never been rough or violent. He isn't now. He gets along with everyone. There are no in-and-out circles of friends with him, either. And I've been right there with him, every step of the way. He's never excluded me, never asked me to stay out of his life. That's why I…I have a hard time believing…the same teenager…my son…did this. I can't fathom… how this happened, why it happened. I am…I haven't been…a bad mother…not some clueless parent. I've been involved, and he's let me be. I don't understand what happened at the high school on Monday. I can't explain why he acted the way he did. There has to be some reason that none of us has figured out yet. And that's why I'm desperate to talk to some of these doctors. There could be some kind of medical reason for it. At least…at least…there has to be something."

She stopped. Her fingers pinched the bridge of her nose. Bryan saw a couple of tears escape and rush down her pale face. Her lips were dry, chapped. Her hand shook as she reached inside her bag and took out a tissue.

"I'm sorry," she said, wiping her face, blowing her nose. "It's been a long few days and I can't…I don't know where I am or what I'm saying or what I have already said. I don't know *what* to say. I can repeat everything going on in Juan's life, in my life—what I've told you and the other agents—but there's nothing unusual. We have a normal life. Day-to-day routines. Activities all the time. Good, positive things. Kids today go in a hundred different directions. Juan is no different. As a parent, you understand what I'm saying."

Bryan wished he did, but he didn't. Since his divorce, his ex had been taking care of everything. Frozen him out of his daughters' lives. He was no more than the stranger who showed up once a month or so to take them out to dinner and a movie. It was pitiful. And he'd allowed it to happen.

"I've already told you that we *talk* to each other," she continued. "We communicate. There were no issues…

nothing. I'm confused. I want to help…but I just can't this way…not by looking at our routines or the kind of life he has." She stopped again and wiped her face.

Bryan watched the shaken woman. Her grief and confusion were tearing the scab off an old wound deep inside him, and he didn't like it. But he couldn't stop it. Hank had been right. He had no business getting so close to this type of case. Nine years ago, he'd been sitting across from his own mother in a hospital waiting room in New Jersey, both of them grieving as she tried to understand why her baby had committed suicide. What were the signs that she'd missed? Bryan couldn't even imagine how much worse everything would have been if they'd been left in the dark as far as specific medical details.

His brother Bobby had died before the night was out, but at least the family knew what was being done to keep the teenager alive.

Bryan's cell phone vibrated in his pocket. He took it out and looked at the display. It was Hank. The bastard was getting too good at knowing when Bryan started teetering too close to the edge, even from a distance. He flipped the phone open.

"What is it?" he said gruffly.

"I'm on the second floor with one of the doctors responsible for Juan Bradley's care. I think you'll want to sit in on this and hear everything firsthand."

Bryan looked at Lexi. She seemed to have herself back together and was obviously trying to listen to his conversation. There was no point in keeping this woman in the dark about her son's care, especially considering the fact that she was an M.D. From everything he'd heard, she hadn't once refused any of the officials' questions. She hadn't pulled any attorneys out of her back pocket or read anyone the riot act of what they can and can't ask. She was cooperating. They could, too.

"Is it bad news?" Bryan asked his partner.

"I don't know. I don't think so. There's just some stuff going on. You can decide for yourself if it's bad or good or weird," Hank said from the other end.

Bryan rose to his feet and walked to the window. "What kind of stuff?"

"Would you stop asking questions and just get down here?" Hank asked.

"I want to know if someone else should sit in on this, too."

"FBI and locals?"

"No."

"Stop playing twenty questions," Hank said.

"I'm busy right now, talking to Dr. Bradley," he drawled for his partner.

"You want to know if you should bring her down for this."

"You're really getting old and senile," Bryan said under his breath. "That's exactly what I mean."

He faced the window and the dark sky outside. It had started snowing. He heard Hank exchange a few words with someone else.

"Sure. We might be able to get some medical-background information from her."

"It might take five to ten minutes to get down there," Bryan told his friend.

"Moving at a snail's pace."

"Just wait for me."

Bryan ended the call and turned back to Lexi. She was watching him. Once again, he found himself thinking about how weak and pale she looked.

"When was the last time you ate something?"

"I don't have to answer that question, Agent Atwood. It's totally irrelevant."

She did have a stubborn streak. "Are you strong enough to go downstairs with me?"

"That depends on the reason."

"To the cafeteria, to get some food in you."

"No," she said. "Don't worry, I'm not on any hunger strike. I'll go and get something to eat after I talk to Juan's doctor."

He changed tactic. "Are you strong enough to go and see his doctor?"

"Right now?" she said, sitting up straight.

"Yes."

"Is he on the floor?" she asked, pulling on her shoes and grabbing her shoulder bag.

"No, we'll meet him in his office on the second floor."

Lexi stood up, only to sit down again. Bryan saw the look. She was trying to focus on everything around her with no success. He couldn't let her pass out on him again.

"Guess what, Dr. Bradley?" he said, walking over and taking her by the arm.

"I'm fine," she whispered. She didn't fight him when he helped her slowly to her feet again.

"I know you're fine. That's why you're keeping me company as we stop at the cafeteria on our way to see your son's doctor."

She opened her mouth to say something but quickly closed it when he darted a threatening look at her.

"You're no good to anyone…including your son…if you end up with a concussion from repeatedly bouncing your head off the floor. You're going to eat something, keep your strength up and then talk to Juan's doctor. Got it?"

She nodded.

"I'm glad we understand each other," Bryan said, leading her to the door.

Nine

Wednesday, January 16, 9:10 p.m.
Colony High School, Orlando, Florida

It was a standing-room-only crowd.

The grandstand seats, the entrance doors—everywhere, people packed the gym. And everyone was on their feet. The cheers were deafening. Streamers of black and red, Colony's school colors, danced in the air above the home team stands. Twenty-four basketball league championship banners hung along the gymnasium walls, speaking of their years of domination in this sport.

Fourth quarter. Just thirty-seven seconds remaining to the end of the game. They were down by two points.

The visiting team had the ball, but with a dive, one of the Colony players batted the basketball away. There was a wild scramble at half court, and the call went

Colony's way. A cheer went up as the home team called time out. They were still in this.

As the teams huddled in front of their benches, Hilary Mitchell, Colony High School's principal, held on tightly to her husband's hand. They'd both graduated from Colony back in '82. Paul, her husband, had played basketball for the high school in the old gym. He'd been a guard, and Hilary hadn't missed too many games back then. She didn't miss any at all now and truly hoped someday their son would be playing on this same court.

The referee's whistle called the ten players back onto the court. No one in the stands bothered to sit down. The benches were empty. Coaches and players lined the side of the court.

Hilary felt her cell phone vibrate. Her mind immediately went to her twelve-year-old son at home. He was at that in-between age where he didn't want a sitter, but at the same time he got worried if his parents were running a few minutes late. As she tried to dig the phone out of her pocket, everyone around them exploded with cheers as one of the Colony players sank a three-pointer. They were ahead by one with twenty-five seconds left.

The cell phone display told her that the call was coming from the main office of the high school. Hilary had locked the outer door herself before the game. Sometimes one of the night custodians called her at this time to check on when they should lock a certain door or if a room needed to be set up for the morning, but she couldn't imagine why anyone would be in there tonight.

Hilary answered her phone, but with all the background noise she couldn't hear a word.

The ball was thrown in and the opposing players moved it down the court. They were going to try to hold the ball for a single shot, but as their guard took the ball into the corner, the Colony defense sprang into action, collapsing on him. In panic, a time-out was called—their last one. Six seconds were left on the clock.

The principal pressed a hand to her other ear, trying to block the noise. "I can't hear you. Say that again."

"I think...down."

"What was that?" she yelled into the phone, barely recognizing the voice as Bob, one of the custodians who was just back last week after recovering from a stroke.

There was more cheering as the teams returned to the court. The crowd in the stands was stomping their feet and chanting *"Defense."*

Hilary sat down and bent her head closer to her knees. "I can't hear what you're saying, but there are only seconds left in the game. I'll stop at the office right after."

"Lock Down..."

This time she heard it. Over the past couple of years, they'd been doing a lot of drills to lock down in case of emergencies. During some of the drills, students were detained in classrooms while police and dogs scoured the campus, looking for drugs or weapons. This was a controversial approach to keeping schools safe, but it was a new world. Despite the fact that there had never been an episode of serious violence at Colony

High School—except for a student riot in 1972—Hilary and the staff were all for the searches.

"We had a drill yesterday morning," Hilary said into the phone, thinking Bob's question had something to do with that.

"No…Police s…"

Suddenly, three popping sounds came from outside the gym doors, like someone setting off firecrackers. An opposing team player was standing on the far sideline, the ball held above his head. The crowd hushed, but only for a moment. Immediately, the sound of screams from the doorways pierced the silence.

Hilary jumped to her feet, the phone forgotten in her hand. The people who'd blocked the main entrance of the gym were surging onto the court. There was instant mayhem. Someone went down. The crowds in the stands shifted as everyone tried to move away from the door. Hilary heard two more popping sounds.

She dialed 911 as she tried to step down onto the court. Her husband, though, was holding her jacket from behind.

Standing on the first row of seats, Hilary could see blood under the digital clock. One of the basketball players and a parent were dragging another player quickly across the floor toward the stands. The blood was coming from him.

Though there was chaos everywhere in the gym, the main entrance was now clear of people. A moment later, Hilary froze at the sight of the boy lurching into the gym. He was carrying a rifle.

This nightmare could not be happening, she thought. It just wasn't possible.

Mike Forbes, a sophomore, the top student in his class, the starting guard on Colony's basketball team, was carrying the gun. He'd been a no-show for the game tonight.

"No, Mike," she whispered.

As everyone watched, the boy stumbled onto the court, turned the muzzle of the rifle to his chin...and fired.

Ten

Wednesday, January 16
West 76th Street, New York

The deadline at the end of the month was looming. There were hundreds of things he needed to be doing. He didn't need his family's help in getting him distracted. He managed just fine by himself, staying neck deep in trouble.

He'd specifically asked his wife to keep their daughter and grandkids at their house in Connecticut. He'd promised to go up Friday night and stay for the weekend. Of course, he'd said the same thing last weekend, but he never made it.

"Grandpa!" The youngest of his grandchildren caught him coming through the door and limped across the foyer toward him.

He put his briefcase down, crouched down and

opened his arms to the four-year-old. David had spina bifida, and wore a brace on his right leg that he swung forward to walk. The child had digestive-track problems, and some hearing, vision and possible sensory processing issues, as well. At his young age, he'd already been through half a dozen surgeries, but none of that dampened the spirit of the little boy or affected his intelligence. He was as smart as a whip.

"I missed you, Grandpa," the bright-faced child said, not releasing him from the bear hug around his neck.

His annoyance melted away in an instant. It would have suited his schedule to be short and make some excuses to the rest of the family and send them packing. But he couldn't. He couldn't do that to this child. He pressed a kiss on the little boy's mop of blond hair.

"Where's the rest of your crew?"

"Mommy and the girls are out shopping. We already had dinner on the way driving down. Did you have dinner, Grandpa?" he asked, pulling back. The blue eyes behind the thick glasses looked right into his.

"Yes, I've had dinner."

The four-year-old tried to pick up the older man's briefcase. It had to weigh as much as he did. "Nanna's been talking to somebody on the phone forever. Will you work on my puzzle with me?"

"Well, I don't know...." He pushed himself to his feet and closed the door. There were phone calls he had to make, e-mails to answer. There was a hundred-page report that he had to read and make some notes on for a nine o'clock meeting tomorrow morning. When the doorman had warned him downstairs that the family was here, he should have turned around and gone back to the office.

"Please?" David asked.

"Okay...but only for a few minutes."

His wife appeared in the doorway to the living room with the phone stuck to one ear.

"I told you if we talked long enough he'd get in," Ann said before putting her hand over the receiver and mouthing a name to him.

He shook his head and made a motion of not wanting to talk to anyone.

She shook her head, rounded her eyes and gave him her standard look of not being happy with his response.

"I'll be thinking of you, honey," his wife said, coming over. "He's right here, Elsa. Of *course* he has time to talk to you."

He only had enough time to peel off his winter coat before she handed him the phone. He made a face, tried to place the name. *Elsa*...and then it was all there. Elsa Harvey. Mitch's wife.

Their wives had been good friends years back. He knew they'd stayed in touch, despite the husbands going in different directions.

He cleared his throat, heading for the room to the left of the foyer that he used as a home office. It was bad enough that Mitch called him daily. Now his wife was on the phone. He hoped Mitch wasn't becoming stupid enough to share anything with Elsa after all these years. The families had never been part of it. They had no clue about specifics.

"Elsa," he said in as cheerful a tone as he could muster, considering everything. "It's been forever since I've talked to you. How are you? How's the family?"

She blurted out an obviously well-rehearsed summary of how each of their kids and grandchildren were doing. He didn't know most of the names, didn't know so-and-so was married and had two children of her own. But he let her chatter away. Her voice was higher pitched than when she'd been younger. He wondered if this was because of something Mitch had told her.

He sat down behind his desk and spotted his grandson waiting in the doorway, watching him. The honesty in the child's face and the look of worship that he always sent him made his palms go clammy. He was relieved when his wife came and took the child by the hand, leading him back to the living room.

"The reason why I called…"

He pulled himself together. "Yes, you were saying."

"I'm really worried about Mitch."

Dozens of objections rose in him. Things like, it wasn't his problem that her husband was a spineless coward who needed someone to hold his hand at the first sign of any problem.

"Worried about what, Elsa?" he asked instead.

"He's missing," she said in a tense tone.

Prickly cold washed down his back. He remembered the last time the pain in the ass had called him. Yesterday morning. There hadn't been any new information, no new incidents, just the same panicky tone.

"What do you mean missing?"

"He didn't come home last night, and this morning he didn't show up at the college."

Christ. He wasn't the jerk's fucking babysitter. He kept that comment to himself, too.

"Did you call the police?"

"I called them. But they said it's too early to report him as missing. They recommended that I should check with friends and family first."

"Where are you?"

"I'm in Arizona, babysitting for my oldest son's children. The parents are in Hawaii for a week."

He sat back in the chair, frustrated that, with everything else in his life, he had to be bothered with this. He wasn't their relative and no longer a close friend, by any means.

"Elsa, I really don't know what I can do for you from New York. I haven't seen Mitch for…"

"Curtis, you've been talking to him every day," she said quickly.

The comment took him by surprise. The shithead had leaked something.

"I checked his cell phone record online. He's been calling you every day. That's why I called you first."

Cold turned to heat. He wiped the perspiration on the back of his neck. Nothing had better have happened to this guy or the same records would be available to any schmuck detective who went looking for Mitch. He didn't need to be involved with police on the eve of his company going public.

"He's been curious about what we're going through with my company right now," he explained, thinking fast. "Everything is happening at the same time, with the pending FDA approval and the stock sale at the end of the month. I think he missed not being in the middle of it. You know…like he was in the old days."

"Could it be that he's in New York to see you?"

"I can't see why he'd do that," he said, hoping he was right. He ran a hand through his thinning hair. "I really don't know where Mitch is, Elsa."

"There are also a half dozen calls to Nevada this past week," she continued on. "The number belongs to one of those self-storage places. I've tried it a few times, but I only get an answering machine. Now, I know you two worked in Nevada fourteen or fifteen years ago, but do you know if he might have left something behind? I don't know…he's never mentioned it, but the storage place is only a half hour from where you used to be. I'm probably just grasping at straws."

What storage place? *They were supposed to leave nothing behind,* he thought bitterly. But that had been Mitch's job, to clear out and destroy all records. And now Mitch was running around like a loose cannon. A piercing headache was suddenly threatening to split his head in two.

"Are you still there?"

"Yes, I'm here, Elsa," he said in what he hoped was a calm voice. "I don't know what to tell you. There's nothing that I can think of, no reason why he should go to Nevada. Nothing that has anything to do with me."

"What am I going to do? I don't want to call the other kids and get them wound up if it's nothing. And he's going to show up—"

"Tell you what. Is there any way you can e-mail me or fax me a listing of everyone that Mitch has called in the past couple of weeks?" He needed to figure out how much damage his old partner had already done.

"Of course. I can print it off the computer and fax it to you."

"Good. Let me make some calls here," he said, anxious to get off the phone. "I'll contact some of the other people we used to work with. Most of them are in New York, anyway. I'll go over your list as soon as I have it, and then I'll call you if I find something. It's probably nothing, Elsa."

"You're probably right," she said gratefully.

After hanging up, he sat and considered the situation. This had the potential for getting out of control… just like the development with the kid in Wickfield, Connecticut, who'd survived the shooting. He needed to handle both problems.

The situation in Connecticut was manageable, though. The right people were in place, ready to do what needed to be done. They were just biding their time, waiting for the right moment to execute their plan.

There was no room for error in any of this. He couldn't afford a screw-up, and none of the others would stand for it. A number of the involved partners had been on the phone to him. Everyone was shaken up. They all wanted it done and forgotten.

For the second time this week, he dialed his man's number. The jobs were across country, and they had to be done immediately. But there were others who worked for him. He'd take care of it. His man had handled this kind of problem for him before.

Hopefully, this would be the last time.

Eleven

Juan's records were being called *misplaced*. *Mislaid*. *Misdirected*. Everything but *lost*.

Lexi listened impatiently to the young resident make his excuses and ask them to stay put while he went to collect the backup files they had on every patient. It took great control not to butt in, not to chew him out for the error. She was pissed off. Medical files don't grow legs and walk away. Someone was responsible for this. They had to backtrack and they'd find them. She kept reminding herself that she was here as a mother and not as a physician working in this hospital. That only made her seethe more. She understood the system. There was no excuse for this carelessness.

The resident had introduced himself as Dr. Barlow.

She figured he couldn't be even thirty years old. It had become the standard practice for the youngest and least experienced to work the graveyard shift in these big hospitals.

Lexi focused on her surroundings. The meeting room where they were asked to wait was only eight by ten, and a round table and four chairs swallowed up most of the space. Three blown-up sepia prints showing the hospital around 1900 were on three of the walls. She glanced over at the Secret Service agents. Two totally different men.

Lexi had immediately liked Hank Gardner's disposition a lot better than Atwood's. There was nothing confrontational about the psychologist, no accusing mannerisms, no superiority complex that seemed to go part and parcel with so many of the people she was meeting lately.

Their looks were far different, too. Frankly, she preferred Gardner there, as well. Hank had a wiry build and was of medium height. His hair was thinning and his wire-rimmed glasses added a scholarly look to his expression. He was soft-spoken. The man appeared to be a gentleman. Completely unthreatening. Unlike Agent Atwood.

Lexi took a chair closest to the door and placed the milk shake she'd been forced to buy on the table in front of her. Even the drink had been a point of contention between them, with Atwood insisting on a meal and her only wanting something that was fast and would get her to the doctor's office quickly. A soda or a bottle of water wouldn't do. No, she had to at least buy a milk shake. Lexi had been tempted to complain that she was lactose intolerant. The argument would have taken energy that she didn't have.

"Well, this explains why they didn't send me any of Juan's medical files," Gardner said, sitting down on a chair next to Lexi.

"The records can't really be *missing*," she said to him. "The hospital's procedures won't allow it. There is too much administrative concern about malpractice to allow something like that to happen."

"One would think so, especially considering the attention this case has been and will be getting. So many different doctors on different shifts have been looking after him. It's likely that one of them still has the files."

She felt like a sponge, absorbing every ounce of information she could about Juan.

"I did get a brief report from one of the doctors about my son's condition last night," Lexi told him.

Gardner turned more fully toward her. She noticed that even Agent Atwood was paying attention.

"Would you mind sharing what you were told?" Gardner asked.

These two had allowed her to come down here and be part of this question-and-answer session with the doctor, so she didn't mind telling them what she knew.

"As you know, the eventual outcome for a patient in a coma is closely associated to the quality of the response during the first twenty-four hours after a suspected injury. I was told that, using the Glasgow Coma

Scale—which scores from three to fifteen, with three being the lowest possible score for a person in a coma and fifteen being a normal-appearing person—Juan scored nine."

"What does that mean?" Atwood asked, crossing his arms and leaning against the far wall.

Lexi paused for a couple of seconds, testing to see if Agent Gardner would answer the question. He didn't, so she continued.

"In patients with a Glasgow Coma Scale of eight to ten, twenty-seven percent will die or remain in a coma, while sixty-eight percent will have a moderate disability and/or good recovery."

She'd been doing more research about this on Allan's laptop last night. She'd hoped for better statistics. She wanted a full recovery. As a physician, though, Lexi knew that the probability was that she would never have Juan back to a hundred percent, the way he'd been. Putting aside the legal battles ahead of them and thinking only of Juan's health, Lexi knew their lives were forever changed.

She was choking up with emotion again.

"None of this is exact science," Gardner put in. "Each case is different. Each patient works to his or her own clock. The medical field tends to be very conservative."

Lexi needed to comment. She cleared her voice and kept the tears at bay. "They took Juan for more tests this morning. I was allowed to accompany him. He responded to environmental stimuli. He opened his eyes and spoke during the MRI test. I believe that's great news for his prognosis, despite the fact that he slid back into a coma."

Neither agent said anything. Neither of them reminded her that she wasn't a neurologist, or that she was building her hopes up for nothing. Or that even if her son fully recovered, he could be spending the rest of his life in jail. They didn't have to; she knew they had to be thinking it.

"Maybe the records are lying around in radiology," Atwood suggested.

Lexi appreciated the quick change of topic.

"If they had them, they'd be done by now, wouldn't they?" he persisted.

"Interpreting the output of a two-hour MRI session takes some time," Hank Gardner said. "It isn't a small undertaking."

"Just because you're a Ph.D., Agent Gardner," Atwood said gruffly, "doesn't mean you have to defend them for screwing up."

Lexi glanced at him. The agent was actually joking. She didn't know he had it in him. The man was intense and restless. Even in this small room, with little space to do anything but sit down, he'd chosen to stand, a brooding and darkly powerful presence against the far wall.

"For your information," Gardner replied, taking the bait, "during a two-hour MRI, approximately half a gigabyte of data is produced—the rough equivalent of four boxes of 3.5-inch computer disks."

"Why so much data?" Atwood asked, back to business.

"Because the actual changes in blood flow that are measured do not represent huge swings. They typically represent around a two-to-four percent change. Of course, there're other imaging technologies that can be used in conjunction to an MRI to provide complementary perspectives, improving diagnosis and understanding." Hank turned to Lexi. "Do you know what other kind of diagnostic tests were done on your son?"

"From the little that I've been told and what I've pieced together myself, there were no neurologic tests done on him when they first brought him to the hospital Monday afternoon."

"And why was that?" Atwood asked shortly. "They had to treat him the same as any other patient."

Lexi glanced at the agent. She had a suspicion that his comment was in her support. She reminded herself that if it weren't for him, she'd be still sitting upstairs in the hallway, waiting for one detective or other to show some mercy and get some doctor to talk to her. Also, he hadn't had to care about whether she ate something or not. But he did. He was gruff, but right beneath the surface, there seemed to be a touch of compassion that he worked hard at hiding.

"There was no apparent head injury," she told him. "His vitals were good."

"No neuropsychiatric tests at all?" Hank asked.

She shrugged. "I don't think so, but I might be wrong. I wasn't allowed to be with him that afternoon. He was unconscious, and his condition didn't change until the brief seconds this morning," Lexi said. "The doctor I spoke to last night told me that, so far, they were focusing on the structure of his brain. They'd planned an MRI and CAT scan for yesterday, but they were only able to get him in for the CAT scan."

"And you didn't see any of those results?" Hank asked.

Lexi shook her head again. "I have to beg to get information out of anyone about my own son."

When she looked up at Atwood, his eyes darted away, but she'd seen the sympathetic look that passed across his face. It surprised her. His expression had hardened again a moment later when he looked back across the table.

"I thought they were looking for his MRI records," he said, staring at his partner.

"As far as I know, all of Juan's records are missing," Hank answered. "Including today's MRI, too."

"We should just have them redo the tests now," Atwood said impatiently.

"They can redo the MRI," Lexi explained, "but not the CAT scan. The radioactivity involved with the CAT scan precludes it from being done again right away."

Atwood moved restlessly to the open door. Standing with his back against the jamb, he glanced down the corridor before looking back at them. He was clearly not a man built for waiting patiently.

"As far as the results, what's the difference between the two tests?" he asked.

"The MRI and CAT scan slice the brain radiographically into slabs," Hank explained. "The MRI does this with magnetic fields—the CAT scan uses X-rays. The MRI provides more detail than the CAT scan."

"The brain damage seen on an MRI—lesions as small as one to two millimeters in size—may escape detection in a CAT scan," Lexi added.

"But the CAT scan is superior to the MRI in detecting fresh blood in and around the brain," Hank Gardner put in, "while the MRI is better at detecting the remnants of old hemorrhaged blood."

This last bit of information reminded Lexi of one thing that had been nagging at her. There were many case reports of mental illness, including obsessive-compulsive disorder, depression, mania and hallucinations, that followed head injuries long after the actual incident. The first two and a half years of Juan's life were a mystery to her. She knew she was grasping at straws, but there was no saying that he hadn't had a serious injury that early in his life.

Their conversation abruptly ended when Atwood pulled his ringing cell phone out of his pocket. He looked at the display and moved out into the corridor to answer it, pulling the door closed behind him.

"May I ask you a question as a psychologist and not as a government agent?"

"So long as it doesn't create a conflict," Hank answered. "I'm part of the investigating team here."

Lexi nodded. "My question has to do with Juan and…and what he did on Monday. He is the perfect young man in every imaginable way. And I'm not only saying that because I'm his mother. There are many who will attest to that. People at the high school, people in the community, anyone whom he's had any interaction with over the past—"

"I know, Dr. Bradley," Hank interrupted her. "I've already heard many positive things about your son."

There was a gleam of hope. Lexi wanted to ask from whom—she needed to hear someone else praise Juan— but she focused on what she wanted to know. "Have you ever seen a teenager this flawless snap like this?"

He opened his mouth to say something, but then paused. She watched him tap his pen a couple of times on the table. The dark eyes behind the glasses turned on her.

"Do you watch the news much, Dr. Bradley?"

"Not regularly. I don't really have time and, to be honest, it's too depressing to listen to what's going on in the world. I don't really watch *any* TV."

"Do you read the newspapers?"

"Yes," she said with hesitation. "Mostly, I keep up with the local news and the medical news. Professional journals are my leisure reading. What are you trying to say?"

"Have you heard anything about the high school shootings that have been happening across the country over this past month?"

A shudder ran through her. She knew where he was going. She just couldn't think of her Juan in the same way as those others. Finally, she nodded.

"Of course. I...I've heard about them through my coworkers and the radio and headlines on the

Internet." She rubbed her neck wearily. "But they were out there, and Juan and I had our own safe, busy life. Those shootings have always seemed distant, not real, somehow. They were nothing that could ever happen in this little corner of Connecticut where we live."

"They were nothing that your son would do."

Lexi felt a knot form in her throat again. She didn't trust her voice, so instead she shook her head.

"To answer your question, Dr. Bradley, the families of all the assailants in the school shootings this past month claim the same thing. They raised perfect children. And then, one day, the teenagers just snapped."

She felt drained, as if something that had been held up in front of her…a warning…but she hadn't seen it. Perhaps she'd ignored it.

No, she told herself. *There was nothing. Juan is not a killer. He's not.*

The door opened and Atwood poked his head in and motioned to his partner. "I need to speak with you."

She was too wrapped up in what she'd just heard to try to consider what Atwood's urgent summons could be about.

Left alone in the room, Lexi stared at the beige walls. Gardner's words continued to play in her head. She wished she knew more about the school violence that had ripped across the country recently. She wasn't sure if his mention of other parents raising perfect children, too, had been said sarcastically or in earnest. Lexi was a proud and protective mother, but there were others who agreed that Juan was one in a million. He was an exceptional human being. She'd known that from the moment she'd first laid eyes on the toddler. He'd been her salvation. Their relationship hadn't only been that of a mother and child. There was a connection that was impossible to explain to anyone who didn't know how empty she'd felt before Juan had come into her life.

Lexi let out a shaky breath and looked around the room. She needed to find out about these other teenagers, the ones she was certain wouldn't match up to her son. There wasn't a single newspaper or magazine in sight. She wished she'd taken her brother Allan up on his offer and held on to his laptop. Ignorance was paralyzing. Lexi felt she was at a point of emotional overload once again.

She reached inside her bag for the cell phone. Allan had stopped at her house during his overnight stay and brought in the mail. Lexi had called in to the post office this morning and put a stop on the delivery of all new mail. Allan had also checked her phone messages. He'd warned her that most of the calls were from reporters who wanted an interview. He'd deleted them. There was nothing she could do about having her address and phone number listed in the phone book right now. Allan had also mentioned that there'd been a number of sympathy calls from her friends and one from a doctor she worked with.

Lexi dialed her home number to replay the messages. There were fifteen new ones on top of what Allan had warned her about. She listened to the older messages first. There was one from a neighbor down the street. There was also a lengthy one from Emily Doyle, the mother of Conor, a very good friend of Juan's. The young woman offered her help in whatever way Lexi needed. She had to wipe away a tear. She'd doubted anyone in Wickfield would ever want to be civil with her again, never mind still treat her like a friend. The call from the other physician was also supportive.

Whatever confidence she'd gained after these messages, she started losing it fast while listening to the new ones left since this morning. Reporter. Delete. Reporter. Delete. TV station. Delete. A radio station in New Haven. Delete. The next one was breaking up, a bad connection. She listened to the short message, not too clear about what exactly she'd heard. Whoever it was seemed to be whispering on the other end. The next one was from a producer at CNN. She deleted that one and went back to the one before.

It was a man's voice, and there were a lot of pauses and static. She went back to the beginning of the message.

Your son...safe...

Lexi stood up. Any number of people could leave her crank calls, harass her for what had happened. Still, none had. She moved to the door, turning up the volume before listening to the message again.

"Your son is not safe. Watch him."

She leaned against the door, numb for a couple of seconds. Was this a threat? Was someone threatening Juan? Maybe one of the family members or friends of those children who'd been shot?

All of a sudden, the room was too small. She couldn't breathe. Lexi didn't bother to listen to the rest of the messages. She opened the door. The hallway was deserted. She saw no sign of the two agents or the night-shift doctor. Worry had planted a seed deep in her stomach and she could feel it driving its roots deep into her.

She had to see Juan.

Lexi darted for the elevators, already knowing that the uniformed officers at the door wouldn't let her see Juan. But she had to go, anyway. She had to try.

Visiting hours were long over. The elevator was empty when it stopped on her floor. She stepped in, pressing the buttons again and again, impatient to get there.

The elevator crawled up to his floor and the doors finally opened. Lexi ran out and turned down the corridor toward Juan's hospital room. The same two uniformed officers were still there. Both of them visibly stiffened as she approached them.

"I'd like to see my son," Lexi said in what she hoped was at least one level below hysterical.

"I'm sorry, but we can't allow that. You need either a detective or—"

"Please," she interrupted. "If you want, I'll stand here and *you* go see my son. I just need someone to tell me that he's okay. That nothing has changed."

The second officer seemed to feel sorry for her. "Look, Dr. Bradley, one of the nurses just checked on him a couple of minutes ago. He's fine."

"Just open the door and let me at least see him from

right here," she pleaded frantically. Something was wrong. Her gut told her so. "I'll just look right from where I'm standing."

"We're expecting some of the investigating officers back here within an hour," the first policeman explained, trying to stay civil. "You can ask them."

"An hour is too late," she snapped.

Lexi held the cell phone out to them. Her body was shaking.

"I just listened to this message. Someone is saying that Juan isn't safe. I...I only need to know that it's a lie...that someone is trying to rattle me. *Please.*" She raised both hands up and away from her body. "Search me. I'm not armed. I'm *just* a mother who thinks her son's life is in danger," she said hurriedly, pleadingly. "I'm certain neither of you two would stand there and do nothing if you thought the life of someone you loved was in danger."

The two exchanged a look, obviously undecided about what she was asking of them.

The agreeable officer finally nodded with a frown. "Look, Dr. Bradley, just don't try anything that will make us have to haul you out of here."

"I swear to you, I won't."

"You stand right where you are," he ordered.

She nodded, planting her feet, hoping that she'd be strong enough to keep her promise.

One stood next to her as the other opened the door. She edged closer. The overhead light was off. The shades were drawn closed. A bedside lamp cast a soft glow across the bed. Tears rushed into her eyes as she saw Juan lying on the hospital bed. He looked peaceful, like he was sleeping. There were no flowers, no gifts, no cards. Nothing to soften the blow of being in a strange place when he woke up. Lexi already knew that she couldn't be objective when it came to her son. She was looking in there as a mother, not as a physician.

"Are you satisfied now, Dr. Bradley?" the officer next to her asked.

How could she be satisfied? That was her son, her baby lying in that bed, and she couldn't even go to him, hold him. She couldn't protect him.

Lexi forced her gaze to go to the IV and the monitoring equipment connected to Juan. From what she could see, no one else was in the room. The bathroom door was open, but there was no other way for anyone to get in. She nodded reluctantly.

The door closed. She whispered a thank-you under her breath and turned away from them before her tears began to run. She was cold. She hurt inside. Her feet felt like bags of sand. She should have expected crank calls. A lot of them. This is the way things were going to be. She was now the outsider. People would try to hurt her. She'd have to pay the price for what had happened. She had no control over the tears that fell freely now. She hated this weakness, the falling apart, but she couldn't help it. She reached for her bag to get a tissue and realized that she'd left it in the conference room downstairs.

She reached the nurses' station just as someone

came out of the floor-duty office. As Lexi took a tissue from a box on the counter, she recognized Linda. She wiped away at the tears. The woman's bright face was like sunshine in a gloomy day.

"So, you're walking around. That must mean you ate something."

Lexi wasn't going to correct her.

The nurse was carrying a tray of medication. With her free hand, Linda pulled a couple of more tissues out of the box and handed them to Lexi. "I saw you go downstairs with one of those agents. Did you talk to the doctor?"

Lexi shook her head. "Not yet. They're looking for Juan's records. They appear to have been misplaced. I'm going back down there now."

"They can't be really lost. But remember, don't let the rest of them see those tears. You'll do a lot better for yourself and your son by staying strong."

Lexi knew she was right.

Linda looked down the hall in the direction of the uniformed officers. "By the time you come back from talking to the doctor, I'll have something for you, too."

"What?"

"I'm checking on Juan now and giving him his medication. By the time you get back, I'll be able to tell you his blood pressure and pulse rate and all the other good stuff that you're dying to know."

She smiled, appreciating the other woman's warmth. Linda hadn't moved away two steps, though, before something crossed Lexi's mind.

"Those police officers just told me that a nurse had checked on Juan a few minutes ago."

Linda turned around, frowning. "Are you sure about that?"

"That's what they told me."

Linda walked back to the nurses' station and looked at the top sheet on a clipboard.

She shook her head. "No, Doc. No one from this station has been to his room in at least an hour. Wait a sec." She poked her head into the duty office and asked someone the same question. She came back, shaking her head.

The feeling of nausea in Lexi's stomach was back. This time it was laced with panic.

"Let's ask them again," the nurse said, picking up her medication tray again and heading toward Juan's room.

Lexi moved ahead of the nurse, reaching them first.

The two officers looked warier than the last time, seeing Lexi coming back. At Linda's question, though, they told her that a nurse had visited Juan's room within the past twenty minutes.

"Was she one of the four that work at my station?" Linda asked, motioning to the nurses' alcove.

"We don't know everyone that works there," one of the officers responded. "She was wearing a badge and carrying a tray of medication like the one in your hand."

The nurse asked what the woman looked like, but Lexi's mind was already on the message she'd listened to on her cell phone. Juan wasn't safe. Would someone go as far as to disguise herself to hurt him? It didn't make sense, but still...

Both officers were trying to describe the nurse at the same time. Lexi stepped past them and opened Juan's door.

"Dr. Bradley, you can't be going in there," one of them called after her.

"Leave her be and stop being so ridiculous," Linda scolded them. "She's a mother, for heaven's sake, and a doctor to boot. She's not going to hurt her own child."

Lexi walked quickly to Juan's bedside. She looked at his face, listened to his breathing. Something wasn't right. He was cold to the touch, but he was sweating. She took his pulse. It seemed normal. She stared at the monitors and fought the feeling of panic growing in her. A phony nurse wouldn't come inside for no reason. Lexi remembered what one of the officers had said. The woman had been carrying a medicine tray. She looked at Juan again, touched his hand. Her fingers went over the bandages where the IV continued to drip into his veins. The IV.

She whirled around, searching for Linda. She was standing at the door, partially blocking the entrance to the room, talking to the uniformed officers. She was clearly buying Lexi some time with her son.

"Linda, I need you here."

The nurse turned around. "Just a minute."

"A minute could be too late," Lexi said aloud. They could have injected any number of substances into him...or into the IV bag. She ripped the tape off the back of her son's hand. "We need to take this out."

"Now, just a minute…" Linda said, coming in.

"Someone is trying to hurt my son. I got a warning on a phone message. I'm removing his IV."

"I don't think you should mess around with the medications he's under. Let me call the doctor on staff first."

"It might already be too late," Lexi said as she disconnected the IV tube.

Twelve

Wednesday, January 16
Reno, Nevada

He wasn't overreacting. He'd been right. It wasn't going away.

Each new incident was more of a bloodbath than the last one. There were four left. But how many would die in the hands of those four? Forty? Four hundred?

The guilt was killing him. He couldn't sit idly while another massacre happened. It had to be stopped.

Sitting on the edge of the worn upholstered chair, Mitch Harvey impatiently changed the TV channel at the commercial break. All the other stations, the half dozen of them, had no interest in the headline news. There was no other mention of what had taken place in Florida on any other channel.

He ran through them again.

There was an old movie on one station. A basketball game on another one. Some stupid stand-up comedy show on the next. Mitch moved up the channels. There was porn on one of the free pay-per-view channels. A channel showing how to play casino games. Next, a sincere-looking guy in a blue gown preaching a hellfire sermon.

He continued to switch the remote up and down until he was back to the same station he'd been on before. It was still showing commercials.

He'd been two miles down the road at one of those UPS drop boxes when the news came through over the radio about the shooting, the details sketchy. Just then, Mitch had seen the billboard for the motel. Free cable and Internet. Both were virtually no use to him. The Internet consisted of a network plug in a desk lamp that didn't work, and the cable channels were shit. Fortunately, the clerk who'd checked him in let Mitch use the computer at the office to send an e-mail.

The news station came back on, and once again Mitch stared at the images of the ambulances at the front entrance of the school. The number of injured and fatalities changed each minute. Two commercials ago, they were talking fifteen. Now the newscaster was saying twenty-one. None of it was confirmed. They knew that the assailant was dead. But as far as the rest of the numbers, no one really knew. The high school wasn't completely evacuated yet. They didn't know if there were bodies in other parts of the school. The gunman might have shot someone else on his way to the gymnasium. Another picture of Mike Forbes, the assailant, flashed across the screen. This one was of the entire basketball team, with Mike's face circled and enlarged on the television screen. A teenage boy's innocent smile.

The anchorman mentioned the name of a school psychologist, supposedly a well-known national expert who was going to come on air after the next commercial break. The next moment, the pictures of the teenagers involved in the latest wave of violence paraded across the screen. Seven. Seven of them involved in this wave of deadly violence since December 11.

Mitch knew all of them.

"Why don't you see the connections?" he asked the empty room.

A picture of Juan Bradley flashed across the screen next. Mitch muted the sound when they started rehashing the same information as before about Juan. They had nothing new on him. He was the only survivor. So far.

Wearily, Mitch ran a hand over his face. He hadn't shaved all week. He looked at the eleven boxes of files that he'd dragged out of the storage space in the outskirts of Reno. They weren't all of it. There was another storage space, too. But he hadn't been able to get to it. There was enough here to make a difference, anyway.

All the files were supposed to have been destroyed. He hadn't done it. Even then, so many years ago, he'd known someday he might need them again. He knew then that they couldn't close the door on everything they'd done and pretend that nothing was different about these kids.

The dust of a dozen years still covered each of them. The mysteries of so many deaths had answers in the pages of those files.

Mitch couldn't leave any of them in the trunk of the rental car, but he'd separated five of those boxes from the others. They contained the information about the teenagers who were still alive, along with the files of others that it was too late for. The only open box contained Juan Bradley's file. His folders lay spread out on the bed.

He'd called Dr. Bradley once already. He'd tried to reach her other ways, too. He'd do it again. She was his contact. She'd know what to do with everything he gave her. She had nothing to lose and everything to gain by helping him. Mitch had no doubt that they would try to eliminate the boy. Curtis would not allow anyone to malfunction and survive. That wasn't part of the plan.

Back in the early 1990s, their project had been well funded. Mitch had met very few of their investors, though. Curtis was the money man, the one who made the deals and made sure their finances met their expenses. Everyone working on this project knew, though, that there were some heavy hitters behind the scenes, people with a great deal invested. There were also political careers on the line.

That was the reason Mitch couldn't trust anyone now. He could not be sure who was a friend or who would empty a gun into his head. That distrust extended to his old partner in New York. Curtis Wells was smooth, but Mitch had heard the lies in his voice.

Dr. Bradley was different, though. She had plenty at stake, and she could do what needed to be done. Hopefully, she could stop what had happened to her son from happening to the others.

The sound of a car traveling along the gravel parking lot in front of the motel rooms made Mitch immediately reach over and turn off the light. He shut off the TV, too. He knew he was doing the right thing. He was ready for it. He'd made up his mind. Better late than never. But he was scared, too.

The car seemed to be moving very slowly. The curtains were drawn, but not completely. Mitch moved to the door and tested the chain. One of the bolts holding the latch was loose. He figured someone putting a shoulder to it could easily break open the lock.

Standing next to the door, he pulled the curtain aside a fraction of an inch and looked outside. A light hanging on the wall at the end of the row of rooms flickered every couple of seconds, shedding meager light on the two cars that were parked in the spaces on this row. Everything else around them was immersed in the darkness. Mitch had asked for a room in the back. He didn't want anyone getting curious over him dragging the boxes out of his car. Looking out at the pitch-black beyond the arc of the light, he wasn't sure that had been such a good idea.

Mitch moved to the other end of the window and peeked out.

The car that had driven by was now stopped at the end of the row. He could just see one of the brake lights from this angle. The car had not parked. The engine was running. Whoever they were, they were just sitting in the middle of the lane. No headlights, from what Mitch could see.

He tried to keep himself calm, but panic set in the minute the driver put the car in Reverse. The car slowly backed up until it reached Mitch's motel room door. He closed the curtain to just a slit, but through it he could see the driver had blocked in the rental car.

They'd found him. Mitch didn't know how. He hadn't told anyone about coming to Nevada, about this motel that he'd checked into only this afternoon. He'd even kept his own family in the dark about all of this.

He could hear his own uneven breaths becoming audible. This was something new. Hyperventilating when he was nervous. Even an asthma attack once about a month ago. He hadn't brought along the inhaler on this trip. Elsa said it was all in his mind. Doctors and a number of tests had told him that there was nothing wrong with his lungs.

You're overreacting, Mitch told himself, taking slow, deep breaths and counting backward.

Deep down, he knew he wasn't overreacting at all.

The car was a dark sedan, and it wasn't moving. Mitch could hear the engine still running. He couldn't see who was inside or what they were doing.

A pickup truck came around the corner, music blasting through the open windows, the sound of the occupants' laughter ringing through the night. Rather than going around the other car, the driver of the pickup slammed on the brakes behind the other car and blasted the horn. From the passenger side, a girl poked her head out, drunk and giggling and yelling at the car in front to get a move on.

The sedan didn't move.

In the midst of the little showdown, Mitch looked behind him. There were no other doors. The window in the bathroom was too small to escape through. He had nowhere else to go.

The truck blasted its horn again. Mitch peered through the opening and saw the sedan move some twenty feet ahead and pull to the side. The pickup backed up and made a sharp turn, parking alongside Mitch's rental car.

A beer can was tossed out onto the ground from the driver's side. The passengers weren't ready to get out. Mitch looked at the other car. No one had stepped out yet. They were waiting.

For once in his life, luck was on Mitch's side. A minute later, another car filled with noisy young people arrived. These people obviously knew the ones in the pickup, and they pulled in next to it. As four young men and women got out, the sedan moved forward another twenty feet.

All the newcomers were unsteady on their feet. Something was said between the driver of the truck and the rest and they all turned to look at the dark sedan, windows closed, engine still running.

One of the four partiers shouted a profanity-laced challenge. The girls were laughing, and the challenger started stiff-legged across the lot.

As Mitch waited, the sedan drove off before the partier reached the car. Drunken cheers greeted the victor as he swaggered back to the arms of his date.

Mitch knew that didn't mean that they weren't coming back. He looked around the room, trying to think clearly. He had to get out of here now, before they came back for him. There was no way he could take everything with him. He rushed to the bed and picked up an armful of files. Quickly, he pulled the four others that still might be stopped. He could only take the ones that had a chance.

The drunken partiers were still in the lot. They looked at Mitch oddly when he ran to his car and climbed behind the wheel.

Thirteen

Juan Bradley's hospital door was open, but a drawn curtain hid everything that was going on inside.

"Who's in there now?" Bryan asked one of the two uniforms.

"The doctor and two nurses from that station." One of the officers motioned to the counter down the hall.

"Where's Dr. Bradley?"

"In that room," the second man replied, pointing to a closed door directly across the hall. "She seems to have lost control. A little wound up, I'd say. Nearly hysterical. Not at all the way she's been the past couple of days. Maybe it's the exhaustion of being here for so long. I don't know if it's safe to leave her there all alone."

There'd been another shooting, this one in Orlando,

Florida. Eight wounded and five fatalities. The shooter was one of the dead. The media was doubling the numbers. Another star student. Varsity basketball player. Good home life, from first reports. A totally unlikely suspect. Hank and Bryan had been on a conference call with Geary about the incident when Lexi Bradley had come back up here. As a result, he hadn't learned what was going on up here until the fur was flying.

"She kept saying something about a phone call. She was really spooked. Something about someone leaving a message for her that her son wasn't safe."

"Why don't you go and check on her while I see what I can find out from the doctor attending the boy," Hank suggested.

Bryan put a hand on his partner's arm. "You'd better come and give her an update as soon as you know something."

Hank nodded. They both understood what she was going through.

Seven shootings and Juan Bradley was the only assailant who'd survived. And now his mother thought her son's life was in danger. Everything was possible.

Bryan knocked and started to go in. She materialized before him, blocking his way. She looked past him toward her son's door. Her expression showed her agitation.

"Agent Atwood," she said quickly. "Did they find anything? Is Juan okay?"

"The doctor and nurses are looking after him now. No one has mentioned any problem with him yet."

Lexi's gaze never wavered from the open door across

the hall. A nurse appeared, wheeling out some equipment. The nurse appeared calm. She even said something to the officers and they chuckled.

"Do you know if they've done a blood-glucose test or any liver-function tests? Whatever was given to him might be reversible if they act fast enough."

She took a step in that direction as if she were going to find the answers to the questions herself.

Bryan moved into her path and blocked her. "Let them do their jobs."

"No. I can't wait for them to do their jobs. They're not doing shit for my son," she exploded. "They stop me, but they let a perfect stranger in his room. If I hadn't gone in there, Juan could be dead. And I don't know how he's doing now. No one has the decency to come and tell me anything. For God's sake, I'm his mother."

"He's stable," a small voice said from behind Bryan.

He looked over his shoulder. The nurse who had just left Juan's room was standing in the hallway. She was speaking to Lexi.

"The doctor is running a number of tests, but your son is doing fine."

Lexi sagged against the door. The lines of worry were still pronounced in her face, but the little bit of information had helped.

"You really believe someone tampered with his IV medication?" Bryan asked when the nurse moved off toward her station.

Her blue eyes were red-rimmed when they looked up at him. "It wasn't my imagination. I didn't make the whole thing up so I could rush in there and get a glimpse of him."

"You did more than that. You disconnected his medication."

"I'm a doctor," she said sharply, temper raising color in her cheeks again. "What I did for Juan I would have done for any other patient. There were witnesses—those police officers—who told me someone, most likely someone unconnected with the hospital, was in Juan's room. I didn't disconnect a life-support system… only an IV."

Bryan was still standing in the doorway. He looked down at her hands curled around the edge of the open door.

"No, you didn't disconnect a life-support system," he said calmly. She was falling apart without his help. He didn't need to push her over the edge. "May I come in?"

Lexi paused. Her blue eyes studied him for a couple of seconds before she turned and walked back into the middle of the room.

Bryan stepped in and closed the door behind him. He watched her hands rub her arms. Her gaze was restless. She started pacing a six-foot stretch of tiles.

"Don't try to lecture me on what I should and shouldn't do," she started. "As a mother and a medical professional, I had reason enough to disconnect the IV."

"I have no intention of lecturing you. You know your business. I know mine."

"Okay, then." She rubbed her neck, let out a frustrated breath. She was all frayed nerves. "The nurse…

or whatever she was…put something in his system. I know whatever tests they run will confirm it. I know my own kid."

He was sure she did. Bryan had read enough about her to understand that Lexi Bradley was pretty grounded and sensible in her everyday life. She was also extremely intelligent and very cautious of public displays. And on top of it all, she had an excellent reputation as a doctor.

"What was this phone call that you mentioned to the officers? Or was it a message?"

She ceased her pacing. "It was a message left at my home answering machine. Would you like to listen to it?"

"Of course."

She pulled her cell phone from her pants pocket, punched in some numbers and put her ear to the phone. Bryan noticed that her hand was trembling. He figured it was either from fatigue or raw nerves.

"Here it is," she said. "Press 1 to repeat the message. The first time around I didn't really get it. I had to listen to it a couple of times."

Bryan listened to the message. She was right. The first time around all he could hear were a few words here and there. Twice more through, though, and he had a good handle on what the caller was saying. But this didn't mean the caller wasn't just some crank.

"And you said this was left on your home number?" he asked after listening to the message another time.

She nodded.

"If you want us to, I can get the number the person called from."

"Yes, I want you to pursue this if it will help keep Juan safe. You said you know your business. Do whatever else that needs to be done."

Bryan used his own cell phone and dialed the number in Washington. It took only a few moments to start the ball on tracing the incoming calls that had been made to Lexi's home number.

"This is a man's voice," she said as he hung up. "Both of those officers out there told me that a woman presented herself as a nurse, but who doesn't appear to have any connection with the nursing staff on this floor, was in Juan's room. That's two people. How do we know that there aren't more? I don't know if Juan is safe here at this hospital."

"We're still not sure if anything *was* done to your son or if the phone call and that nurse are connected. He might be just fine and there could be a perfectly reasonable explanation for that nurse's visit."

She sank onto the edge of a chair. "As much as my instincts tell me you're wrong, I really hope you're right. I just want my son to be safe."

He believed her. And he hoped he was right about the boy being okay. The sooner Juan Bradley was awake and could talk to them, the sooner Bryan hoped they might understand how these shootings were connected. That is, if they *were* connected.

Lexi ran a tissue under each eye. He could see she was trying to gather her strength, control her emotions. Bryan watched her for a couple of moments in silence until she finally looked up.

"I never had a chance to talk to the doctor downstairs. Did you?" she asked.

"No."

"Will you please let me know if you find something?" she asked in a much calmer tone. "You're the only one who seems to have an understanding of what I'm going through."

He felt the muscles in his face grow taut. What he understood was his business, and he didn't like having her notice it. "I don't know why you say that. We all want to understand what is happening. There are a lot of unanswered questions about these shootings."

"It's not that." She shrugged. "I don't know, but there's something right beneath the surface with you, Agent Atwood. There's a look that I can't describe. And you're here. Talking to me. You don't have to be. You could have sent one of your people to question the crazy mother. But you didn't."

Her eyes looked like crystals when they filled with tears. She was paler now than before. He searched for the right words to deny her words. He didn't need feelings causing conflict in investigating this case.

She stabbed at a tear on her cheek and waved both hands in the air. "Please don't change, Agent Atwood. I need someone who will deal with me the way I deal with them. Honesty both ways. That's all I'm asking. And I promise not to create a problem...with you doing your job."

Again she knew what he was thinking.

She pushed to her feet. "Unless you have other questions for me right now, I'd like to go downstairs and get my bag. I think I left it in the conference room where we were waiting."

Bryan nodded, realizing he was still holding on to her cell phone. He handed it to her.

"They'll find who made the call," he said.

She went ahead of him out of the room. In the hallway she paused, looking at the Juan's door. It was closed. With the exception of the same two officers, no one else was in sight. She looked over her shoulder at him.

"I'll need to know what they found out."

"Why don't you go downstairs and get your stuff? Agent Gardner was trying to get some answers. I'll make sure he talks to you when you get back."

"Thank you, Agent Atwood," she whispered under her breath. "You're a good man."

Bryan watched her walk to the elevator.

"Shit," he murmured under his breath. Lexi Bradley had the wrong effect on him. He found her attractive. She made him care. He rubbed his neck. That meant vulnerability. He had to stop. When the elevator door closed behind her, he turned to the two policemen on duty. "Are the doctor and nurses still in there?"

"Only one of the nurses is left. The doctor was with Agent Gardner before he left the floor."

"And where's Gardner?" Bryan asked.

"He's in that room." One of them motioned to two doors down the hall. "He asked if you could stop to talk to him."

Bryan was glad Hank had a chance to talk to the

doctor. He wondered if they'd recovered Juan's missing files. Inside the room, he found his partner on the phone. The psychologist's tone was outwardly calm, but Bryan knew him well enough to know that Hank was definitely pissed off.

"I *will* explain it to Agent Atwood, but I believe he's going to share my sentiments. I *don't* understand your reasoning." Hank motioned to Bryan to close the door.

Whatever was said on the other end only received a noncommittal grunt from Gardner in response. "I'm sure Atwood will contact you himself."

Bryan's curiosity was definitely piqued.

"What was that about?" he asked as soon as the other man ended the call.

"The nurse visiting Juan's hospital room has vanished," Hank explained. "No one knows who she was. So far, no one in any department is taking responsibility for sending her up here."

"What does hospital security say?"

"They're bringing someone in to set it up for the cops in the hall to look at personnel photos. Nothing beyond that. But I don't expect them to find her on the list of employees."

"Why?"

"Because it appears that she might have done something to Juan, possibly injected some toxin into the IV bag."

Lexi's instincts had been right. "What do you mean, *something*?"

"I mean, the mother knew what she was doing. So

far, the tests they've run haven't shown what it was that phony nurse gave him, but the kid is showing symptoms of foul play."

"What's going on with him?" Bryan asked.

"Hypoglycemia, rapid heart rate, sweating. My guess is that if he were conscious, there'd be other symptoms…like headache, fainting, slurred speech. Symptoms of seriously low sugar."

"Low sugar? You mean, as in diabetic stuff?"

"So you *were* listening during biology class."

Bryan wasn't feeling amused. "Did Juan have any record of diabetes or any problems like this before?"

Hank shook his head. "His blood test from this morning was fine. What they just took out of him shows a major drop in blood sugar. We can't prove it yet, but the doctor's guess is that he might have been injected with a couple hundred units of Humulin N, a long-acting variety of insulin. They're trying to stabilize the blood sugar right now, but Juan would have been dead by the morning if his mother hadn't rushed in there. The IV bag is in the lab right now. We'll know pretty quick if it was juiced up with insulin."

This wasn't coincidental stuff, nor was it a simple attempt at revenge. An average person wouldn't go this far for retaliation.

Bryan wondered if the information the nurse had given Lexi in the hall had been a lie to calm her down. "How is Juan doing now?"

"He didn't slide into respiratory arrest. So that's good. I told you that they're working on the blood sugar. There's a nurse staying with him, monitoring that. The doctor needed to make two more patient visits, but he should be back to check on him in a few minutes. With any luck, the kid shouldn't be any worse than he was."

"Have the uniformed officers at the door been briefed about who to let in that room? This might not be a one-time thing."

"They've been given specific orders. And I've asked the FBI and the local police force to immediately increase the security in the hospital."

The numbers ran through Bryan's head again. Seven shootings and Juan Bradley was the only survivor. What happened if all of the violence *was* connected? If these shootings were somehow being orchestrated, then someone might want Juan dead. Especially if they were planning more killings. But what wackos would be doing this? He remembered the phone call on Lexi's answering machine.

"Someone did leave a warning message on Dr. Bradley's home number. I listened to it myself."

"So?"

"Our people are putting a trace on it," Bryan said. "What was going on with the phone call when I came in?"

Hank sat down on the edge of the hospital bed. "I think you'll want to sit down for this."

"What?"

"I was on the phone with Geary," Hank told him. "I called *him*."

"To tell him about the attempt on Juan's life?"

"That and the fact that I learned from that doctor downstairs that our right hand doesn't exactly know what our left hand is doing," Hank told him.

"What *exactly* is going on?" Bryan asked.

"Juan Bradley's records."

"They were missing."

"Twice," Hank added. "His test results from Monday have vanished into thin air. But the ones from this morning were sent to Geary's people without you and me ever being told."

Bryan was really getting annoyed. He sat down on the edge of the closest chair. "We were told a couple of hours ago that those records were missing."

"The hospital records are the ones that are missing. But, apparently, they've been sending duplicate records of everything to Geary as soon as they've become available. He's had all of them, right along."

Bryan felt his temperature rising. "We were on the phone with him less than an hour ago. We told him about the missing files. He never bothered to tell us he already had them."

"That would be correct," Hank responded, biting off each word. "When I asked him about it, he said he didn't think that was relevant, so he didn't mention it. But that's not all of it."

Since 9/11, there had been major shakeups of the federal agencies in terms of personnel and significant transformations in policy and duties. But one thing that hadn't changed was the fact that every branch still looked after its own interests first. In most working situations, as much as they pretended otherwise, there was still a very proprietary attitude about information. Cooperation and information-sharing was still a joke. This was yet another perfect example.

"What else is the sonovabitch hiding from us?" Bryan asked.

"It's not what he's hiding, but what his department plans to do," Hank told him. "The decision has been made by Geary or someone above him that Juan Bradley should be transferred to a certain VA hospital for observation and for his own safety. The troubling part for me is that his mother will not be allowed to accompany him there. Also, she is not to be told about the specifics of the attempt on his life tonight."

"She was the one who pulled the IV," Bryan protested. "She already knows there's something wrong. She's an M.D., for God's sake."

"I pointed that out."

"I can see them wanting to move him if we can't protect him here, but why keep the parent away? She's done everything we've asked her, been cooperative every step of the way." Lexi Bradley was upset now, but she'd be destroyed if they moved her son somewhere where she had no access to him.

"I told Geary that as a psychologist and as the ranking medical member of the team, I wasn't supporting his actions regarding keeping Dr. Bradley away. Oh, I assured him you won't be happy with this, either."

"And what was his response to that?"

"He thinks we should fly to Florida tonight and put our focus on interviewing some of the witnesses of the most recent shooting."

"That's bullshit," Bryan said, pushing up to his feet. "We aren't done here. We haven't even spoken to Juan yet. They called the wrong agents if they wanted people whose chain they could yank so easily. I think it's my turn to call Special Agent in Charge Geary."

Fourteen

Hank Gardner left the room just as the phone conversation between Bryan and Geary started getting colorful. The psychologist had no doubt that his partner would have his way, at least for the short term, anyway. After putting Geary on the defensive about withholding information on the medical tests, Bryan was moving on to the legal, ethical and public relations issues involved in keeping Lexi Bradley from her son. Earning a law degree before joining the U.S. Secret Service had always served Bryan well. Having personal connections with certain presidential cabinet members and high-ranking administrators in the Justice Department didn't hurt his clout, either.

In the hallway Hank saw one of the nurses talking to Dr. Bradley and pointing toward Juan's room. Well, that took care of the other part of Geary's plans. None of the hospital staff had been told what was and wasn't confidential. He wasn't about to interfere, either.

Lexi turned to him just as he was passing the two women. "Anything new, Agent Gardner?"

He made the decision in a space of a second. "In fact, there might be. I just had a call from Dr. Barlow. He says that there's something at the MRI lab concerning Juan's test results that he wants me to see."

"Can I come down there with you?"

Having heard Bryan's argument about her qualifications as a doctor and her rights as Juan's mother, Hank nodded. She could be a valuable resource regarding her son's medical background. "Absolutely."

She visibly brightened and fell in beside him. They waited by the elevator. "Linda was just telling me that Juan's condition is stable."

Hank nodded. "Did she tell you anything else?"

"She told me what I had already suspected." Lexi looked around behind her toward the direction of the nurses' station and Juan's room. "She isn't going to be in trouble for it, is she?"

"Not as far as I'm concerned." He shook his head. "You said it yourself. You already knew."

The elevator was taking forever to arrive, and Hank didn't want to miss the opportunity of taking Dr. Bradley down to the MRI lab with him. Geary had mentioned on the phone that Nick Luna, the long-haired agent they'd met in New York, was already on his way to the hospital to secure Juan's transfer. They were assuming that Bryan and Hank were all packed up and ready to leave for Florida.

"Are you strong enough to take the stairs down?" he asked her.

"Of course," she said enthusiastically, leading the way to the staircase door. "But I have to warn you, I'm not too familiar with the lab areas of the hospital."

The hospital was a catacomb of hallways and stairwells that didn't necessary connect or follow a logical pattern. The stairs they took didn't lead to the basement but to an area that was under construction, and Hank and Lexi had to stop and get directions. As they walked, Hank asked her a few questions about her practice. Just as he expected, she was extremely competent and professional. Their conversation, though, wasn't totally devoid of Juan. She was very proud of her son's accomplishments, and she made sure to add that to any answers she gave.

Perhaps it took them a few minutes longer than if they'd taken the elevator, but they managed to find the way to the basement, where there were adequate signs directing them to the MRI lab.

At this late hour, the reception area was empty and the lights in the waiting room were dimmed. The muffled sound of a vacuum cleaner somewhere in the distance was the only familiar noise. Hank glanced at the half-dozen doors that led out of the room and off the hallway leading through the imaging center. They waited in silence in the darkened area for a few moments.

"Where is Dr. Barlow meeting us?" she asked.

"He said in the waiting room," Hank answered. "I assume that's right here."

She poked her head over the divider to the receptionist's area. "There's usually a direct line to the labs from here, but I don't want to touch the wrong thing and activate their alarm system."

Hank agreed. "He called me on my cell phone. I can call him back."

Just as Hank was reaching for his phone, though, a double door at the end of the hallway opened and Barlow came through it.

"I thought you would have found your way down here by now," the young doctor told him. He stopped, obviously surprised at seeing Lexi.

Hank knew the two had met when the young doctor had made the first mention of Juan's records missing.

"You remember Dr. Bradley," Hank said, preferring to keep it on the professional side. "I believe her insights regarding the patient's medical history would be invaluable."

The young man nodded noncommittally and led the way back through the double doors. Hank let Lexi go in ahead of him.

"As I mentioned to you before, all the imaging records that we've taken of Juan since his hospitalization seem to have disappeared. That is, with the exception of what was faxed to your New York office," he added.

"Yes, we know that," Hank answered.

"In this patient's situation, there were no head injuries that we know of, so it's very difficult to treat him without the results of the diagnostic tests," Barlow explained. "The hospital has been in contact with the FBI, trying to get copies of those records back, but we've had no success, as yet."

Hank didn't miss the curious look Lexi sent over her shoulder at him.

"I perfectly understand your concerns, Dr. Barlow," he said. "When you called, you said that you were able to find something, though."

"Yes. I asked one of our consulting radiologists if she could just poke her head back in here tonight. She's the absolute expert. She's the one who took us into twenty-first century methods, diagnosis and equipment," he said, opening the door to one of the labs. An older woman with silvery hair and a pinched face was doing something on one of the computers.

"Agent Gardner, Dr. Bradley, this is Dr. Wolf," Barlow said, making the introductions.

The semiretired radiologist was all business. She showed no indication of being surprised at seeing the patient's mother there.

She gave Hank and Lexi a quick overview of how the imaging files were saved and where they were stored in the hospital mainframe.

A glass wall separated the room from the testing area, where an MRI machine sat in partial darkness. Other than the four of them, no one else appeared to be in these labs.

"I don't know if Dr. Barlow mentioned it or not, but they were unable to retrieve the imaging files from the system earlier today," the radiologist explained.

Hank didn't say anything, but he didn't recall that specific information.

"You mean the original images?" Lexi asked.

"That's correct."

"How could that happen?" Hank asked.

"My suspicion is that someone used remote access to perhaps copy and then delete the files," the older woman responded.

"Are the files that accessible?" Hank asked. "Isn't there a security system to stop hackers from getting in?"

"The hospital has an excellent security system on its network. But just as your banking records are available to you online, a lot of health records and tests are available for physicians to view online…not to mention government agencies operating under the original Patriot Act," she said curtly. "Be that as it may, as far as hacking into the hospital system, no network is completely invulnerable. How many times have the CIA, or the FBI, or the Secret Service or Homeland Security's systems been breached in the past five or ten years?"

Hank remembered what Barlow had said. These systems were hers, and despite retirement, she still defended them. "You're absolutely right. None of us are safe these days."

"Are Juan's records the only ones that are missing?" Lexi asked, forcing everyone to get back to the specifics of why they were there. "Or was this a random act by some stranger wanting to mess things up, for whatever reason?"

"Good question. This list contains everyone who was tested today," the radiologist said, picking up a printout from the desk. It took her a minute to cross-check the names on the chart with what was on the computer. "It appears that Juan Bradley was the only error…or whatever. I can go back and check the names for the day he was checked in, too, and see if he's the only patient with missing records. But there's something else that I'd like to show you first. Perhaps you'll find it more helpful to you."

Lexi worked her way to the right side of the computer station. Hank was able to move in closer, and he watched the radiologist change screens and start typing away.

A fake nurse, a suspicious phone call and now tampered records. The threat on Juan was becoming more real with every passing moment. Striking back at an assailant in a case of school violence was a possibility, but engineering such detailed actions seemed unlikely. Hank had never seen anything like this before.

Moving the teenager to a safe environment with tighter security was one part of Geary's plan that Hank was now in full agreement with.

"This is what I'd like you to see," Dr. Wolf said, leaning back in her chair.

Hank shifted closer behind the radiologist so he could have a clear view of the computer screen. Dr. Barlow moved next to Lexi.

An MRI image loaded on the computer screen. Hank looked at the small text box in the corner where the date and patient's name was listed. The file was dated today.

"This is Juan's MRI. I thought you said it was deleted," Lexi said aloud.

"The test had to be performed twice this morning, because the technician wasn't happy with the clarity of the image," Dr. Wolf told them. "Possibly because of the patient moving."

"I was here," Lexi explained. "Juan woke up during the test and complained of a headache."

"That would do it." The radiologist nodded, satisfied. "What we're seeing here is the original image that was sent to the recycle bin. We all know…or don't know…what happened to the second one. Lucky for us, the hacker had no way of knowing that the test was performed twice."

Hank tried to look closer at the screen. He'd studied many of these images over the past few years, but he was no expert. Still, there were shadows on the image that looked peculiar. "How bad is this image?"

"It's not perfect, but it definitely gives us something to look at."

"Dr. Wolf did a preliminary review of it before you two came down," Dr. Barlow explained. "There are some very interesting areas to see."

"You found something?" Lexi said.

"Perhaps," the radiologist said modestly. "I only had time for a quick sweep. I looked for anything that stood out, something that was obviously not in place." She motioned to some chairs behind her. "Pull those in closer and sit down. You'll have a much better view that way."

Both men did as they were told, but Lexi remained standing, one hand resting on the workstation, practically leaning over the computer. The light from the screen threw a pale halo on the young woman's face. The loading images were reflected in her blue eyes.

Hank tried to imagine what was going through the mother's mind right now. The stress that she was under had to be monumental. Her son was in a coma, he'd been the perpetrator of a school shooting and now she was being told that there could be something out of the norm in the teenager's brain image.

Admiring Lexi's strength, Hank wondered if this new finding was perhaps the explanation she'd been after.

Hank turned his attention to the screen and noticed that the radiologist had already zoomed in on a specific section and was working on the clarity of it. He inched closer. He'd worked enough with M.D.s and radiologists and had seen enough images to know that the shadows that were becoming clearer with each click of the mouse were definitely not normal.

"What is that?" Lexi asked, leaning in.

"Is this what you saw before?" Hank asked at the same time.

"Yes," the radiologist answered. "I'm trying to improve the image, but it's still unidentifiable."

"Those dark lines look like…wires," Hank said aloud. The enlargement of the specific sector sacrificed the quality of the image. The radiologist backed up the zoomed area, trying to find a balance. "But they look…I don't know…segmented. Is that the pixels of the image?"

"I can't tell yet," the radiologist responded. "But there is something there."

"Juan had no brain injury or surgery," Lexi offered.

"I assume he's had no implants, either?" Hank asked.

"No." Lexi shook her head adamantly. "I adopted Juan when he was almost two and half, but there was nothing in his medical records about any of this. Are you sure this is Juan's file?"

The radiologist pointed to the tag on the file. "As far as I can tell."

"Have you ever seen anything like it?" Hank asked her.

"It's difficult to tell. I wish we had a better image," she answered. "I can tell you what it *looks* like."

Dr. Wolf turned her attention back to the screen. She pointed with the cursor.

"Do you see these? They look like coils, possibly chips. This is not exact, but they slightly resemble a NeuroCybernetic Prosthesis System."

Hank knew the term. It was a device that was commonly referred to as a "pacemaker for the brain." It had only been approved for use in the past decade or so. Lexi was staring at the screen and frowning.

"I have a vague recollection of the details of that," Hank said. "That's a treatment used for epilepsy, isn't it?"

"That's right," Barlow answered him. "The tiny device consists of a series of coils placed around the vagus nerve. It connects to a generator the size of a stopwatch that is surgically implanted under the skin of the chest."

Lexi shook her head slightly.

The young doctor continued, not taking his eyes off the computer screen. "The generator sends a thirty-second burst of electricity, followed by a five-minute lull, continuing in alteration. These bursts will disrupt seizure patterns. But that's not the vagus nerve."

"This is impossible," Lexi said passionately, straightening up. "He has no scar anywhere from any implant. Furthermore, in the past twelve years, Juan has never suffered from seizures. This has *never* come up, and there is no reason anything like this would have been implanted in his brain. But even if he had a problem, why would any hospital eliminate that from his medical record? This makes no sense."

"I agree. It doesn't make sense," Dr. Wolf said. "What I said was that what we see in these images slightly *resembles* a NeuroCybernetic Prosthesis System. It's something else. Keep in mind, what we're looking at is magnified. These things—and they certainly are artificial—are smaller than the width of a hair."

"It does look like some kind of implant," Barlow agreed. "But what is this?" He motioned to a dark area to the left of where they could make out the string-like device.

"Perhaps bleeding. It might be some kind of injury. It could be a blood clot," the radiologist explained. "Is he on TPA?"

"Mild dose. There was a lot of guesswork prescribing that one."

Tissue plasminogen activator was a common drug used for stroke victims to dissolve blood clots. Hank remembered reading in *Nature Genetics* that TPA could also damage nerve cells. There was certainly a lot of controversy regarding the drug.

"It could also be tissue damage," Barlow told them.

"Whatever it is, could it be caused by the device?"

"Anything is possible here," the radiologist commented. "What I don't understand is why the technician taking the images Monday or the one from this morning didn't point this out to one of the doctors right away."

Barlow had made some excuses about the workload. Hank stayed out of that conversation, as he could imagine anyone in Dr. Wolf's position thinking the quality of the work wasn't up to the standards that she'd demanded while still at the hospital.

The psychologist's attention turned to Lexi. She was again leaning over the workstation, studying the images. She was all concentration.

"What do you think, Dr. Bradley?" he asked quietly.

"Headaches," she whispered. "These must have been the cause of them."

"I didn't see anything in the pediatrician's files about it. Did Juan have frequent headaches?" Dr. Barlow asked.

"Only recently. During the past week or so prior to the shooting. I didn't do anything about it. I had him take Tylenol and asked him to stay home on Monday. I thought it could be from a virus going around the school." She pointed to the dark shaded area on the screen. "This could be new. Maybe this is when everything started."

Her fingers traced the rest of the image on the screen. "Whatever this is, it had to be implanted before I got him. I have the birth record from the hospital where he was born. I also have all his immunizations and the list of some routine illnesses common to many children. There is nothing that indicates anything like this."

"He wasn't in a hospital until he was two and half," Hank commented.

She shook her head. "He lived on an Indian reservation. His mother worked in a *maquiladora,* a sewing sweatshop in Mexico. I was told she died when Juan was less than six months old. The father was a Hualapai Navajo. He supposedly died in a car accident right before Juan turned two. The toddler was temporarily living with an aunt in Coconino, Arizona, before I adopted him."

It was curious how someone like Lexi Bradley would have even crossed paths with Juan. But the question was totally unrelated to what they were focusing on now.

"How detailed a medical record was kept on each child in that reservation?" Hank asked.

Lexi didn't immediately answer. She was clearly past denying that these weren't her son's imaging files.

"Obviously not too good," she whispered under her breath.

This was certainly a new window of opportunity in investigating this case, Hank thought. He stood up, all of the sudden feeling antsy. Too many questions were rocketing through his head. There was so much that he needed to find out about the other teenagers.

Lexi stood up, too, looking at him.

"We need better images if we're going to figure out what's going on in this area of the patient's brain," the radiologist said, gesturing toward the computer screen.

Barlow turned to Hank. "We either have to get the files back from the FBI or I have to bring Juan down here for another MRI."

"Can't you get the files from the FBI?" Lexi asked.

"I can't see why not. I'll make a couple of phone calls after I talk to my partner, Agent Atwood, upstairs," Hank explained. "We should have an answer either way very soon."

Dr. Barlow's beeper went off. He looked at the display. "I have to get back to the floor," he told them. He turned to Hank. "Will you let me know what you find out?"

"I will."

"Mind if I walk upstairs with you?" Lexi asked the physician. "I was hoping to pick your brain on a couple of things regarding Juan's condition."

Hank could tell an element of trust had already been established between the young doctor and the boy's mother.

After they left, Hank turned to Dr. Wolf. "Based on the little we've seen, what do you think is the next best test that should be given to Juan?"

"Medically speaking, another MRI so soon would not be good for the patient." The radiologist turned her chair around to face him. "But if we have to plan another MRI, then my recommendation would be an MRS instead."

Magnetic resonance spectroscopy. Hank knew this was a new tool. No one he knew had ever undergone this test.

"If we use this in conjunction with the MRI, we can get an image of the intracellular relationship of brain metabolites."

Hank remembered reading somewhere that patients with schizophrenia were good candidates for this test. There was so much that he didn't know about it, though.

"Tell me exactly what that will do for us," he said.

She took off her glasses and held them in her lap. Hank guessed that she must have been a very pretty woman when she was younger. Blazing a trail for other women in a field like radiology had given her face a taut, nervous edge, though. She didn't look like a woman who let her guard down too often. No, he thought, a woman this bright and accomplished probably scared the hell out of most men her age.

"Studies show that in an injured brain," the radiologist explained, "the relationship between the amounts of certain compounds change in predictable ways, which can be picked up, noninvasively, by MRS. While MRS is in its early stages, it holds great promise in the field of brain injury. It may give us some of the answers we're looking for in this boy's case, without having to do exploratory surgery."

"And Yale–New Haven has an MRS machine."

"We're pioneering its use," the older woman said proudly. A small smile softened her face.

"Thanks. Sounds like a good route." Hank gestured toward the screen. "Can you print these images for me?"

She promised to send the files upstairs to him.

He left the radiologist and took the stairs again. There was a lot that Hank needed to talk to Bryan about, but there was a lot of information that he needed to sort through first.

Over the past two decades, there'd been a great deal of experimentation done in the neuroscience field. A lot of therapeutic research had focused on inserting electronic devices into a subject in an attempt to manipulate the brain reception and transmission of signals to neurons.

The frontline in that research involved efforts to use a microchip to send signals from one healthy cell to another, bypassing any damaged tissue that might otherwise block the message. Another artificial device was being designed to help Alzheimer's patients regain the ability to form memories. Similar techniques were also being considered to treat Parkinson's disease, and methods were being developed to tap into the motor-control regions of the brains of victims of paralysis.

A lot of these projects were being funded by the government. Others were supported by private organizations and universities. None of them involved healthy teenagers, though…or infants or toddlers. And if Juan Bradley had been implanted with something, it clearly would have been before Lexi adopted him.

Even with the poor imaging, the four of them had been able to see a questionable area in Juan's brain. This meant that Geary's medical analysts in New York had already seen the same thing.

Hank already had an answer for Drs. Wolf and Barlow about the missing records, though. The FBI wouldn't send the records back. He was beginning to think they wouldn't allow another test, either. Juan Bradley would be airlifted out of this hospital ASAP.

The questions remaining had to do with how successful Bryan had been in convincing the top dogs to allow Dr. Bradley and the two of them to stay with the teenager until they had some answers.

Fifteen

"My superiors in this investigation believe that they can't sufficiently protect and treat your son at this location. Juan is being airlifted to a military hospital in Maryland tonight."

Lexi hadn't seen this agent before. She would have remembered him. She'd gone downstairs with Hank Gardner, only to come back up and find this guy here waiting for her and acting like he was in charge.

The agent had introduced himself as FBI Special Agent Nick Luna. The young man was dressed in tight, faded blue jeans and a black leather coat, and except for the identification card he wore on a lanyard around his neck, it looked like someone in a movie wardrobe department had dressed him for Al Pacino's role in *Serpico*. Luna conveyed an "I'm your best friend" attitude that made her suspicious from the moment she saw him. She tried to keep a positive attitude, though. After all, they were moving Juan to keep him safe. Someone was actually showing some concern.

"Where in Maryland is he being taken?" she asked.

"A hospital near Baltimore where he can get the best care in a secure environment."

That was not too specific.

"Where *exactly*? What hospital? I need to let the people in my practice know where I'll be and how I can be reached."

"I can understand that." The FBI agent glanced quickly at his watch and then checked the display on his cell phone. "We'll give you the specifics once the transfer is complete."

Suddenly, Lexi had a very uncomfortable feeling.

"I'm going with him," she said.

"We're making arrangements for you to come later and visit with him, Dr. Bradley. But as far as accompanying him in the airlift, I'm afraid that's not possible. Because it's a military facility, there are clearance issues and red tape that need to be taken care of."

"Then take care of it right now," Lexi blurted out, her patience running thin. "How long is all of that going to take?"

"I'm sorry, Dr. Bradley." He shook his head. "Tomorrow will be the earliest you—"

"Look, Agent...Luna," Lexi interrupted sharply. "I'm his mother. He's only fifteen. He's still a child in many ways."

The agent had asked her to meet with him in a small conference room down the hall. She'd refused.

She figured he wanted to minimize any scene she might make or at least not have an audience for whatever bomb they were going to drop on her now. She'd been agreeable for two days. Enough was enough. She noticed Linda and another nurse looking at them from their station. "You're not so far away from the time *you* were fifteen, Agent Luna. You should understand."

His eyes narrowed. "The Connecticut Attorney General," he said, an edge emerging through the suaveness, "has already been in consultation with the Justice Department on the topic of trying your son as an adult. We're well aware of his age."

Staring into the young man's brown eyes, she wondered how she'd succeeded in reaching a working relationship with the other two Secret Service agents, while this one had her blood pressure about to go through the roof.

Lexi's hand found the lawyer's card in her pocket. "I'm focusing on Juan's care right now. That should be your only concern, too," she reminded him. The future was just an unpleasant haze.

She watched as the man's composure quickly returned. That casual, friendly attitude was only a veneer, she thought. Just beneath the surface, this guy was as edgy as a fox.

"Of course, ma'am. I'm here because we are concerned. And the sooner we settle this pointless argument, the sooner we'll have Juan on his way."

There was nothing pointless about her request. And she didn't believe anything he said. Hank Gardner was still downstairs. She wondered where Agent Atwood was. She would take his gruffness and attitude anytime over this one's.

Lexi took out the attorney's card and looked down at the name and phone number. Judy McGrath's home number was carefully printed in neat handwriting on the back of the card.

"Before anyone moves my son, I'd like to contact my attorney and have her join us here to go over all the details."

The young agent shrugged and looked away. "You do what you have to, Dr. Bradley…as we will. Now, if you'll excuse me."

As he brushed past her, Lexi felt a sense of dread cut into her like a chill wind. She didn't believe they would actually wait for her lawyer to arrive.

A man and a woman, both in street clothes, stepped out of the elevator. Luna approached and greeted them. They all headed for Juan's door. From the other end of the hall, an orderly was pushing a gurney toward her son's room, too.

Lexi didn't know the name of the hospital or the exact location. Maryland was all Luna had said. Once they moved Juan, she might not get authorization onto the grounds of a military hospital. She was in deep trouble. She pulled out her cell phone to call the attorney.

Considering her luck, she should have known. The phone was totally out of charge.

Sixteen

Express Copy was the only twenty-four-hour copying place Mitch could find near the highway. Located between Reno and Sparks, the store was visible from the exit off Interstate 80. Mitch pulled into an empty lot across the street and studied the brightly lit store for a couple of minutes. The Yellow Pages he'd ripped out of the phone book outside a convenience store by the last exit lay on the passenger seat.

He looked back at the exit from the highway. No black sedan. There hadn't been any sign of it since he'd left the motel. He'd lost them…for now.

Mitch thought about calling Elsa. He glanced at the clock display on the dashboard. She was probably sleeping. Taking care of the grandchildren was a tough job. When Elsa was down there, she went to bed whenever they did.

"She'll be worried, though," he murmured to himself. She had to know by now that he wasn't home. She was a good woman. They'd been married…how long? Thirty-seven years in June. He should call and leave a message, anyway, maybe at home. That way, when she called looking for him, she'd get the message.

What would he say? Christ. What *could* he say to her? That he'd been part of something that had gone crazy? That his dreams of doing something great had turned to shit? No…worse than shit. He was responsible for killing people. There was no other way to put it. He'd killed children.

It wasn't what they'd set out to do. How had it gone so wrong?

Mitch felt himself growing nauseous. He tried to block out the images of all those dead children…and others. He rolled down the window and took deep breaths of air. The smell of greasy fries wafting across the road didn't help. He looked back at Express Copy.

He didn't like the floor-to-ceiling-glass front panel of the store. The insurance agency that shared the building was dark. He looked up and down the strip. The Comfort Inn had just a few cars in the lot and the two fast-food places on this side of the highway overpass were closed. He could see a kid leaning on a mop handle in the one next to the motel. He was talking to the manager, who had just disappeared into a room off the kitchen, obviously taking care of paperwork. The street was dead quiet, no passing cars. Even the traffic on the highway was surprisingly light.

Still, Mitch was wary of the openness of the large windows of Express Copy. Only one person seemed to be working the late shift. From where Mitch was sitting, he could see a balding, middle-aged man loading paper into one of the big copying machines.

Mitch looked behind him down the street. No one was coming. He grabbed the top file off the backseat. He had to make the effort. It was clear they were after him. When they caught up to him, he was a dead man. He couldn't fold his hand and give up, though, not after coming this far. There was still a chance that he could make a difference. If he could save even one life. Even one…

As he opened the car door, an eighteen-wheeler hauling a pair of trailers roared across the overpass. The sound made him jump back against the car in a rush of panic and he dropped the folder, the pages fanning out at his feet. For a moment, he thought he was having a heart attack. When his pulse slowed a bit, he bent and scooped up the pages.

"You're doing the right thing, you ass," he muttered. "Show some guts."

For the first time in years, he felt like a weight was being lifted from his shoulders as he hurried across the deserted street.

A loud chime sounded as he walked through the door. The balding man looked up at him from where he was crouched beside a copying machine.

"Can I help you?"

He had a gruff voice, like sand over glass.

"I need to fax something," Mitch told him, stepping to the side of the counter and pretending to look at a business card display.

"Is it international?"

"No." He shook his head. "Domestic. I'm faxing these to Connecticut."

"How many pages?"

Mitch looked down at the file in his hand. "Thirty pages, maybe a few more."

"I've got four big jobs that need to be ready to go for the morning. I have to start them first. Afraid I won't get to it for maybe an hour."

"Mind if I do it myself?"

The clerk pushed slowly up to his feet. "Do you know how to use one of those?" He pointed to a fax machine on a counter against the wall.

"Sure."

"I can't charge you any less for doing it yourself."

"No problem," Mitch said, quickly moving in that direction. A car passed on the street, but it drove by too fast for him to get a look at it. He didn't think it had come off the exit ramp.

He took a slip of paper out of his shirt pocket. There was a number listed on it. He started dialing.

"You don't have to feed it one page at a time," the clerk chimed in from the machine he was working on. "You can put the whole stack in."

"I know. I've used one of these before," Mitch said, glancing in the direction of the street again. The lights from the store reflected off the windows of his car across the road. There was nobody else around.

He opened the file on the counter. Old paper clips and rusty staples held some of the pages together. The pages had become mixed when he dropped them, but he wasn't worrying about keeping everything in the right sequence. He piled the loose pages in the fax machine while going to work on removing the staples and clips.

It seemed to take forever before the dialing went through and the sheets started to feed into the machine. An error flashed across the thin screen. The fax was incomplete.

Why was there an error?

He glanced at the slip of paper in his hand again and punched in the numbers.

The large copying machine that the store clerk had been working on started suddenly. The machine was working loudly now, collating the print job as the papers spilled out into the trays.

"Do you need any help with those?"

"No," Mitch called back. "I'm all set."

He stacked in few more pages into the machine. Some of the ones from before appeared to be going through.

Mitch's cell phone started ringing in his pocket. He ignored it. He'd been ignoring it since he'd left California last night. Or was it the night before? He was losing track of time.

"Is that you ringing?" the clerk asked.

He wasn't going to answer the phone and he wasn't

going to answer the store clerk, either. He tore a large staple out of a stack of pictures. He didn't know how these would go through the fax.

The chime on the door sounded. Mitch paused for a moment as a cold sweat broke out along his spine. He found himself blocking the machine with his body. He didn't want to turn around to see who had come in, but he didn't want the newcomer to see what he was doing, either. He hurriedly moved the pictures to the fax machine. The pages he'd put there before were running through.

"Well, this is a busy night for a Wednesday," the clerk said in his gruff voice. "Can I help you fellas?"

"No, thanks," a soft, low voice replied. "This is what I've been looking for."

It was a man's voice. He'd found what he was looking for. Mitch didn't have to spend too much time contemplating what that meant. He knew.

The shot in Mitch's back felt like a sharp punch. Like a hot poker, the bullet burned through him, the force of it smashing him up against the counter. He was startlingly aware of his head banging on the fax machine as he slid to the floor.

He never saw the killers, but an image of Elsa's pretty face flickered before his eyes and then merged into a flashing, brilliant eternity of fiery autumn color.

Seventeen

Bryan Atwood glanced over at the cluster of pictures on the desk where Hank was sitting. The diurnal occupant of that space had two rather mischievous-looking boys. Even the posed studio portrait of the two could not mask the obvious trouble they had in them. They looked like they'd barely been settled for the photographer to snap the picture. The family photo cleared up the matter entirely. Dad looked like he could play linebacker for the Ravens and had the same devilish grin on his face. Mom looked like she couldn't decide whether to be amused or angry. Either way you read her expression, there was a definite besieged look in her eyes.

Hank, holding the phone to his ear, followed Bryan's

gaze to the photos before saying, "When was the last time you saw the girls?"

"We went out for dinner on Christmas Eve."

"Did Jenny go out with you, too?"

Bryan shook his head. Despite the divorce, there'd been one tradition that Bryan and his ex-wife had kept...until this year. They would put their differences aside and take the girls out to dinner on Christmas Eve. "She was spending it with her boyfriend's family."

She hadn't told the girls yet, but Jenny had told Bryan that her boyfriend had popped the big question. They were planning on getting married this coming summer.

Truly, Bryan had been happy for her. He was also happy for his daughters. They were the kind of kids who loved family and family rituals. The only person he didn't feel happy for was himself.

Hank looked back down at the papers on the desk in front of him. Bryan forced his focus back to the job, clearing his mind of everything but what they had to do.

The hospital staff had been very accommodating about letting them use one of the administrative offices for the night. Rather than flying back and forth across the country, Bryan and Hank decided to try getting a lot of their legwork done from here.

Bryan had been on the phone with Geary for some time earlier, discussing the missing medical records, the phony nurse, the threat on the boy's life. He was reasonable enough to see the wisdom behind some of the decisions that had to be made tonight. The most important, of course, was that Juan was on his way to

Baltimore right now. Geary told him that the mother would be able to join her son there in the morning. There was no point for Hank and Bryan to stay with the teenager until he was conscious. Geary's biggest concession—and Bryan had heard him biting his tongue as he said it—was that he and Hank were to proceed with their portion of the investigation as *they* saw fit. Neither New York nor Washington would second-guess them, but they needed to keep Geary apprised of their actions on a daily basis.

Bryan finished jotting down the information he'd been able to get from Clark County Coroner's Office for the December 20 shooting in Las Vegas. He was also promised by the third-shift supervisor that the autopsy reports would be e-mailed to him tonight.

"I have to go to the car for my laptop. Do you need anything?" Bryan asked, pulling on his overcoat.

Hank was on hold with someone working at the District Nine Medical Examiner's office in Orlando. He'd been able to get past the after-business-hours answering machine and find a live person who wasn't the third-shift janitor. Mike Forbes, the shooter at the high school in Orlando, was scheduled to be autopsied first thing in the morning. Before they started the procedure, Bryan's partner had said he wanted to make sure the medical examiner knew what to look for.

Hank touched the growth of beard on his chin. "Yeah, you can get my overnight bag. It's on the backseat."

The room was windowless, but the last time Bryan had a chance to peek outside snow was falling hard and fast.

"Has Luna contacted you since they left?" Hank asked.

Nick Luna was part of the escort service taking Juan Bradley to Maryland.

"No. He said he'd call as soon as they settled Juan at the hospital."

"How about Dr. Bradley? Have you talked to her?"

"You saw her last. Luna was supposed to give her all the details. I assume she's already on her way to the VA hospital in Baltimore."

Whoever was on the line with Hank came back on, and Bryan grabbed the car keys and went out. It was better this way, he told himself. It was better for everyone having Lexi deal with other agents who were investigating the case.

The elevator brought him to a lobby that appeared deserted, with the exception of a security guard who nodded to him as he passed. Glancing through the double doors, Bryan could see the snow was coming down hard and piling up in the street. No one seemed to be on the road. No plow had come through, either.

Bryan turned to the guard. "Is there a way that I can get to the Howard Street Garage going through the building?"

The burly young man behind the counter shook his head and started to explain how he could get closer by using a second-floor walkway, but Bryan's attention was immediately drawn to a movement on a bench at the far end of the lobby. He'd missed her the first time.

Bryan thanked the guard and walked toward the bench. She obviously hadn't seen or heard him, either.

With her coat draped over her shoulders, she was leaning forward, her elbows planted on her knees. Her face was propped in her hands, her eyes closed.

"Dr. Bradley," he said softly.

Her hand slid from under her chin. There was a moment of obvious confusion in her face. She blinked a couple of times, seemingly trying to see if she were awake or asleep.

"I must have dozed off," she whispered.

"The exhaustion is finally getting to you."

She shook her head, stretched, looked up at him again.

"You're too tall," she said under her breath, rubbing her neck.

Bryan decided she was still half asleep. "You aren't going to pass out on me again, are you?" he said, sitting down on the seat next to her.

She rubbed her eyes and stifled a yawn. Strands of her blond hair had come out of the band and fallen on her shoulder. She looked sleepy. An image popped into his head of her blond head lying on a pillow, of her opening her eyes for the first moment of the day. He could see her stretch and sit up in bed....

Slow down, he told himself, stifling the image. *Keep it professional.* He forced his glance out at the snow.

"What time is it?" she asked. Before he could check the time, she glanced down at her own watch. "Ten after two. I called them more than an hour ago."

"Called who?"

"A cab," she said, getting up to her feet and looking up and down the snowy street.

"Where's your car?"

"At my house. My brother drove it from my office to the house when he was visiting last night," she answered. "I came here in a police cruiser on Monday. I haven't left since."

Bryan didn't know what the exact weather forecast was, but what he could see from here wasn't too promising.

"It doesn't seem they've done much work clearing the streets yet. Where were you going to try to get a cab to take you?"

"An hour or so north of here," she whispered. "Well, I was hoping."

"You might be stuck here for the night."

"I can't," she said turning to him. "They took Juan two hours ago. That arrogant agent...what was his name? Nick...Looney..."

"Nick Luna." He smiled.

"That's him," she said, running a hand through her hair. The band holding it back fell to the ground. She bent down and picked it up. "He wouldn't even tell me the name of the hospital that they were taking Juan to."

"That's not confidential information. Not as far as you're concerned."

"Thank you," she said, throwing her hands up in frustration. "I called my lawyer. She called someone in Hartford, I don't know who. I don't know if that was the reason for it or not, but Agent Luna stopped to see me again before they left with Juan. He said that as soon as Juan was checked in, they'd call me with the exact details of where he is and how I can get clearance to visit him."

"He didn't give you the name or location of the hospital?"

She shook her head. "He said he'd call me with that information. I gave him my cell number, which, by the way, is no good since my phone is totally dead. I also gave him my home number, but that doesn't do me any good when I'm stuck here at the hospital."

Bryan thought she was working herself up for good reason. There was no cause for Luna to be such a hardass with her.

"My understanding is that Juan was flown to the Baltimore VA Rehabilitation and Extended Care Center. I'll get you the street address and arrange for security clearances."

She sent him a look that made him feel like a miracle worker. "Why can't everyone be as agreeable and nice to work with as you and your partner?"

"Oh, well, I'm known internationally as 'Agent Agreeable.'"

She actually smiled momentarily.

"I'm very grateful for the way you and Agent Gardner have treated me."

Throwing Hank in the pot with him was a good thing. It made everything less personal. Much better.

"Agent Luna is still a rookie. He'll learn with time the best way to deal with people. I know you only want what's best for your son." He looked outside at the wind that was now whipping up the snow. "I don't

know how much success you're going to have getting
a cab to take you anywhere. The storm is turning into
a blizzard."

"They took Juan in a helicopter. Do you think
they've already arrived in Baltimore? Is there any way
to check to see if they're there already? I don't like the
idea of him flying in this kind of weather."

"These pilots wouldn't fly if the weather was too bad,
but I think they probably got out ahead of this. Seriously, I'm sure your son will be fine." Seeing her anxious
look, he added, "Luna is supposed to call me, too, as
soon as they arrive. That should be any time now."

She pushed her arms into her jacket and looked
toward the guard's station. "I need to look at a phone
book. Maybe there's a car rental place near here that I
can walk to."

"At two-thirty in the morning, in the middle of a
snowstorm, in downtown New Haven?"

"I need to go home, get my car and be on the road
to Baltimore."

"What town do you live in?" Bryan couldn't believe
he'd asked the question. He knew she lived in Wickfield, and that was an hour away. He wasn't going to
offer her a ride.

"I live too far away," she answered softly, an ap-
preciative smile tugging at her lips. "That's okay,
Agent Atwood. I'll find a way." She headed for the
guard's station.

Bryan's cell phone rang. Before he could reach for
it, Lexi was back standing beside him.

"Maybe that's Agent Luna," she said hopefully.

He looked at the display. The call was from their headquarters. He answered the phone. On the other end was the agent whom he'd asked to trace the calls to Lexi's house.

"The call you asked about originated in Reno. It was made from a public phone at the intersection of Arlington and Liberty."

"Hold on," Bryan said into the phone, and turned to Lexi. "Do you know anyone in Reno?"

She thought about that for a couple of seconds and shook her head. "I don't think so. At least, not anyone that I'm close to."

Bryan spoke into the phone again. "Anything else?"

"One thing," the agent at the other end continued. "Since 1:14 a.m. our time, someone at an Express Copy store in Sparks, Nevada, has been repeatedly trying to fax Lexi Bradley's number some documents. Our assumption is that either they're trying to send a very long document, or that it's a programmed machine and it keeps encountering some kind of problem with her unit at home."

Bryan turned to Lexi. "Do you have a fax machine at home?"

"Yes, I do."

"Do you know if it has paper in it?"

"It did…the last time I was home," she answered. "Why?"

"Do people often send faxes to you at home?" he asked instead.

"Not really. Everything is usually sent to my practice. I only have it there for emergencies."

"Is anyone staying at your house? Could they be expecting a fax?"

"No. What's going on?"

It was not such a long shot to think that whoever had called Lexi to leave that warning about Juan might now be trying to fax her something. If his memory served, Sparks and Reno were only about ten miles apart.

"Call back the copy place in Sparks and get an ID on whoever it was that requested the job," he ordered the other agent. "Call me back when you have a name."

"What's this all about?" Lexi asked again.

Juan's computer and the contents of his desk at home had been taken by the local detectives on Monday. Lexi, though, wasn't under investigation. Without a proper court order, they had no right to enter her house and confiscate or even look at any of her documents. Still, she'd been cooperating so far. Bryan considered whether checking those faxes would be worth the two or three hours of his time that it would take to drive her home and get back.

"Before I change my opinion of you, Agent Atwood," she said sternly, "I want you to tell me what's going on."

Bryan had no problem being honest with her. "We might be chasing nothing, but someone from the same vicinity as the person who called you with the warning about your son has been trying to fax you something. I'd like to drive you home and, if it's okay with you, take a look at what was sent. Of course, you can look at it first."

She didn't even take a second to mull over his request. "Where are you parked?"

Eighteen

Thursday, January 17
West Seventy-sixth Street, New York

Curtis woke up with the cell phone vibrating under his pillow. His hand found the device, and he looked at the clock on the bedside table. It was 3:14 a.m.

He slid from under the covers and looked over his shoulder at his wife. She was turned away from him and snoring softly in her sleep. The phone stopped its vibration.

There was no voice mail box for this phone. There were no documents anywhere tracing it to him. The disposable device was used only for one purpose.

He padded barefoot to the bathroom and closed the door. As he'd expected, the phone started with its vibration again. Curtis didn't bother with the light, but turned on the fan and sat on the edge of the tub.

He opened the phone. "Yes?"

"The Nevada account is closed."

He didn't need a translator to tell him what that meant. The pang of sadness was unexpected. Mitch's face, the way he remembered him some fifteen years ago, ran across his mind's eye. His old partner was truly a genius, and those had been his best years. Those were the days when the man had poured his heart and soul into the project. Mitch had truly believed in what they were doing. He thought their experiments would begin a new chapter in the shaping of human intelligence. Their advances would expose a dimension that no one knew existed.

"Was there any paperwork?" Curtis asked.

"Boxes. He'd left them in a motel room. They were all destroyed per your instructions."

It was not like Curtis to second-guess himself, but a thought occurred to him that perhaps it would have been better not to destroy the files. At least, not until he had a chance to look through them. It would have been a good thing to see what it was exactly that Mitch had saved. Also, how did he know that this constituted all of the remaining files?

"How about the storage facility?" Curtis asked. "Could there be anything left?"

"We couldn't get in. But I'm sorry to say there was a terrible accident at that facility. It's burning to the ground as we speak."

Curtis rubbed his forehead with his free hand. His eyes were getting used to the dark. He stared at his image in the full-length mirror on the far wall. His back was bent. He looked like an old man. He cleared his voice and forced himself to focus.

"Any other instructions?" the voice asked.

"How about the cleanup?" he asked. "You didn't leave anybody behind, did you?"

"All taken care of. He was replaced with a...a clerk who happened to be available."

"That's good work," Curtis said. They couldn't find Mitch's body on any murder scene. There was too much that tied the two of them together. "No shortcuts. Is that clear?"

"You're the boss."

"What about the Connecticut account?" Curtis asked.

"We're working on it as we speak."

"Any leaks?"

"Nothing that we can't take care of," the man on the phone said confidently. "Everything should be cleared up by morning."

This all sounded too easy to believe. It was far too good to be true.

"How about the Connecticut personnel?"

There was a pause on the line. Curtis cursed silently. He'd been right to assume that everything couldn't be buried so tidily.

"The personnel there is being relocated."

"Where to? And how the hell are you going to take care of it? That was part of the deal. We had..."

"Easy does it," the other man warned.

Curtis didn't appreciate the sharp tone.

"We'll have a location as soon as they complete the move."

"And then?" Curtis asked.

"I thought you told me you don't want to know," the man replied snidely.

Curtis Wells decided he didn't like this man. There was a growing arrogance that was coming across loud and clear. He stood up.

"Just finish the job you're being paid to do. I want all accounts settled by tomorrow."

Snapping the phone shut, Curtis stood in the darkness and stared for a long time at the old man in the mirror across the bathroom.

Nineteen

The plows were clearly not keeping up with the heavy, wind-driven snow. Drifts were beginning to pile up, and visibility was minimal. It was like looking through a swirling black sea.

No one except them appeared to be crazy enough to be on the road. Lexi had given up her white-knuckled hold of the door handle while they were still traveling west on Route 34, a winding road that passed alternately by wooded watershed areas, strip malls and old industrial-era neighborhoods. Bryan Atwood was a competent driver, though, and the SUV he was driving was practically a tank. He was also taking his time.

Neither of them talked. Sometime before they reached Route 8, Lexi started dozing off. He'd flipped on the switch for the heated car seat, and she felt the warmth seeping into her. This was the most comfortable she'd been since the last time she'd slept in a bed.

He was right. She *was* exhausted. Still, she couldn't let her mind shut down for too long. Even as she dozed, nightmares about Juan haunted her.

In her mind's eye, Lexi could see a teenager firing a gun at his classmates. But not even in the state of half sleep could she force herself to see her son's face as the killer's. In the next second, she was going through door after door in the hospital in pursuit of Juan's gurney. But he was always just out of reach. Then, in the next instant, she was back at her house. Juan was there, lying in a bed in the corner of the living room. He was in a coma.

Suddenly fully awake, she stared at the wipers moving back and forth on the windshield. Lexi had been so wound up about what had taken place at Wickfield High School and how Juan was doing now that she'd spent no time really contemplating their future. Life would never be the same as it had been for them. She was knowledgeable and realistic enough to know that if, by some miracle, he were found innocent of all crimes, she'd still never have Juan back the way he'd been. His mind, his motor skills, his level of activity—in addition to everything he'd accomplished socially and in the community—would be different. They would both have to cope with the changes…learn to live some new way of life.

She closed her eyes and fought back the new surge of emotions. This new layer of reality was as terrifying as all the rest of it.

Lexi forced herself to focus when she sensed the car

was slowing down. They were stopping at Morris township just south of Wickfield. He'd gotten off the highway somewhere and come up through Watertown. She'd missed that entirely. She looked at the dashboard clock, amazed how she'd lost track of time.

No one had called Agent Atwood's phone. She thought about the cell service along Route 8. Lexi knew there weren't many cell towers along there, but she didn't know what kind of service government agencies used.

"I must have slept more than I thought," she whispered.

"You really needed it."

He'd shed his jacket. His tie was gone, and his shirt was rolled up to his elbows. She was surprised to find his missing jacket draped over her. She hadn't really had anyone looking after her in the past...how many years? Probably never. The men in her life had mostly been in the "pre-Juan" days, and even then she'd always been able to take care of herself.

"Thank you," she said, straightening her car seat more to an upright position and carefully folding his jacket.

"Don't mention it."

She rubbed her face and stretched her shoulders. She looked over at him. Sitting behind the wheel, with the soft glow of lights from the dash displays on his face, he wasn't as imposing as he'd been in the hospital. With his hair standing up in spots from running his hand through it, he looked far less fierce...though not exactly domesticated. Lexi remembered what he'd told her earlier about having children, so she forced her thoughts not to wander too far into the area of the personal. It was hard to imagine him with a family, though.

"I didn't miss a call from Agent Luna, did I?" she asked.

"My cell phone has been out of the service area for the past fifteen minutes. I'll call him when we get to your house."

"You guys don't have super-duper, good-anywhere satellite service phones?"

He glanced at her, and she raised an eyebrow.

"Of course," he replied, straight-faced. "But I left that phone and my laser weapon in my other jacket."

She smiled and looked at the road ahead. "Seriously, I appreciate you calling for me."

"Seriously, it's no problem."

She gave him the directions to where she lived. The roads were not good as they drove the last few miles to Wickfield. The SUV skidded once going down a steep hill, but he managed the corrections easily. Lexi lived at the end of a cul-de-sac not too close to anything and on top of a hill overlooking the town. She wondered if the SUV would be able to make it into the neighborhood.

The nap, if it could count as that, had done her a world of good. She'd learned during her residency after med school the value of a power nap. Lexi found herself thinking more clearly. The sense of desperation she'd been fighting was less now. She was already planning on a few things that needed to be done as soon as she got home. Calling Allan was at the top of her list. She needed to check on her sister-in-law Donna. It didn't matter what time it was. Allan was used to his crazy sister calling him at all hours of the night.

Her stomach growled. Lexi couldn't believe it. She was actually hungry.

He glanced at her. "Do you have any food at your house?"

"I'm a mother of a teenager. There's always plenty to eat."

As they approached the outskirts of town, she saw the flashing yellow lights of a township plow moving some hundred yards ahead. The road was clear here because of it.

They drove by her office, next to the post office. She didn't point it out. They were at the height of the cold and flu season. Even on regular days and with Lexi there, they needed to overbook the appointments. She couldn't even imagine how overworked everyone at the practice must have been this week.

She pushed that part of her life away, though, and focused on her son.

"Did Agent Gardner tell you about what we thought we saw on Juan's MRI?" she asked him.

"Yes, he did."

"They were going to run some more imaging tests on him at Yale–New Haven to see what exactly we were looking at. Hopefully, they'll do that in Baltimore."

"I'm sure they will. They'll give him the best care possible."

Lexi couldn't believe she'd thought poorly of Agent

Atwood at first. He was being more considerate than she deserved. "Thank you for saying that. It's hard for me to think of him so far away, even for tonight."

He sent her a sideways glance.

"I believe whatever it is that we could see in Juan's brain is the cause for the way he acted this past Monday," she told him.

He neither agreed nor denied her claim, and Lexi thought that was a very positive step. Perhaps she wasn't grasping at straws. Perhaps they were already considering that themselves.

"Have you run across any cases of illegal experiments being done on young children?"

He stopped at a stop sign at the green. This was the very center of town. He turned to look at her. "What makes you think what he has implanted in his brain was done illegally?"

"It had to be. Why would they hide it?" She looked into his eyes. "And it did happen before I got him."

"I believe you."

"Turn right here."

The plow had gone straight, and even though this road was a main thoroughfare, it didn't appear to have been plowed in some time. The SUV powered its way through, though.

"Look, Agent Atwood, something is very strange. I'm a doctor. I looked at Juan's medical records with a fine-tooth comb during and after the adoption process. There was nothing about it anywhere. There was no record of any hospitalization immediately after birth.

He's had no surgery whatsoever since the adoption. That means whatever they did to him before was never documented. Now, why would someone do that?"

"I don't know."

"We're talking about the United States, not some developing country." She shook her head. "By law, everything is listed on those adoption medical records, whether it's AIDS or colic. If this was a corrective procedure for some kind of neurological disorder, they wouldn't hide it."

He didn't answer. Another positive step, she thought.

"But there was something there on those MRI images."

"Hank agrees with you."

Lexi thought about her attorney. She'd forgotten to mention anything about what she'd seen in the MRI lab to Judith. That was another phone call that she had to make before getting on the road to Baltimore. They actually had a defense. She could feel her energy picking up. She just had to get Juan healthy.

"We're not ignoring anything as a possible explanation," he told her. "We just want to find out what happened and what caused your son to go into that high school and start firing that gun."

She nodded and told him where to make a turn. The side road hadn't been plowed at all. The SUV followed the tracks of another vehicle, however, that had passed through not too long before.

There was at least a foot and a half of the white stuff on the ground already. The schools would be closed today, for sure. The thought of Juan on days like this, grunting with satisfaction as he rolled over and went back to sleep, made Lexi look out the side window and choke back a tear. She had to keep telling herself that he'd be okay.

"After the winery, make the next turn and you'll be on my street."

He nodded.

"I can't thank you enough for what you're doing, driving me all the way here. In this weather."

Before he could say anything, his cell phone rang. The phone was propped in a cup holder between the two front seats. Lexi had to tuck her hands under her legs to keep from reaching over and answering it for him. She hadn't even realized he was wearing an earpiece in his left ear until he started talking.

"We just pulled into Wickfield… Real bad… What did he say?"

As the agent continued to talk, Lexi found every inch of her body straining with tension. She waited, listening to every word, trying to fill in the gap of every pause. With each comment, she tried to decide how it might have something to do with Juan.

"Did you get the specifics?" he said into the device.

Lexi was impressed when he turned where he was supposed to.

"You're breaking up," he said.

This was one of the last streets that Wickfield Township plowed. Seeing the tire tracks of another car on the road ahead was surprising. Her neighbors were the kind that didn't go anywhere for two days before or two days after each snowstorm. Even the newspaper delivery ceased to exist on days or nights like this.

"How did that get missed before?" he asked into the phone.

Lexi turned to him. He was all concentration and had two hands on the wheel as the SUV slid and balked at going up an incline.

"Did they involve one specific agency? One non-profit organization?"

They had to be talking about Juan. He was adopted through a nonprofit organization.

"I didn't hear what you said. Let me call you back. We're almost there." He turned to look at her.

She nodded and pointed to her house straight ahead. Lexi's house sat far back from the road, but with the leaves on the trees gone, she could see it was in darkness. Atwood ended the call.

Lexi pointed toward her property. "Someone must have driven up my driveway since the snow started."

The tire tracks led directly up the driveway and disappeared around the side of the house by the garage. Each two-plus acre lot had its own driveway. There was no reason for anyone to have gone there. Even the newspaper deliveryman only drove by and threw the paper onto the end of the driveway. She noticed that perhaps only an inch of snow had filled in the tracks. From this angle, she wasn't able to see the front of her garage.

"Has anyone been checking on the house for you

while you've been gone?" Bryan stopped the car by her mailbox. "Didn't you have family here to help you after the shooting?"

"Yes," she said, glancing at the house. "My brother, Allan, was here from New Jersey. He stayed overnight a couple of days ago. He checked on things for me. But that was it. I even had him call and cancel the woman who comes in to clean the house once a week."

Other days that she and Juan went away, their neighbors, Mr. and Mrs. Myers, would be keeping an eye on the house. But with Juan stealing the gun from their basement, Lexi figured that that was not too likely at present.

"You're sure he didn't come back?"

Lexi was perplexed. "No, I talked to him earlier. He's back with his family."

"Does anyone else have a key to your house?"

Lexi thought about that for couple of seconds. "It's not a matter of having a key. Anyone can get into the house if they know the code to the garage door opener. I think a few of Juan's friends know it. One or two of my friends have it, too. And the neighbors. And there are doors to the house that have never been locked," she added.

The agent was looking intently at the house. There were no lights or visible movement.

"You know, I'm getting wound up about nothing. It could have been anyone. It might even be the police keeping an eye on things," Lexi said.

"That's possible."

"Seriously, with the exception of some lunatic who was running cars up and down on the green a couple of years ago by remote control, Wickfield is a pretty safe town," she said. "I don't think anyone around here even locks their doors."

Neither of the neighbors on either side had any lights on. And the single streetlight on the cul-de-sac had been out since a lightning storm last summer.

"Okay. Let's go inside and look." Bryan turned the SUV into her driveway.

"The phone call you just got," she asked him. "Has there been any news from Agent Luna?"

"You do have a visitor," he said, slowing down the car before coming to a full stop.

Lexi stared ahead at a black Escalade that was parked in front of her garage. The car was facing out. The headlights were off, but the vehicle was running. She could see the exhaust coming from the rear of the SUV.

"I don't know who that could be."

As she glanced at him, he reached across his body and a pistol appeared in his hand.

"Take my phone," he told her. "Call 911."

She stared at the gun for a second before moving quickly for his phone.

Just as she did, the headlights of the black SUV lit up, blinding her momentarily.

"Get out," he shouted.

Lexi barely had a chance to react to Bryan's warning. The Escalade was coming straight at them. She felt her seat belt unbuckle as she grabbed the door handle.

A split second later, she landed on her back in the snow, with Agent Atwood on top of her.

The sound of the crash was an explosive, jarring bang, accompanied by the screech of metal against metal. She closed her eyes at the feel of the glass showering over them. From the far side of their SUV, the roar of an engine and spinning of tires on the snowy driveway could be heard as the Escalade raced down the road.

By the time Bryan rolled off her, there was nothing but silence and the feel of the wet snow on her face.

Twenty

Buffalo, New York

With the blizzard having passed, the hospital helipad
had been reopened only an hour earlier, which was a
good thing.

Standing inside the glass-enclosed receiving passage-
way with a steaming mug of coffee in his hand, Orrin
Dexter watched the lights of the aircraft as the medevac
chopper approached the newly plowed landing area and
centered itself above. Four feet of snow had been pushed
into ten-foot piles surrounding the pad, and his view of
the helicopter door was cut off as it slowly set down.

His own flight from Ithaca to the VA Hospital in
Buffalo had been an adventure, so he could only
imagine what these guys had flown through. The storm
had blanketed the East, from Chicago to southern New
England, where it was still snowing. They'd flown from

Connecticut, tracked north to miss as much bad weather as they could, but it must have been a bumpy ride. Night flying in a storm like this was never fun.

Still, he was glad they were here. This might be the breakthrough they'd been searching for.

As soon as the chopper was secure, the crew of orderlies and nurses who were gathered in the outer receiving area moved as a unit down the short, covered path to the pad. They were pros, and though he couldn't see the transfer of the patient, in a moment they were all moving quickly back toward the hospital.

A young, long-haired man led the group. His black leather coat gleamed in the overhead floodlights. The sliding doors opened and the cold air hit Dexter. The patient still appeared to be unconscious.

"Dr. Dexter?" The agent flashed the ID around his neck. "I'm Special Agent Nick Luna, with the New York office."

It had been this man's superior at the FBI office in Manhattan who'd called and told Dexter to get ready to go to Buffalo.

"Glad to see you, Agent Luna." The patient and the entourage passed and the two men fell in behind them. "And I can't tell you how glad I am to see this young man."

"My SAC at headquarters told me you've been expecting this for some time."

"More hoping for it than expecting it. There were rumors of it fourteen years ago. We tried to get in on it, but the whole thing went underground. Vanished."

"That's hard to believe."

"Well, it wasn't for want of trying."

They passed through the ER and moved down a corridor to a waiting elevator. A number of the entourage dropped off as they crowded in. In a moment they were speeding toward the sixth floor. They were silent on the elevator. The work Dexter had spent his life focused on at Cornell was not for the ears of just any hospital orderly or nurse. His research on nanotechnology had been cutting edge—and top secret—since his graduate days in the early 1990s.

Over the past decade and a half, he and his hand-selected team had moved the science from the theoretical to the actual, but there were still a thousand obstacles…or rather, a thousand advances still to be made.

He looked down at the teenager strapped to the gurney. He'd seen the MRI images. It was unbelievable.

The doors of the elevator opened and the patient was pushed out ahead of the two men. The FBI agent pulled Dexter aside.

"Doctor, I need to call in and let my boss know that we've completed the delivery, but first I have one question—How do you think this could have remained secret for so long?"

Dexter watched his patient disappear into the waiting room. He didn't want to lose any time, but he knew it would take the hospital personnel a few minutes to situate the boy.

"As I said, there were only rumors."

"But at that time there can't have been too many people with the expertise to—"

"There were only a handful of us. Nanotechnology was only in its infancy, and advances were being guarded as closely as the location of a gold strike in the Wild West."

"But if what they were doing was really so advanced—"

"Advanced?" Dexter frowned down at the agent. "You probably grew up with computers in your home, but you have to keep in mind that it wasn't until 1989 that Intel brought out the 80486 microprocessor and the 1860 RISC/co-processor chip. If the implant in this teenager's brain is what I think it is, these guys were doing things that most of us were still only dreaming of…and that's just on the mechanical side."

"What do you mean?"

The scientist looked at the man in disbelief. How could anyone be so ignorant of the most important biotechnical events of a century?

"I don't have time to give you a history lesson, but just consider this. It wasn't until 1972 that the anti-rejection drug cyclosporine was discovered. It wasn't until 1992 that the first heart-lung transplant was done successfully in the United States. In the early nineties, the chance of surviving brain surgery, never mind implantation, was only about twenty-five percent."

"I see. So what they were doing is pretty amazing."

"Yeah." Dexter started down the hallway. "What's most amazing, though, is something we never would have guessed."

"What's that?"

"That these guys, whoever they are, were testing their research on live subjects." The scientist stopped and looked straight at the agent. "On babies."

Twenty-One

Wickfield, Connecticut

"They were definitely trying to make it look like a robbery, but it looks like you messed up their plan."

Jeremy Simpson stamped the snow from his shoes. He'd been double-checking the parameter of the house and garage.

"The door to the greenhouse where they came in has no lock that works," he said. "They could have just walked right in, but they still broke the window next to it."

Bryan nodded. Despite the continuing blizzard conditions outside, two uniformed police patrols had made it to the house in less than fifteen minutes, and the Wickfield detective had not been far behind.

There was no doubt that Lexi and Bryan's arrival had surprised those going through the house. The intruders must have seen Bryan and Lexi when they stopped in front of the house and made the run to their SUV for the getaway. They'd taken the door right off the car Bryan had been driving.

The local detective crouched down next to the afghan the intruders had spread on the living room floor and the collection of things they'd thrown onto it. "They gathered up whatever was within arm's length. Framed pictures, a clock, a silver bowl, an old VHS player…fake fruit."

"A real hot item for resale," Bryan said, frowning.

"There's a video camera bag on the floor next to the table where some of this stuff must have been sitting," the detective said, pointing to the corner of the room.

That wasn't everything that was on the blanket, but Bryan agreed one hundred percent with the young detective. Petty thieves didn't drive new Escalades, nor did they destroy valuable electronic equipment instead of taking it…as they'd done in the small office off the front hall.

"Dr. Bradley's office was clearly their target," he told Simpson, leading the way.

The uniformed officers were outside, collecting evidence. They'd set up screens over the footprints and the tire tracks and were taking photographs. After seeing her office, Lexi had gone upstairs to check what might be missing from any of the bedrooms.

Simpson had already glanced at the office briefly.

"The telephone and fax machine were destroyed. Her laptop is missing."

"That might have been already gone," Jeremy said thoughtfully. "Dr. Bradley might not know it, but I believe I saw her laptop on the list of items the FBI took custody of Monday night when they took her son's computer for evidence. There were a total of three computers taken out of this house that night."

The rest of the office was a mess. Everything on the desk had been swept to the floor. The drawers had been opened, files haphazardly pulled out and dumped. The intruders had done the same thing to the file cabinet behind the desk. Even the books on the shelves of her floor-to-ceiling bookcases were all over the floor.

"We've found three sets of footprints outside. The State Police have sent an expert to dust for fingerprints here."

Bryan guessed they wouldn't find anything. There was one thing these people were after when they broke in here, and they'd obviously found it. In his gut, he knew it was the fax from Nevada. Why else wait until tonight?

He'd spoken with Geary about the break-in right after Lexi called 911. Bryan had gotten the distinct impression that the SAC did not believe there was any connection between the Nevada calls and the shootings.

"Has Dr. Bradley figured out if anything else is missing?"

"I'll go upstairs and check with her," Bryan offered.

Coming into the house the first time, Bryan had left Lexi by the car and had gone through the house, room by room, making sure there was no one and no surprises left behind. This second time through, though, he had a better chance to actually look at everything.

The spacious house was a remodeled colonial with few new additions, and it matched everything he'd seen, heard and read about the mother and son. It was meticulously clean and organized. Very few knick-knacks, no teenage sneakers tossed in a corner. There seemed to be a shelf or a drawer for everything. Upstairs, he poked his head into the first bedroom. Juan's room. Car and music posters lined the walls. Academic and athletic awards were displayed in a bookcase.

"You're up here," Lexi said, coming up behind him. "Did you have any cuts from the broken glass?"

He'd been showered with the pebbled glass when the windshield had exploded into a thousand pieces. He had clothes in the car and had changed when she'd gone upstairs.

"No. Nothing." He turned around. "Does he keep the room like this himself, or do you have someone follow him around and pick up after him?"

She stood next to him in the doorway, looking sadly inside. Bryan guessed during the FBI sweep on Monday night, a few things had been taken from Juan's room, too. At least, they hadn't left a mess.

He'd heard the water run downstairs. She must have taken a quick shower. Her hair was still wet, pulled into a ponytail. The small cut on her forehead was oozing a little blood. She followed the direction of his gaze and patted it with a tissue in her hand.

"I have a cleaning person who comes in for a

couple of hours once a week. But she doesn't do any picking up after Juan. That's all him. He's always been like this. Never messy. Always organized. And that's not only at home. The same thing is true with his school and sports and other activities. You can ask anyone, and they'll tell you the same thing. Have you heard from Agent Luna yet?" she asked, changing the subject.

"Not directly," he told her. "But he contacted Hank, and they've landed. Everything is going per plan. I didn't have the best connection with my cell phone when I talked to Agent Gardner. Can I use your phone to call him back?"

She nodded and looked at her son's bedside table. "I assume the police were the ones who took Juan's phone. There's another phone in my bedroom." She led the way down the hall.

"Have you figured if anything was taken from upstairs?" he asked.

She shook her head. "I don't even know if they came upstairs or not. My pearl necklace is still sitting on my dresser, and I had sixty-seven dollars in cash that is sitting next to it." She stopped in the doorway to her bedroom and pointed. "Nobody touched any of it. There's the phone."

Photos of Juan at various ages covered the walls and shelves. Lexi's file had made no mention of a husband, and from what he'd gathered talking to different people at the hospital, there seemed to be no current boyfriend, either. The closest family was her brother and his wife who lived in New Jersey. Her son seemed to be her entire life. He walked toward the phone.

"You don't think someone needs to be here for what Detective Simpson and his men are doing, do you?" she asked, leaning a shoulder against the doorway.

"Are you going somewhere?" he asked, sitting on the edge of the bed, reaching for the phone.

"Baltimore," she said. "I doubt if there are any flights leaving from Hartford in this weather. I'd rather have a car there, anyway, so I'm driving."

"In this weather?"

"You drove in it, so can I. I have an all-wheel drive vehicle sitting in my garage."

"Detective Simpson told me downstairs that the governor is declaring a state of emergency. The worst of the storm is yet to come. They're going to shut down the state roads and highways. Only emergency vehicles are allowed to be out at all."

"Being a physician has its advantages. I'm considered emergency personnel," she said confidently. "Look, I've driven in this kind of weather my whole life. Also, I'll be heading south. The weather can only get better as I get closer to Baltimore."

Bryan decided this was as good a time as any to tell her. "Juan isn't in Baltimore. He was taken to Buffalo."

She was speechless for a couple of seconds. She walked inside the bedroom, sat down on a love seat across the way from him and stared at him. She looked like she was trying to decide if he was telling her the truth.

"Agent Luna said they were taking Juan to Baltimore."

"There must have been a change of plan." He shook his head. "My connection with Hank kept breaking up, but that much I heard clearly."

She turned and pulled up a road atlas from the bottom shelf of a bookcase next to the love seat. She paged through it quickly.

"I can give you more information once I talk to Hank." Bryan didn't know if he was repeating himself, but she definitely had a one-track mind when it came to her son.

"That's about four hundred miles," she said, looking horrified. She glanced at her watch. "If I leave now, I can—"

"Please, just sit there. Don't move," he ordered. "Let me make this call first."

Lexi turned her attention back to the atlas. Her look told him that he'd better be quick or she'd be gone.

"Do you have a name and address for this hospital?" she asked.

"No," he barked. "Hold on until I'm done with this call."

She glowered at him and glanced down at her watch again.

Bryan turned his attention to the phone in his hand. There was a banner running across the display. "Forwarded fax. What does that mean?"

She reached over and took the phone out of his hand and looked at the same message. "I set this up last year when I thought my fax and answering machine was on its last legs. I forgot all about it," she told him.

"What it means is that whenever my fax at home acts up and doesn't accept a document after three tries, the fax automatically gets forwarded to the number at my practice."

They were finally getting a break. Bryan pushed to his feet. "Did your downstairs fax machine say that? Is there any way the people who broke into your house could have found that out?"

"Not unless they saw the message on this receiver. Juan's phone is gone. And there's a phone in the kitchen. That's still there. If someone looked at it, I guess they could have seen the same thing there, too," she said.

Bryan took Lexi's hand and pulled her to her feet. "You take me to your office and let me check out that fax, and I'll promise to take you to your son myself."

"Today."

"Today," he repeated.

She was out the door before him.

Twenty-Two

In spite of her talk, Lexi's car wasn't anywhere near as good in the snow as the SUV they'd been driving before. Sitting behind the wheel, she was relieved to at least make it out of the driveway. Still, after all her bravado about being able to drive to Buffalo in this weather, she *had* to save face by making it to her office in downtown Wickfield. She had to do it without sliding off the road, too.

From what Detective Simpson had told her before they'd left, the forecast was that the slow-moving storm was dumping another eight to ten inches on northwestern Connecticut before moving off midday. Lexi looked at the clock on the dash. The green LED display read four fifty-eight. Midday was still too many hours away.

"Did Agent Gardner have any more news of Juan when you called him?" she asked. Bryan had made a call from her kitchen while she'd been starting the car. She assumed he'd called his partner back at the hospital. He'd been very quiet since getting into the car.

"The helicopter has landed at the Buffalo VA hospital. The transfer went very smoothly."

"How is Juan?" she asked. Her cell phone was out of charge. Her answering machine was in pieces. Even if Agent Luna had left her a message, she would never know.

"The same. They told Hank that he did pretty well with the flight."

With these people, being in a coma was obviously considered doing "pretty well."

"Can I be more involved with my son's care once I get to Buffalo?" she asked him. The car was crawling down the steep hill.

"I don't head this investigation, but considering your background, I would consider you an asset."

She appreciated the expression of confidence, but something in his response made her cast a side glance at him. "But you don't look convinced that they would."

"I think you should take one step at a time," he said reasonably. "I'll try to do everything I can from my end to keep you close to Juan."

As a person of science, Lexi considered herself reasonably skeptical, but she wasn't an untrusting person. At the same time, she was not one to rely on just anyone when she could manage for herself, particularly not someone she'd just met. Life had given her a few hard lessons in that area.

She'd lost her mother at age seven, and she and her

brother had dealt with her father's ongoing bouts of depression until he'd passed away while she was in medical school. And then she'd been diagnosed with cervical cancer at an age when most were planning their future careers and families. She'd had to get through that on her own. Allan had been working in South America that year. Donna and the girls were with him. She didn't think it was fair to disrupt their life. She'd learned at a very young age that independence was the key to survival.

In the case of Agent Bryan Atwood, she found that she *was* trusting him. She *was* allowing herself to rely on him. She believed he'd do what he was promising her. At the same time, she already understood his reserved nature. He was man of few words. He definitely didn't offer information; she had to probe.

They turned out of her street, and she found the road clearer. The town had at least tried to plow here. The snow was falling heavily, and the windshield wipers were having difficulty keeping up with the wet snow.

"When we were on our way to Wickfield, you mentioned something on the phone to your partner that sounded like…maybe that you're investigating the organization that helped me with Juan's adoption?"

He waited a couple of seconds to answer her. Lexi wondered if she was crossing the line as far as what he could or couldn't tell her.

"Did I?"

"I've answered a zillion questions of various law enforcement officers, but none have asked about the adoption. If you do need any of those records, I have them all. I can show them to you. Names, agencies, phone numbers. It could save you some time," she explained. "In fact, I keep a copy of all the records in a safe at work."

He still didn't say a thing.

"You're trying to solve a case. I'm trying to help my son. I think we both know that Juan's actions this past Monday were not that of the standard teenager wanting to take revenge on his classmates and teachers, and going crazy." She darted another glance at him. "I haven't called my attorney since we left the hospital. I'm cooperating, trying to help you. I'd appreciate the same treatment."

"I told you before, I'll take you to Buffalo today."

Lexi shook her head, disappointed.

"Law enforcement bullshit," she cursed, hammering the wheel.

"What law enforcement bullshit?"

"This investigation is ongoing," she said, using a mock official tone. *"So you can't know anything since you aren't one of us."* She glowered at him. *"That* bullshit. Damn it, I'm trying to help you! That's why I'm taking you to my office, handing you whatever this fax is that you're looking for. I'm not stupid. I know I could hand this over to my attorney and use it as a bargaining chip in Juan's case."

He stared at her intently for a long moment, and Lexi wished she knew what was going on behind that brooding expression.

"And as far as someone taking me to Buffalo," she continued, letting the steam escape for a change. "I could hire a driver to take me. So there. This is all shit… shit…shit."

"You just ran a stop sign," he told her.

"So ticket me," she snapped back.

Thankfully, there was no traffic on the road, and no traffic cops, either.

Lexi was disappointed that she couldn't break through Agent Atwood's shield. She took a couple of deep breaths, adjusted her steely grip on the wheel, and looked around at the houses perched closer together as they neared the center of Wickfield.

"By the way," she said. "I've decided it can't be me. You must always be like this."

"Always like what?"

"Like the way you are now. Brooding to the point of grouchiness. When you talk, it's always to the point. You ask a lot of questions, but you feel it's beneath you to answer. I'd bet money that you're this way with your wife and children, too. It's not healthy," she said before he could put a word in edgewise. "Especially with teenagers. That's no way to develop trust, no way to build a relationship."

Lexi stopped herself, realizing what she was saying. She was giving him a lecture about parenthood when her son was accused of a violent crime. Her exhaustion of the past few days was turning to frustration and anger. She couldn't let herself burn the one bridge that was standing, though.

She couldn't look at him, but she decided not to run the next stop sign. Her office was just around the next turn.

"I'm sorry," she whispered. "I'm the last person who should be lecturing anyone about parenting right now."

"Oh, you're talking about parenting. I thought you were talking about me."

Lexi felt her ears burning. She had to wait for two trucks, one plowing and the other spreading salt and sand, to go by before she could turn into the alley that led to the lot behind the building.

The snow on the front walkways was still undisturbed. And there were no cars, no footsteps, nothing marring the pristine snow in the back of the building, either.

"Even though this is an official investigation," he said wryly, "I suppose I can say, judging from the looks of things, that the intruders at your house haven't been here."

He was right. It was clear that no one had been anywhere near the building since the snow started. Lexi was suddenly glad that Peter, the guy who plowed their lot in the winter and took care of the landscaping in the summer, hadn't come in yet.

Her car balked at the deep snow in the lot, slipping and sliding until she finally managed to park near the back door that the doctors and office staff used to get into the building. She reached over the seat for her hat, gloves and jacket. Bryan put a hand on her arm.

"You need to know something. Even though I'm

very aware of how cooperative you're being, there are things I just cannot tell you about this investigation. How confidential do you keep your patients' privacy?"

Lexi looked at him. "Very."

He didn't say anything more, but the look he sent her said it all.

Lexi pulled on her hat and gloves. She didn't bother with the jacket. "All I have to say is that you'd better hope you never have a heart attack on an island where I'm the only doctor."

She took her keys and stepped out of the car. She was almost certain she heard him chuckle.

Lexi pushed through the snow ahead of him. At the door, she put the key into the lock.

"How many ways are there to get inside the building?"

"To get inside the building? Four. To get inside my office? Two," she explained. "The patients come through the front door and take the elevator or the stairs to our office. Until next spring, while we're doing some renovations, only the staff come in this way."

"How is the security system?"

"The building has locks and an alarm system." Lexi turned the key in the door. "We have another alarm system for our office."

"You should let me go in first and make sure no one else is here," he told her.

She shook her head. "Just in case someone was camping out here since before the storm started?"

He didn't seem completely convinced, staying very close to her as she went through the steps of unlocking the outer and inner doors and disarming the building security system.

"Does this have a motion sensor?"

"No," she replied. "The office does, though."

"Why don't you arm this one again?" he suggested as soon as they were in.

Lexi nodded and complied. Starting for the stairs, she turned on the lights as she went through. The familiar surroundings and smells boosted her confidence. She was as much at home here as she was at her own house. It was Juan that made the other a home.

"Does this hallway lead to the front door?"

"Yes."

She led the way. The small elevator was halfway down the hall. Jack Zebo had his dentist's office on one side of the hall and on the other side was the Black Pearl Antique Shop. Lexi watched Bryan take out a pocket light and look through the glass doors into each of the rooms as he went. When he was satisfied, they backtracked and went up the stairs to the second floor.

Lexi unlocked that door, stepped inside and disarmed the alarm.

She nodded down a narrow corridor. "These doors are my partners' offices and beyond them are examination rooms. The receptionist and bookkeepers are located opposite the elevator."

"With your permission, I'm going to poke my head into each of these rooms."

"Go ahead," she told him. "I'll turn on the lights from here."

She switched on the lights at a panel near the back door and then followed him, stopping at the door to her own office. She glanced inside. It felt like a lifetime since she'd been here.

Her gaze fell first on an eight-by-ten framed photo sitting on her desk. Her boy. The picture had been taken at the end of last summer when she and Juan and her brother's family had taken a vacation for a week on Cape Cod. Juan had let his black, wavy hair grow until it reached his shoulders. His dark eyes were full of mischief as he pretended he was taking a bite out of the foot-long blue fish that was still dangling from his fishing line.

Tears rose up in Lexi's eyes, and she quickly looked away, trying to focus on the rest of her office. She'd expected piles of paperwork on her desk, but everything was neatly organized with paper clips and notes attached to each file and piece of paper. She had no doubt that Pat, their office manager, had been staying late every night to take care of these things.

Bryan appeared in her doorway. "Looks good."

Lexi felt a little flustered the way he filled the doorway. "You didn't expect to find someone hiding in a closet, did you?"

He nodded, looking past her. "Nice office."

She turned around and tried to look at it through his eyes. The room was small, neat and packed with professional books and journals. It represented too much of her type-A personality.

"Thanks. It's me." She figured he probably couldn't even fit behind the desk.

"The FBI didn't take all your computers," he commented, pointing to the laptop sitting at the corner of her desk.

"That's because this one is mine. I only bought it at Christmas, and it's never left this office."

He smiled and walked in, looking at the frames on her desk and walls. "You don't have to get upset. I'm not going to take it away."

She didn't know how to take his attempt at humor.

"You wanted to look at the incoming faxes," she said.

He motioned to her to lead the way, but there wasn't enough room to go by without brushing past him. He was too tall and broad. There was something about his smile that made him look almost boyish…and very handsome. It was a stupid feeling, but she was actually flustered.

She gathered her protective cloak of professionalism around her. "After you," she told him.

He stepped out into the hall. Lexi went past him and led the way to the receptionist's area.

"This is the main fax machine for our practice." She took stacks of paper out of the tray. "It's an absolute workhorse. Even if it runs out of paper, it saves the incoming document in its memory."

She pressed a button on the machine, paging through the messages on the display screen. "Everything that's been sent has been received…."

"My technician said there was an aborted fax to your house. Are you sure it didn't get forw—"

"Hold it. Here it is." She finished going through the list. "Just the one forwarded fax."

She put all the faxed documents on one of the desks and went through them. Bryan was right beside her, looking over her shoulder. Lab reports, letters from other doctors, insurance statements, billing documents, more lab reports. There was nothing that didn't belong.

"That fax didn't come through," she said, looking up at him, disappointed.

"The problem must have been at the other end."

"Is anyone checking out the number that it was called from? Maybe there's still someone there who would answer the phone."

"We're already checking that angle out."

Lexi wondered if he was still planning to take her to Buffalo. She wasn't going to ask, though. She knew somehow he'd keep his word.

"This person, whoever he is," Bryan said reflectively, "has tried to communicate with you through a phone call and a fax. I assume you're listed in the phone book."

She nodded. "I use the same number for both."

"How easy is it to find your e-mail address?"

Lexi turned and leaned against the edge of one of the desks. "We have a Web site for the office. It's listed there. Also, if someone knows what hospitals I'm affiliated with, they could get it from the online directory of any of them."

Lexi guessed anyone who'd been reading the regional papers since the Wickfield High School shooting knew just about everything there was to know about her.

"And when was the last time you checked your e-mail?"

"Monday morning. I checked my mail here at work," she said, pushing away from the desk and heading back toward her office.

On impulse, she made a detour into the small kitchenette next door to the receptionist's area and checked the fridge for anything edible. She had to be feeling a lot better, because she was absolutely starving. An unopened container of yogurt, left over from someone's lunch, was the most appetizing thing she could find.

"I'm glad to see you're not anorexic."

Bryan was filling the doorway again, watching everything she did.

"No chance of that." She took out a couple of plastic spoons from one of the drawers. "I'll share it with you."

He shook his head. "You'll need your energy working with me."

She liked the sound of that. In her office, she sat behind her desk and turned on the laptop. Bryan grabbed one of the metal folding chairs from the kitchenette and jammed himself right next to her.

While the computer was booting up, Lexi took her cell phone out of her bag and plugged it in to be charged. She turned back to her computer to find him studying the pictures on her desk again.

"He looks like he was a happy kid."

"He was. He will be again," she said adamantly.

"Who's he fishing with in that picture?"

"That's my brother, Allan," she told him. She pointed to another picture. "And that's his wife,

Donna, and their two daughters. They're nineteen and twenty-one."

"Is that the only family you have?"

She shrugged. "As far as siblings, yes."

The laptop was taking its time, and Lexi found his scrutiny of her private life somewhat unnerving. She decided to turn the tables a little. "How old are your children?"

"Fifteen and seventeen."

"Boys?"

He shook his head. "Both girls."

She imagined he'd be a big teddy bear to his girls. "What are their names?"

"Amy and Andrea. Amy is fifteen, Andrea seventeen."

"Where do you all live?"

"I live in New York City. The girls live with their mother in a small town just north of Philadelphia."

Lexi gave him a quick look. "It must be hard to keep two residences. It's tough on everybody. I have friends that have to do that because of their jobs. At least New York and Philadelphia are close."

"I'm divorced."

"I'm sorry," she said, turning her attention fully back to the computer. She opened her e-mail account. She had 169 unread messages.

"I guess I'll need a little time to sort through all of these," she told him.

"Would you mind if I made a pot of coffee and used your office phone to make a couple of phone calls?"

"No, make yourself at home."

Lexi found she could breathe easier after Bryan left the room. It had been too long since she'd felt this disconcerted around anyone. And knowing he was divorced only made her feel more...awkward.

Lexi forced her attention on the list of e-mails. She sorted and filtered them by the names that were already in her address book. Twelve of them stood out as first-time correspondents. She browsed each one quickly, hoping that Agent Atwood's hunch was correct. She heard the water running and knew she'd be smelling the first scent of coffee any minute.

The seventh e-mail she opened made Lexi sit upright in her chair.

Dr. Bradley,
You need this information.
Case number #269J
Subject name: Juan Marquez
DOB: 12/7/1992
Laboratory-based pediatric research applying genetic nanotechnology, using molecular sensors to view changes in brain-chemical levels as well as creating fibrous scaffolding within the brain lobes. Made out of the protein actin. To enhance development of multiple intelligences in subject.

Lexi reread the lines. Juan's last name prior to adoption was Marquez. His birth date. There were no attachments to the document. Nothing more. She went back to her list of unread e-mail. There was another one from the same Hotmail address. She opened it.

Whoever had written the e-mail wanted to meet her in Reno Thursday night.

Twenty-Three

"Bryan, you're a veteran of government law enforcement. You've been with the Secret Service long enough to know how these things work," Geary said over the phone. "This project has been reclassified. We know now that it's not a standard high school shooting. A new team of agents will be working on it. You and Agent Gardner will both be commended for your efforts this week, but the nature of the beast calls for a different kind of expertise."

Bryan had called Hank while he was making coffee. The first words out of his partner's mouth had been to tell him they'd been dropped from the investigating team. Bryan called Geary to try to get more information out of him. He'd closed the door to the kitchen before making the second call.

"Hank and I understand that the needs of investigations change," he told the SAC. "That's no big deal. Still, considering we were yanked off our own projects and put on this, we deserve more of an explanation. Hank told me that all the teenagers, including the one involved in the incident in Orlando last night, were adopted. Is this something you already knew? Is any information available on the agencies? Are we talking about some kind of weird testing that might have been done on some kids that were being put out for adoption?"

There was a pause at the other end. "I told you before. We have other agents that are being assigned to this case. I don't see any need for you to be briefed on the results of the investigation."

"I don't think you understand me very well, Geary," Bryan said in a low voice. "There have been some serious lapses of communication in the course of this investigation. I want you to tell me what's going on. If you don't have the authority to tell me, then I'll need to take this to the next level."

He didn't like the idea of being cut out of this investigation. He'd felt out of the loop a number of times over the past couple of days, and he didn't understand that. Geary was either incompetent as a SAC or something was flat-out fishy about the way he and Hank were being treated. He didn't think the former was true, but the latter certainly stank.

Bryan and Geary reported to a different hierarchy of management, but if they kept going up the ladder, Bryan knew he could reach a little higher than this guy. The investigation had lacked adequate communication, at the very least, and Geary knew it. An FBI SAC with plans for moving up couldn't afford to have Bryan bring attention to this. No, the way he and Hank were being treated was bullshit, and he wasn't about to put up with it.

"I'm not going to get into a pissing contest with you, Bryan," Geary said, his tone suddenly conciliatory. "Personally, I have no problem with you and Hank remaining on this team. We all know that you two certainly have the qualifications to be a part of any investigation. The fact is that this case is not a new case. It goes back some fifteen years."

"What are you talking about?" Bryan snapped. He was getting pretty damn tired of all the song and dance.

"What I'm about to convey is confidential."

"I'm listening."

"Let me be clear. None of this can leak to Dr. Bradley."

Bryan understood one of the reasons why he was being pushed to the outside. Someone must have been whispering in Geary's ear about him and Hank being civil to Juan's mother.

"Look, Geary. I'm not a rookie. I understand procedure," he said impatiently. "And I'm getting pretty tired of you dancing around this. Either you tell me what's going on or I'll make some calls and get some answers myself."

"That's not necessary," Geary said shortly. "I said before, I don't want to get into a pissing contest."

Bryan looked at the coffeemaker. It was finished brewing, but it didn't feel right pouring himself a cup when he couldn't offer Lexi any just yet. She'd been the one who was close to starvation.

"This sounds like science fiction," Geary started, "but it's all real. A lot of it I don't understand at all. It's about nanotechnology and the ability to insert tiny programmed machines the size of molecules and smaller into the body to diagnose, treat or monitor the progress of a disease like cancer or Parkinson's or Alzheimer's."

Bryan sat down on one of the chairs. "I'm no scientist, either, but I know that this is nothing new. There's been research done on this kind of thing for a few years now. It's in the tech and biomedical magazines all the time. They see these nanoparticles as little construction units that will be able to self-replicate from materials in the body, as well. It's all pretty theoretical. So what about it?"

"It's not theoretical anymore. There have been a lot of discoveries in the past ten years. The way it was explained to me, though, was that the major hurdle for all these breakthroughs has been the problem of rejection. Our bodies spit these things out. If our bodies don't get rid of them right away, then they accumulate in the organs and become toxic. Scientists haven't been able to figure out how to keep these nanoparticles in the body long enough to do their job."

Bryan thought about whatever Hank and Lexi had seen on the MRI image.

"This seems like legitimate medical research. How does it tie in with these kids and the shootings?"

"Our theory is that these teenagers had a nano-device implanted in their brains some fourteen or fifteen years ago. As primitive and simple as it must be, it was incredibly advanced for the time. Each of those kids still have the device in their heads. Those of them that are still alive," Geary told him. "What we want is that technology. We want those scientists."

"There's a step that you're skipping," Bryan cut in. "I've been involved with enough top-secret projects to know that what you've told me doesn't warrant either the priority or the secrecy. It's a straight criminal case if these scientists never cleared the red tape for such experimentation. What else is there, Geary? Whatever it is, it has to be much bigger."

Bryan pushed to his feet. He walked around the table, trying to decide if he should threaten the SAC again or not.

"Whatever I told you so far was factual. The rest is speculation."

"I'd like to know the speculation, as well."

"If you do, then you have to stay with the project."

"I didn't ask to get off of it," he reminded Geary. "And I plan to stay on."

Bryan knew he sounded arrogant, but at this point he didn't care. His interest was piqued. And perhaps having Lexi relying on him to get her to Juan motivated him, too.

He considered what Geary had told him. They still hadn't even discussed the possibility of these shootings continuing.

"How many kids were involved in the initial research?" Bryan asked.

"We don't know."

"Don't you think that's important? If there are more out there, then we need to know what the actual threat is."

"The MRIs of Juan Bradley's brain were the first hint that this research had even involved humans," Geary answered.

"That's why you've hustled him off to Buffalo."

"We've got the top people in the field there to see what we can learn from him."

"Christ."

"And here I was told that you'd be reluctant to work on anything that had to do with teenage violence. I thought you'd be happy to get off of this case."

"That was Tuesday. Today is Thursday," Bryan told him. "I'm staying on the investigating team."

"And does this include Hank?" Geary asked.

"He can answer that for himself. My money says that he'll stay involved," Bryan explained. "Still, you haven't told me why this is such a priority."

"Intelligence."

"I don't get it."

"Human intelligence," Geary said. "Now, don't forget, we're stepping into an area of speculation that couldn't be confirmed fourteen years ago and can't be confirmed now."

"Go on."

"There were rumors back then that a group of independent scientists with business backing had developed a technique, using nanotechnology that was way ahead of anything in the mainstream, to increase learning capacity. Actually improve intelligence. They were supposedly making super brains."

"All the seven recent shootings were done by top students."

"That's an understatement," Geary agreed. "A lot of these shooters were extremely intelligent, but that has been overshadowed by the tragedy of the violent acts they've committed."

Hank remembered what Lexi had been telling him about how smart Juan was, about his organization skills, his abilities in so many areas.

"We've been putting together a profile, just for the recent shooters. Of the ones we've looked at, every one of them tested as highly gifted at some point. Most, at one time or another, were in the position to skip grades and some did. Several had photographic memory. We don't know much about their infancy since none were adopted until after the age of two, but one hundred percent had full language development at the time of adoption, perfect motor skills. One hundred percent of them were ambidextrous. I can go on and on about music, the arts, about their learning curve for any new topic. Actually, all anyone has to do is look at these teenagers' school records. It's amazing how easy everything came to them. We can only imagine what their potential for learning would have been if they'd been kept in a dedicated environment."

"And you think this was all because of these nanomolecules that were inserted in their brains?"

"We're speculating," Geary repeated. "We really won't know any of this until some serious testing is done on Juan."

"Has his status changed?"

"No, he's still in a coma, but we're watching him carefully. There's increased brain activity, and our medical people in Buffalo believe it's just a matter of time before he pulls through."

"I'm taking Dr. Bradley there today. She wants to be with her son," Bryan told him. "And I'm warning you, don't make it difficult for her to be there, or see him, or be involved at some level. She's been cooperating fully. And, ironically enough, she might be our only connection to these people who you're after."

"She's been getting some crank calls."

Bryan knew Geary had to know everything that was going on with Lexi, as he'd been using Homeland Security resources. Still, he assumed the SAC would want to hear it from him firsthand.

"It's a lot more than just crank calls." Bryan explained about her house being broken into last night and her office at home getting trashed. "Someone is trying to communicate with her. I'm having the local police in Nevada check the store where we think a fax might have been sent from. Right now, she's checking her e-mail to see if there's a message from this guy. And there are others who are trying to stop this communication. Probably the same ones who made the attempt on Juan's life at the hospital."

"This might be a wild-goose chase. Totally unrelated."

"If it is, then we'll eliminate it as a possibility," Bryan asserted. "At the same time, we have no clue about how many children were involved with this testing. Seeing the bloody record of the last seven shootings, and the sudden frequency of them, I don't think we can afford to sit back and assume that there are no others out there."

He could hear Geary let out a heavy breath. Bryan guessed the SAC had pulled an all-nighter as well. It was six-thirty in the morning, and he'd answered the phone at his office.

"I don't like getting a civilian involved."

"I don't, either," Bryan told him. "And I won't unless that's the only option."

"When you take her to Buffalo, she's going to notice we're doing things differently with her son."

"She's a professional. I'm sure she will," Bryan said. "That's why I think it's in our best interest to be up front with her, tell her what's going on."

"You mean, brief her on what we've just spoken about?"

"Yes, I do," Bryan said. Lexi had more at stake in this than any of them. Her son's life was on the line. "I believe you can count on her keeping everything confidential."

"Our objective must remain classified."

Bryan knew exactly what Geary meant about that. The government obviously wanted to find and squeeze the criminals behind this experiment with the intent of gaining control of the technology. That had to remain top secret.

"Whatever," he said. "The only thing she's interested in right now is her son's recovery."

"As you say, *right now*…but later on, we don't want any—"

There was a soft tap on the door.

"Hold on a second," Bryan interrupted.

He opened the kitchen door. Lexi stood in the hallway, two sheets of paper in her hand and a bundle of mail under her arm. "I did have e-mail from him. I think this was what you were looking for."

He took the papers from her hand and stood back, so she could come in. Bryan read the two messages. He read them aloud a second time to Geary on the phone.

Lexi poured two cups of coffee. When he was done reading them, she looked up at him.

"Take me to Juan this morning so I can see him. Then I'll go to Reno and meet with this guy…whoever he is."

Twenty-Four

The cup of coffee sat cooling and forgotten next to her hand.

Sitting at the small table of the kitchenette, Lexi listened to Bryan relate everything he'd just heard from his superior about Juan's situation. She frowned and shook her head as he told her about the government's speculation of what might have happened to these kids some fourteen or fifteen years ago.

Pieces started to fall into place for her.

There'd been so many signs over the years that she'd ignored or taken for granted. Juan had been able to sight-read music when he'd been only four. He'd learned to speak three languages fluently just by going to summer "cultural enrichment" camps with dozens of other children whose end-of-the-summer accomplishment was saying "hello" and "goodbye" and hitting a decent backhand. From the time he was a preschooler, Lexi never had to look up a recipe. She had to make something only once with him, and he'd remember the ingredients and their respective quantities forever. He never had to be told anything twice. Multistep directions were a breeze. His outstanding academic progress was such a small part, too. There were hundreds of other instances when his memory or intelligence had delighted her.

She had a million questions about how much of Juan's abilities could be tied to this and what his prognosis after the episode would be. If the shaded areas that they'd seen on the MRI were indeed mechanical, what was to be done about them? Was there any way to remove the nano-particles without doing any long-term damage to his brain? Had irreparable damage already been done?

Bryan had warned her before even starting that he couldn't answer any of the questions that she would surely have. The next source of information was a physician and scientist named Orrin Dexter. He'd been flown in to Buffalo from Cornell to oversee Juan's progress. Bryan promised that she'd have a chance to speak with him.

"When are we leaving? How are we going to get to Buffalo?" Lexi asked, already impatient to get there.

"We're flying there. And I'll know when as soon as they call me and let me know there's a plane and pilot ready." He got up and took her cup, too. He dumped the contents in the small sink and poured them both fresh cups of coffee.

Lexi appreciated his thoughtfulness. "I guess this is no commercial flight."

"Bradley Airport is shut down because of the weather. All commercial flights are grounded on the East Coast from Washington to Logan. A military plane is being requested. That's our only chance. Even at that, I wouldn't build up any hopes for leaving too soon."

"Maybe we should drive," she suggested, already knowing what the answer would be. It was crazy to try to do four hundred miles in this weather.

"Maybe we shouldn't," he replied. "Even if we need to wait three hours, we'll still get there sooner if we fly."

His cell phone rang. Cell reception was much better here in town.

"Maybe this is the call about the flight."

He looked at the display and Lexi immediately knew this had to be a personal call. The frown immediately disappeared, and his face actually relaxed. The transformation in him was subtle and priceless.

He answered the call. "Good morning, beautiful."

Lexi picked up her cup, trying to decide if she should walk out and offer him some privacy. At the same time, she was curious about whom he was talking to. Maybe a girlfriend. His voice was much gentler, full of affection.

He leaned a hip against the kitchen counter by the door, facing her. "No school today?"

The caller had to be one of his daughters.

"No snow where I am. It's absolutely beautiful here." His gaze moved over Lexi's face.

It was stupid, totally her imagination. Still, Lexi couldn't stop the heat from rushing into her cheeks.

She got up and made a pretense of topping off her coffee cup, even though it was already full. She looked inside the fridge, knowing there was nothing edible left in there.

"I'm in Connecticut," he said into the phone. "Okay, fine. There's probably a couple of feet of white stuff outside."

She darted a glance at her escape route. Bryan's outstretched legs were blocking the doorway. Lexi didn't feel very comfortable going past him. She decided that he could always walk out if he needed some privacy. She walked to the stack of mail, still tied up with a rubber band, sitting on the counter where she'd put it when she came in.

"I was going to come down on Sunday," he said into the phone. "I miss you both. It's been too long."

All the mail was from yesterday. No one had gone through it, yet.

"When is Andrea coming back?" he asked.

His daughters' names were Andrea and Amy. Lexi remembered that one was fifteen, the other seventeen, but she didn't recall which was the older and which the younger.

"No, I haven't been there for years," he said into the phone. "Is it an all-day thing?"

Lexi sorted the mail into piles. She couldn't stop herself from listening to the conversation. It was that father-daughter thing, endearing in a way. She thought about her own father, a hardworking, old-style country doctor who'd never been able to bounce back after her mother's death. Despite his problems, though, the two of them had been very close.

"I'm definitely going to try," he said into the phone. "In fact, if you two can drag yourselves out of bed early enough, maybe we could even try to do breakfast before the museum."

Lexi tried to shake herself off Bryan's conversation and focus on the pile of letters before her. Something kept nagging at her. Something obvious that she wasn't able to see. She couldn't figure out what it was, but she kept staring at the letters.

She heard Bryan end the call, and she took a sip of her coffee.

He came and stood next to her. "That was my younger daughter, Amy. She's fifteen."

The same age as Juan, she thought. All of a sudden, everything cleared in her mind. The phone call, the e-mail, the fax. Mail.

"Mail," she whispered.

"What did you say?"

"Mail," she repeated, looking up at him. "He's tried everything else. That guy could have sent me mail… from Reno."

"Who's collecting your home mail while you've been at the hospital with Juan?"

"It was piling up in my mailbox until my brother's visit a couple of days ago. I called and had the post office hold the rest for me."

She looked at the clock on the wall. It was 8:05 a.m. "Do you think anyone could be at the post office?"

"I haven't been listening to any news or even looked outside lately. It could be the weather is so bad that they haven't opened."

"I'll give them a call."

"What about other types of packages?" he asked before she could reach for the phone. "What happens if you got a Federal Express or a UPS package?"

"In the old days, they used to leave it in between the front door and the storm door," Lexi told him. "But Wickfield is too small a town for those drivers not to know what's going on with my family."

"They'd hold on to the package and leave a delivery slip."

Lexi grabbed the phone book, looking up the numbers. "I'll give both places a call."

Bryan's cell phone started ringing again. This time, rather than eavesdropping, she dialed the number for the post office. The phone kept ringing. No answer. There was no way of knowing if they were closed or too busy to answer the phone.

"Have you called Agent Geary yet with this information?" Bryan asked whomever he was talking to.

Lexi decided that she might have dialed the wrong number and started all over again. After four rings, she gave up on that and started dialing the delivery services.

"I was coming out there, but we'll definitely reevaluate the Reno leg of the trip," he said. "We do need to send in some of our own people."

They were talking about her. Lexi made no pretense of not listening to the conversation. She turned around, the phone still stuck to her ear, watching Bryan taking some notes on a piece of paper.

Someone at the UPS depot in Watertown answered, and Lexi quickly came up with a story of not knowing if they'd tried to deliver anything to her address from Reno. Due to the bad weather, she explained, she was afraid the slip they usually left behind might have blown away. She gave her name, address and phone number.

"Do you have any witnesses?" Bryan asked.

The person she was speaking to was checking the computer. Lexi hoped whoever had called Bryan wasn't reporting another school shooting. Based on what he'd told her, they had no idea how many children might have been involved in this experiment or how widely they were spread across the country…or the world, for that matter.

"I don't care if it's a long shot, we have to pursue it," Bryan said sharply. "Also, I need the time of death."

There *was* a killing. Lexi leaned against the fridge. The person who'd been on the phone with her came back on the line. "We do have a letter pack that was scheduled for delivery to your house this morning. But I don't think our trucks will be getting out for a while. We're short on drivers, and the roads are not that good."

"Check all the recent credit card receipts at the store, just in case," Bryan was saying.

"Do you have a counter open where I can come and pick up the package?" Lexi asked.

"Yes, with proper identification, you can pick it up here at our Watertown customer center location."

She knew where that was. It was a twenty-minute drive in good weather. She didn't want to guess how long it would take her on a day like today.

"But you can't pick up a package tonight until 6:00 p.m. We're here Monday through Friday until 9:00 p.m."

"Why?" she asked. "You just told me the trucks aren't going out. It's not like you have to wait for them to return."

"I'm just telling you the hours of the operation."

"Were there any surveillance cameras?" Bryan asked.

Most of Lexi's attention was on what Bryan was saying. As a result, she was being insensitive to some poor soul who'd simply managed to get to work on a miserable day...or who'd been there all night. If she were to drive there, she was certain they'd hand her the package.

"Can you read me the name of the person who shipped this to me?" Lexi asked, wanting to make sure that the trip would be worth it.

"I'm sorry. I can't give that information out over the phone."

Lexi then got a lecture on how they couldn't verify her identification until she got there, and there was nothing more about the package that they could reveal over the phone.

Lexi figured she might have burned her bridges.

"Call me back," Bryan told the other person.

They both ended their calls about the same time. He spoke first.

"You're not going to Reno tonight."

"What happened?" she asked.

"There was a homicide in the same copy store where someone was trying to send you a fax," Bryan told her. "The killer or killers tried to make it look like a robbery."

"That's horrible."

Bryan nodded and looked down at his notes.

"What time did it happen?" she asked.

"The police there think it was a little after ten, their time. That's a little after one here."

"That's about the same time the fax was aborted."

"You're starting to sound like a cop," he said. "The two might very well be related."

"And someone was hurt," she said quietly, already having heard that much. "Someone not involved?"

Bryan nodded. "The clerk who worked the third shift was killed. A man in his late fifties."

"But he couldn't have been the one that was sending me the fax, could he?"

"We really don't know yet. It could be that someone showed up at the store and dropped off the job and left," Bryan said. "Preliminary reports say there was only one person there. But they're just starting to dig into everything as we speak. Also, there are witnesses who still need to be interviewed. And paperwork that they have to sort through and surveillance videos to look at. There's a lot to do."

She rubbed her arms. "But you're sure that this was a cover-up."

He shrugged without answering.

"Maybe it really was a robbery," she said, "and the timing of it just happened to coincide with that fax. Maybe we're trying to make more of it than it is."

She didn't want everything to be so complicated. She didn't want anyone else getting hurt. No more murders. Someone wanted to get her involved, but Lexi didn't know if she was strong enough to take it right now. She didn't know if she could be of any use.

She put the coffee mug down and took a deep breath, forcing herself to recognize the bunch of crap she was telling herself.

She *was* strong enough, and she *would* get involved. She was doing this for Juan and herself and for other teenagers who might be victims of the same thing as Juan. Kids who were still alive but might not be tomorrow or the next day. This was who she was. This was who she and Juan both were. They wouldn't get knocked down easily, and if they did, they wouldn't stay down for long.

Someone had chosen her to make a difference. She wasn't going to disappoint.

Lexi looked up and found Bryan watching her. He hadn't answered her. He didn't have to.

"How are you holding up?" he asked gently.

She nodded and grabbed her mug of coffee off the counter and drained half of it in one gulp. "I'm fine… and I'm ready."

"I haven't heard anything about a flight to Buffalo yet."

She put the cup in the sink. "I'm ready for a drive to the frontiers of Watertown, Connecticut. There's a package there waiting for me that was sent from Reno."

Twenty-Five

Leslie sat at the back of the school bus, her head down as she pretended to fiddle with her iPod. She was so glad they were going on this field trip to the Hopi reservation today. She didn't know if she could have gotten through the day otherwise.

She should have called in sick, she thought.

But she couldn't have. Her father would have grilled her why she wanted to stay home. Especially since they'd already paid the ten dollars for the trip. She could hear him. *Look, Leslie. I know it's been hard since your mother died, but she wanted you to go to this school....*

She took a deep breath. She didn't like keeping stuff from him. He really was a good dad, and he was trying so hard. But it wasn't her place to tell him about Doreen.

She and Doreen had been up all night, crying. Her older sister might legally be an adult, but obviously handling the pain and the loss of having an abortion wasn't any easier just because a girl was eighteen.

Leslie had told her sister plenty of times that Leonard Maxwell was trash. That boy only wanted one thing, and "long term" wasn't it. Every girl in the high school knew it. Doreen was an idiot not to see it.

Not that it made any difference. Leslie was not particularly in favor of abortion, but there wasn't much choice in the matter. Their father would have killed her, adult or not. And they would have tossed her ass right out of the Magnet School, even if she was a real good student and had only a few months until graduation. They'd heard it often enough…attending the Phoenix Union Magnet School was a privilege that was extended to bright, goal-oriented students who were dedicated to advancing their learning and becoming "beacons of light" for the Phoenix community.

No, Leslie thought, having that baby was not exactly a choice that would have gone down well at home or anywhere else.

Besides, what was done was done, and Doreen was still her sister. They were family. Their mother had held their hands the day she died and made them promise to watch out for each other. No matter what.

So Leslie sat up with her sister and cried with her and held her when the cramps were very bad, and that would have been a little difficult to explain to their father.

As she stared down at the iPod she'd gotten for

Christmas, a tear dropped from Leslie's cheek, and she quickly wiped it away. She had hoped to see Josh today. She would have liked to have seen him waiting for her outside the front entrance, to have him hug her and tell her that everything would be okay.

She frowned and pushed the earpiece in. So where was he? He was supposed to be on this field trip. He was supposed to be sitting right here next to her, holding her hand. He never missed a day of school. Even though he said yesterday that he was still having headaches, it wasn't like him to miss—

"Leslie, isn't that Josh coming across the parking lot?" Her friend Annie turned around in her seat and jabbed a thumb toward the window. "I thought he wasn't in school."

Pulling the earpiece out, Leslie leaned forward and looked out the school bus window at Josh, stumbling across the lot. The teenager wove between the parked cars, bouncing off each one as if he didn't even see them.

"Jeez, Leslie. It looks like your boyfriend decided to come to school stoned."

"Shut up, Annie. You know Josh doesn't smoke."

"Well, whatever. He doesn't look too good."

Leslie stared out the window. Something was definitely wrong with him. If he came to school stoned, they'd toss him so fast he'd bounce like a stone skipping across a pond.

Just then, Mr. Alvarez and Ms. Roberts saw him, too. The last of the kids to get on the bus were standing in a group by the door, and they all looked around at

Josh. Leslie pulled down the window as Mr. Alvarez called to him.

"Josh," the teacher started. "You know you can't come late to school and still expect to go on a field trip."

At that moment, Ms. Roberts plucked at Alvarez's jacket sleeve and said something in a low voice. Leslie could see Mr. Alvarez frown and hand his clipboard to Ms. Roberts before starting across the lot toward Josh.

There was definitely something wrong with him, Leslie thought. This was not like him at all.

The kids on the bus were making cracks about Josh. It was clearly a big joke to them that he'd be in trouble. He was at the top of all of his classes and made them look bad. But now he'd be in for it, big-time, and they were loving it.

"Big joke," she shouted, starting to get up. "Why don't you all just shut your mouths."

Before she was even out of her seat, Leslie heard the popping sound. Looking out the window, she froze. Mr. Alvarez was sitting on the pavement, holding his stomach. As she watched, the teacher slumped over onto his side.

Josh was standing in front of him with a silver pistol in his hand.

"No," she whispered. This couldn't be happening.

When Josh started toward the school bus, the gun still raised, the kids standing outside scattered in every direction, screaming for help. When he started shooting, Leslie couldn't move. She just stood, frozen, and stared in disbelief. He was shooting at the kids who were running. Inside the bus, everyone was trying to hide under the seats, shrieking and crying as they pushed one another for a hiding space. The front windows shattered. Someone was pulling at her from behind and screaming.

Ms. Roberts scrambled onto the bus and was pulling the doors shut when Josh reached it. Leslie could see him outside, calmly aiming and firing at the teacher. The window on the door exploded, and the woman spun back onto the empty driver's seat, screaming and grabbing her shoulder.

This made no sense. He *liked* Ms. Roberts.

Leslie shook her head repeatedly at Josh as he stared in at Ms. Roberts through the empty window. The teacher was crying and writhing in pain.

Then Josh started along the bus, shooting through the side. Kids were really screaming now, crowding up against the far wall, as if that would help. Glass was flying, and she could feel each shot vibrate in her body. When he reached the window where Leslie was standing, he suddenly stopped shooting. She knew he could see her. He was looking right at her.

But it wasn't Josh. This wasn't the boy who waited for her after chemistry and ate lunch with her every day and walked halfway across Phoenix on Saturdays to see her when she had to help her aunt at the grocery store. This wasn't her best friend since sixth grade. She was looking into somebody else's eyes.

"No, Josh," she whispered, shaking her head again. From the corner of her eye, she saw the principal and a guidance counselor come out the front door of the school. Josh must have heard them, because he turned around and faced the school, the gun pointed at the two adults. They all stood there for what felt like eternity.

When Leslie heard the siren, a flash of hope coursed through her. It only lasted for an instant, though, because at that very moment Josh raised the silver pistol to his temple and fired.

Twenty-Six

Watertown, Connecticut

The car was running, and from where Bryan was parked in the snow-covered parking lot, he had a clear view of Lexi through the double set of sliding glass doors. She was standing at the counter waiting for someone to come out and help her collect the package.

More than a dozen parked cars were buried in the snow to the left side of the huge distribution center warehouse. The fleet of brown delivery trucks lined up by the loading docks were also covered with snow. Two plows were working to clear the snow, and six or seven eighteen-wheelers were visible at the far end of the lot. Only one other car in the lot had just a coating of snow on the windshield. This one was parked some hundred yards away, next to the chain-link fence. Bryan couldn't see anyone inside. Bryan figured that had to belong to the person working the counter. There was no sign of any black Escalade with a dent in the side, at any rate.

Gusts of wind were now blowing the snow around, and it looked like real blizzard conditions had developed. He'd spoken to the dispatcher who was arranging the flight to Buffalo for them before leaving Wickfield, and he'd told Bryan that there was no chance they could take off in this weather. The fourteen-mile trip to the UPS service center had taken them more than an hour. Snowplows had been the only other vehicles they'd seen on the road. And even they were barely crawling in this weather. They definitely weren't keeping up with the snowfall. The wind-driven drifts would only make things worse.

Bryan flipped open the cell phone and called his partner. Hank answered right away.

"Are you still working from the hospital?" he asked.

"No, I've graduated to a spare desk at the FBI field office in New Haven," Hank answered. "Much better access to everything."

"Did you get your overnight bag?" Bryan had left that with one of the building security guards before leaving with Lexi.

"Yes, it reached me safe and sound, not that I've had a chance to take five minutes and clean up yet," Hank grumbled.

Bryan could tell that was a good grumble. His partner was busy and he knew Hank liked it that way.

"By the way, Bryan, good job twisting Geary's arm.

I was really getting into this case, and I was pissed when he called and wanted us off of it."

"There was no arm twisting. He saw the light."

"Hallelujah."

"He did call you back, didn't he?" Bryan asked.

"Yes, he did. And he definitely sang a different tune," Hank told him.

Bryan gave his friend a short report on what had happened with the fax and the e-mail Lexi had received. He also told him about the break-in at her house and the homicide in Nevada. He finished by telling him where he was and how they hoped their next clue was inside the package she was picking up.

Relaying everything made Bryan uneasy enough to look around the lot again. The bad weather was to their advantage and hopefully kept the others from following them.

"Once she picks up the package, I'm going to call headquarters with the tracking number. They can trace it back and see how it was paid for. Hopefully, whoever this guy is, he used a credit card."

"A name will make everything so much easier," Hank said.

"The trouble is that the ones who are trying to stop him from communicating with Lexi already seem to have the name and know where he is." Bryan preferred not to automatically assume that the caller was already dead.

The timing of the fax and whatever happened at the copy place in Nevada was way too close to be a coincidence. But if he was dead, then where was the body?

"I've been collecting information on the adoption circumstances for all seven teenagers," Hank told him.

"Find anything?"

"Not yet. The seven of them come from three different states and the paperwork was done by seven different agencies."

"What are the three states?" Bryan asked.

"Nevada, Arizona and New Mexico."

"Very convenient, considering how close they're all together." Bryan saw Lexi speaking to a woman dressed in a brown jacket at the counter inside. He was prepared to go in and flash his badge and Homeland Security credentials and flex his Patriot Act muscles if she needed him to. For now, though, she'd asked him to stay in the car.

"Are they all low-volume adoption agencies?" Bryan asked.

"Nope. Different sizes. Nonprofits and for-profit agencies, both. All reputable places, by all accounts."

"These kids have to have something in common," Bryan said into the phone.

The person at the counter had disappeared again. Lexi turned to the glass door and gave him a thumbs-up sign.

"How about the hospital where they were born?"

"That would be too easy," Hank told him. "But no luck. In fact, three of these kids were delivered by different midwives on two different reservations."

"Well, that's something."

"Yeah, that clears up everything," Hank said wryly.

"I hope you plan to keep digging at that," Bryan said.

"There has to be some record of something that sent these kids to a hospital or a clinic, even for a short period of time."

"You're assuming that this operation was totally contained to one area," Hank said. "We haven't really gone back to look at anything prior to the December 11 shooting. We also haven't looked at any recent teen homicides that didn't take place in school. This could be much bigger than we've been thinking. It could be that the scope of this investigation needs to encompass different age groups of kids, as well. What we know right now—as far as the numbers and frequency of the shootings—could just be the tip of the iceberg."

Bryan didn't doubt anything his friend had just said. But for a change he was trying to remain optimistic. These shootings were so different from the ones that had affected him so adversely when he and Hank had been developing the profile. Back then, he'd had other things on his mind. Things like his teenage brother's suicide.

Lexi was right. As tragic as the losses were, the fact that these kids were being driven to commit acts of violence by a specific implant made it so much easier for him. Now he had perpetrators to pursue, not just angst-ridden, self-destructive teens to try to understand. This was straight law enforcement work. That's why, Bryan decided, he was doing so much better than expected working on this case.

"Hold on a second," Hank said. "Something is happening...."

The woman at the counter was back. Lexi was digging through her pocketbook.

"Turn the news on," Hank told him, his tone gruff. "There's been another one."

"Christ," Bryan muttered under his breath. There'd been a shooting in Florida last night. Now this morning. The frequency of them was increasing dramatically. He turned on the radio, switching channels to find a news station.

Lexi stepped out of the building with a package under her arm. As they'd expected, the package was a large cardboard shipping envelope used for sending documents. She'd had the counter help drop it into manila folder they had brought from the office. Bryan wanted to keep from adding her fingerprints to those already on the package. There was a bounce in her steps. She looked happy.

Bryan found the news on a New York AM radio station. She opened the door and got in just as a reporter was relating the events.

"The assailant—reportedly a top student at the school—killed two and wounded six before taking his own life right outside the Phoenix Union Magnet School, moments before the bus full of students was to take Arizona high schoolers on a field trip. We'll have more on this latest in the growing epidemic of school shootings as the details become available...."

"Not another," she whispered in shock.

"It sounds that way."

"Are you still there?" Hank asked from the other end of the phone.

"I'm here," Bryan said.

"CNN has a chopper showing live video of the school. Looks like a mess. Not many details."

"We need to confirm right away if this one is related to the others."

"Leave that to me. I'm already on it," his partner assured him. "Call me back if the letter Lexi is picking up has anything useful."

"She's right here. Hold on a second. Let's see what we've got."

Bryan switched off the radio. She passed on the folder containing the package to him. He held it on his lap so she could see everything as he opened it. The sender's name was handwritten, and it was totally illegible. The package itself was thin and light.

"The method of payment is not a credit card, but an account number," Bryan said into the phone.

"Why don't you read it to me, and I'll start the ball rolling on it from this end."

Bryan read off the account number and the tracking number and everything else that he could make out on the exterior of the package.

"Hold on," Hank said when he was finished.

Bryan could hear a muffled voice in the background.

"We just got some additional information from Geary," Hank said. "About the shooting this morning in Phoenix."

"What have you got?"

"The assailant, a fifteen-year-old named Josh Maury, was adopted." Hank read him the rest of the report, including the parents' names and home address. The teenager's birthday was also in December.

Bryan relayed the information to Lexi.

"How many is that?" she asked.

"Eight that we think are connected."

"I'm waiting for the report on place of birth and adoption agency and the rest of the medical records," Hank explained.

"Should we open this now?" Lexi asked, looking impatiently at the envelope.

In a perfect investigation, Bryan would have waited until the envelope could be taken to one of their labs and dusted and analyzed while being opened. They didn't want to overlook anything that might be used later as evidence. But this wasn't a perfect world, and Bryan didn't know when the weather would ease up enough for them to do that. The increased frequency of the shootings made the need for immediate action essential.

Snow was beginning to block the visibility out the side windows. Bryan didn't like the fact that they were vulnerable sitting there in the lot. At the same time, he didn't trust the cell service enough to get on the road and still keep the connection with Hank.

Taking a penknife from his jacket pocket, he carefully slit the top of the package and looked inside. There was only a single sheet of paper inside. "It's a handwritten list of names," he said into the phone.

"How many?"

"Eleven," Bryan counted.

"Read the names."

He started giving his partner the names.

"The sixth one," Lexi cried out before he'd gotten to the third name on the list. "Juan Marquez. That's my son. These have to be the names of the teenagers who've been involved with the shootings. Maybe their names before the adoption."

Bryan nodded and then finished reading the names to his partner.

"The first six are in sequential order to the shootings," Hank said from his end. "He must have made the list and mailed it prior to the Orlando, Florida, shooting."

"I assume Michael Saul is the birth name of Michael Forbes," Bryan said, looking down at the list. The teenage shooter from Orlando was the tenth one on the list.

"I'm looking him up right now. I was going through his adoption records right before you called," Hank told them.

Other voices could be heard at the other end. It appeared that Hank was getting some help at the FBI field office.

"Saul *was* the preadoption family name listed for Mike Forbes," Hank affirmed in a minute. "And the same goes for the other shooters."

This was better than anything Bryan might have hoped for. They actually knew the name and scope of how many teenagers were involved with the experimentation.

"Who are we left with?" Lexi asked.

Bryan read down the list again, leaving out Juan's name.

"We have three from this list that we have to find," Bryan said. "Billy Ward, Roy Carter and Donald Gray. Will you call Geary with the names?"

"Right away. I'll also contact the Nevada, Arizona and New Mexico state departments of Vital Statistics, Family Services, Child Welfare...whatever. We need to start tracking any records they have on these kids."

"How about a social security number search?" Lexi asked him. "I had to get one for Juan the moment the paperwork started. I used his original last name as a middle name on the records. I was told a lot of parents do that."

"Did you hear that?" Bryan asked Hank.

"Yeah, I did. We'll get on that, too."

"Thank you, whoever you are," Lexi whispered, staring at the envelope. "You're saving lives by doing this."

Twenty-Seven

Thursday, January 17, 1:42 p.m.
Manhattan, New York

Riding the elevator up to his office, Curtis Wells was feeling pretty good.

He brushed some of the melting drops of snow off his black cashmere overcoat. It was still snowing, though not as hard as it had been, he thought. It was difficult getting around the city, but not impossible. Actually, in all his years of living and working in the city, Curtis couldn't remember too many times when New York traffic had come to a complete standstill because of a snowstorm.

New Yorkers just knew how to deal with whatever was thrown at them. Be it blizzard, power failure or transit strike, people still got around, went to work, met for their appointments. Restaurants found a way to stay open and serve food. City dwellers were much better off here during a heavy snow than just about anywhere else on the East Coast.

Another great thing about this city. Only in New York could you find a first-rate restaurant around every corner, and Curtis had taken advantage of that this morning. He'd had his secretary change the lunch reservation to a nearby restaurant for the four Japanese investors who'd arrived last night. He was meeting with them for a business lunch before the two o'clock press conference. The end result had been a huge success. Curtis even had about ten minutes to look over his notes before taking his show public.

When he'd started in this business, Curtis had never imagined he'd be making millions in the fight against cancer. But that was exactly what he was doing…or rather, what he was about to do. Every technological and business venture he'd been involved in had led him to this.

This was his time. This was when he cashed in.

Quantum dots. Who knew that something so small could be so effective in the fight against disease? The nano-size crystals that he'd been funding scientists to develop were now at the breakout point. The tiny particles, injected into living cells, actually created probes that detected DNA sequences associated with cancer. It was the cutting edge…the place where he'd always wanted to be.

Quantum dots were a tiny product that would produce big returns. Very big. And today, the next step.

Curtis was presenting their product and business plans to the general investment community and the public.

It didn't matter that they were still waiting for FDA approval. That was going to happen. Besides, a little pressure from the American public on the importance of this technology was a good thing for everyone. It was especially good for him.

Coming back to his office after lunch, Curtis nodded to his secretary as he passed by her desk. She was on the phone.

The presentation was to be virtual-reality and three-dimensional. Very high tech. A team of game programmers from Microsoft had adapted special technology for this presentation, and Curtis planned to impress…no, blow the doors off reporters and investors with the colors and sounds and the futuristic feel of the production. He was going to take his audience right into the human cell. The techies from Microsoft would be on stage with him to make sure the show went the way it should. His brief introduction and the presentation itself would steer the questions directly into the areas he wanted to cover during the question-and-answer period.

He was in the perfect mood—pumped up just enough to give one of his most brilliant performances. He didn't need any distractions, nothing to take his mind off one of the most important moments of his career.

He'd left his notes in the middle of his desk, but as he walked into his office, the envelope in his in-box caught his attention. Block letters in red marker spelled "Confidential."

He knew that handwriting.

Curtis picked it up, the presentation forgotten. He swiveled his chair around to the glass wall of his nineteenth-floor office. The envelope was light. He turned it over in his hand and then hesitated, looking out for a moment at the snow falling on the city.

The concept that Curtis was presenting today had a lot to do with the research that he and his partner had started more than two decades ago. Even in recent years, Mitch knew what Curtis's company was doing, but never once had he objected or asked for some credit for the developing product. That was one of Mitch's greatest faults. His generosity. He could have been standing next to Curtis on that podium today.

But Mitch was gone. He was dead.

Curtis looked down at the envelope. It had been shipped from Reno last night. He ripped the tab and pulled out the contents. Two sheets of paper. That's all there was.

The first page was a short handwritten note from Mitch. The second contained a list of names. Curtis perused the list first.

Back when they'd been in the midst of testing their theories, Curtis had had no interest in knowing the names of these children. They were only case numbers to him. Subjects used for important experimentation. The work was supposed to help improve their chances in life, not injure them. During the first week, though, they'd lost five and a half percent of the subjects.

So they'd remained numbers for him. Still, this past

month, Mitch and his frequent phone calls had forced Curtis to become familiar with some of the names.

He looked down at the long list again. Fifty-seven names. He knew this was the original list. All of them were undoubtedly here. Mitch was nothing if not thorough. There were dates before most of the names. He knew that had to be the date they'd lost the subject. Five names were highlighted in yellow and had no dates before them. Mitch must have made the list before the last two shootings.

Curtis frowned and considered those shootings. They were becoming the top news item of the day. Even the Japanese investors, who were no strangers to teenage burnout and suicide that was in their own country, had been talking at lunch about what they'd heard on the news this morning. Except for the early business reports, Curtis hadn't looked at the news himself. He didn't want to know anything beyond what the headline provided as it scrolled across the bottom of the screen. He definitely didn't want to pay attention to the names. He knew that these two teens had to be theirs.

He looked down at the list. That meant there were only three left. As he'd said to his former partner, things were taking care of themselves.

He started to crumple the list in one hand, but stopped and looked over Mitch's note. It was undated.

Curtis,

Too many lives have been lost for me to let all the research be shredded and burned. If we'd taken our time, stayed with laboratory subjects before moving to human test subjects—if we hadn't allowed ourselves to be rushed by investors and politicians—some good might have come out of our work. It was good work at the beginning.

In case you decide to do the right thing, here is the list. You know what the right thing is. Each life is precious. Too many of them are gone. Save the ones you can. Do it for you and me. For God's sake, save us all.

Mitch

Curtis read the letter again. Did this mean that there were still files out there? Was it possible that everything his people destroyed in Reno last night hadn't been all of it?

"They're ready for you in the meeting room, sir."

Startled, Curtis spun around in his chair. He hadn't heard his secretary poke her head into the office. He crumpled the pages in his hand.

"Are you okay? Can I get you anything?" the young woman asked, looking concerned.

"No, no," he said hoarsely. "Tell them I'll be there in a minute."

She went out. Curtis stared at the two crumpled pieces of paper. He was in trouble. The nightmare was back.

He hadn't been able to kill Mitch, after all.

Twenty-Eight

Lexi had never been nervous about flying. But the snow-covered runway and the gusts of wind rocking the small jet from side to side were making her knuckles white and tying her stomach in a knot even prior to takeoff.

The fold-out doors to the cockpit had been left open. A pilot, co-pilot, Bryan and Lexi were the only ones on the eight-seater jet. The snow continued to fall, and through the front windshield she could see a plow working to clear the single runway. Bryan told her the wind had subsided enough for them to take off safely, but Lexi had a sense that the decision to go had less to do with the weather and more to do with the series of phone calls that Bryan had been involved with since they'd opened that envelope in Watertown.

They'd stopped back at her house for five minutes so that she could pack an overnight bag. Then they'd come directly to the small private airport just north of the town, where the jet was waiting. Even though the aircraft did not have Air Force markings, the pilots both turned out to be uniformed officers.

Bryan hadn't shared much of the information from the telephone conversations with her, but Lexi already knew he was not happy about some of the decisions being made by his superiors. He'd still been on the phone when they taxied to the end of the runway. Lexi had a feeling that at least some of those arguments had to do with her; she'd heard her name mentioned a few times.

She looked ahead, but she could barely see the end of the tarmac. When the jet started down the newly cleared runway, the incredible power of the aircraft pressed her hard into her seat. The sensation was far more pronounced than anything she'd ever felt flying in a commercial airliner. In seconds, it seemed, the front wheels lifted, and then they were in the air. She breathed a sigh of relief but stopped as the jet bumped and shook as it rose into the sky. In less than a minute, she could see nothing but white out her window. The ground had disappeared.

"You both okay back there?" the pilot asked, turning around and smiling briefly at her.

Lexi nodded, taking from his calm that they must have reached a safe altitude. She looked over at Bryan sitting next to her. He was still on the phone. She had known him for so little a time, and yet she understood that his mood always seemed to be reflected in his expression. Right now, he looked positively pissed off.

"Excuse me, sir," she joked. "The captain has not turned off the No Electronic Devices sign. You'll have to turn that off and talk to me."

His blue eyes turned to her, and he shook his head with obvious frustration. A moment later, he snapped the phone shut.

She touched his hand. "What is it?"

"Talking to you is exactly what Geary wants."

"Who's Geary?" she asked.

"The FBI Special Agent in Charge. He's the team leader for this investigation."

She remembered hearing his name. "What is it that he wants you to talk to me about?"

"He wants me to explain his plan to you," he said. "He seems to think that there's a much better chance of you going along with it if it comes from me."

"What does he think? That you're special?"

He narrowed his gaze and looked into her eyes, then he actually laughed. "Actually, now that you put it that way, yes, I am."

She punched him on the arm. The muscles were like rock. She liked the sound of his laughter. Lexi thought this was the first time she'd heard him do that. Really laugh.

The plane angled sharply to the left and right, dropping and then rising again. Lexi grabbed for Bryan, catching his forearm, and he held it firmly in place with his other hand. Something in his response, so immediate and natural, warmed her inside, and she suddenly felt very conscious of his touch.

The pilot said something to the co-pilot, who turned around.

"A few more minutes of climbing through this turbulence and the ride should smooth out," the co-pilot told them. "Then we'll be above it."

True to his word, after a couple of more sharp bounces, the ride became calmer.

"Thanks," Lexi whispered to Bryan, trying to withdraw her hand.

His hand remained on hers, his serious eyes looking into her face. "What Geary wanted me to do is to ask you to go to Reno tonight."

The e-mail she'd received earlier today flashed back in her mind. The person behind the calls, letters and e-mail had wanted to meet with her tonight.

"But we're going to Buffalo right now," she said, needing to make sure.

"I told you we are," he said patting her hand before withdrawing his.

Suddenly, they broke through the clouds and into the bright morning sunlight. Above, the sky was blue. Beneath them, the clouds were gray and unbroken for as far as the eye could see.

"And they want me to go to Reno after Buffalo because they think this guy will contact me," Lexi continued, restating what they already knew.

"That's what they say," he said thinly. "But you're a civilian. There has already been a murder out there. In fact, we're operating on the assumption that the murder has a direct bearing on this case and the fax your contact was trying to send you."

He looked out the window for a moment but continued to talk.

"Never mind the break-in at your house and the threat on Juan's life at the hospital in New Haven. Personally and professionally, I think it's insane to get you involved," Bryan said adamantly. "No, we can send an undercover agent, pretending to be you. There is no way this guy knows for sure what you look like."

"The nurses at the hospital told me that there was a picture of me on the news and in some of the papers."

"We can use a look-alike. It's been done plenty of times before," Bryan said.

She thought about that. It was possible they would have only one chance at find out what this stranger at Reno was doing. She understood Geary's point in wanting to make sure they succeeded. At the same time, she understood...and appreciated...Bryan's concerns.

"You know, I don't seem to be any good to Juan right now, though I desperately want to be there when he comes out of this coma. But at the same time, I certainly am no lawyer or wheeler-dealer," she said hesitantly. "So what I'm going to ask, I'm more or less winging. I'm hoping this is how things will work."

Lexi gauged his expression. It was very important to her to have Bryan in her corner. So far, his support had been invaluable, and she didn't want what she was about to say to come across wrong.

"Go on," he encouraged.

"If I were to go through with this...go to Reno as this guy Geary wants and do whatever these guys at the FBI ask me to do...does that mean I can have some bargaining power when it comes to how Juan is treated? Legally, I mean. Can I make some deals? Lessen any charges?"

What she was saying sounded like something you'd see in the movies. Lexi wasn't sure this kind of stuff was done in real life. Suddenly, she wished she had talked to the lawyer.

"Of course," he said, putting an end to her uncertainty. "You've already been very instrumental in this investigation. But all I can say is, don't get ahead of yourself. You should remember that, based on everything we've gathered, it's really doubtful that there will be any criminal charges brought against Juan. You saw the results of the MRI. You and I both know that Juan could very well turn out to be the victim of something himself. He could be cleared of any wrongdoing without you having to do any of this."

"'Could be' is not a guarantee. And I don't want to risk it," Lexi said. "I'll do anything. I'll go to the ends of the earth to give my son another chance. This offer of getting involved, being part of the investigation, is actually a gift, an opportunity for me to do something. I don't feel useless."

"Lexi, what they're asking you to do is dangerous."

"Tell me what's *not* dangerous these days," she said, matching his tone.

"These are violent criminals we're dealing with here. They're professionals."

"I have you with me, Agent Atwood, to take care of the bad guys." She shook her head. "There's something else… Aside from Juan, I need to do this. Not only for myself, but for all those teachers and students who have died or been wounded in all this recent school violence. These kids, like Juan, couldn't have known where they were going or what they were doing. They couldn't have known the danger they were in. Besides, who says this list we have in our possession is all of them? We have to find this guy. I feel responsible to do my part of it. He's chosen me to contact. I have to be there."

He still didn't seem happy with her answer, but he didn't try to talk her out of it anymore. The brooding expression was back. She wasn't going to lose this opportunity, though. She believed everything she'd said. And another thing that Lexi hadn't said was that she needed to do this to help diminish the guilt she was feeling for what Juan had done. It was crazy, but she figured this was what parenthood was all about. You celebrated and mourned your child's successes and losses as if they were your own.

"How do I go about making these deals…telling whoever is in charge what I want?"

"I'll take care of all of that for you," he said gruffly.

Lexi had no doubt that he would. She didn't know how and when it had happened, but she trusted him, pure and simple.

"But you *will* be going to Reno, too, won't you?" Lexi asked after a couple of moments of silence. She could hear the note of hope in her voice.

"You can bet on it," he said in the same gruff tone.

"Thanks," Lexi whispered, biting her lip to stop a

smile. She was more than relieved to hear that he was going. And despite his scare tactic regarding the danger involved, she wasn't nervous at all. "The only news that can top this is getting to Buffalo and hearing a positive report on Juan from this Dr. Dexter."

She thought he grunted. He *was* like a big teddy bear—his fur definitely got ruffled when he didn't get his way.

Lexi looked out the window. For the first time in days she felt that positive sense of *doing* something, of being in charge of her destiny. It felt great to imagine there was hope.

They were flying just above the tops of the clouds. The ride was occasionally bumpy but it was nothing compared to the roller-coaster they'd put up with right after takeoff.

She'd meant to call Allan and her attorney before leaving the house, but with everything else going on, she'd never had a chance. Right now, she didn't think there was anything more Attorney McGrath could do for her, anyway. She was in it with the authorities up to her neck. They all would simply have to wait and see how the investigation would turn out.

Lexi looked back at Bryan. "Do you know if it's still snowing in Buffalo?"

"Before we left Wickfield, the pilot mentioned there are only flurries out there."

He was talking to her. She appreciated that he wasn't holding a grudge because she'd disregarded his concern.

"How long do we have at the hospital?" she asked.

"Not too long. Maybe an hour," he said. "A helicopter is picking us up at the airport and taking us to the VA hospital. These guys will take us on to Reno. Listen, why don't you try to rest."

"I'm fine," she said brightly. "Really."

She looked out the window again and thought she saw small patches of clearing. Yes, she was actually seeing buildings and snow-covered earth and roads far below.

"Can I ask you a personal question?" he asked.

Lexi looked over at him and shrugged. She was amazed at how quickly she was feeling comfortable with him. He felt like an old friend. She couldn't allow herself to think anything beyond that. But even as a friend, there was so little they knew about each other.

"Why did you adopt Juan?"

The question took her by surprise. Did he mean, why did she adopt a half Mexican, half American Indian toddler? Was this about the color of his skin? It wasn't. It couldn't be, she told herself.

Lexi had to fight the usual defensiveness she felt when asked these kinds of questions. She wasn't used to talking about herself. She didn't share her past easily with people. And her claws came out instinctively when someone was talking about Juan.

She looked at him. Bryan was studying her face.

"My question has to do more with *why* you decided to adopt…not so much why Juan."

She guessed he must have read the look on her face. "Many people adopt. There are lots of single parents. It's not really that strange anymore."

"I don't think it was ever strange," he told her. "My curiosity is more about you. If you don't mind me asking, how old were you when you adopted Juan?"

"Twenty-seven. I'm forty-one now," she told him. Lexi had no problem revealing her age. She was proud that she'd made it this far.

"See? That's impressive. How many twenty-seven-year-olds are ready for that kind of responsibility?"

This was the most talkative he'd been. Actually, the most interested, she corrected. Lexi realized what he wanted. He wanted to know why a twenty-seven-year-old woman would decide on adopting a toddler instead of having children of her own. He wanted to know why she didn't have a husband and pursue the dreams so many other young people had.

Only a handful of people knew why. Lexi wasn't embarrassed about it; she just preferred not to talk about it.

She didn't know when and how her past had become so top secret. She'd felt uncomfortable when Bryan had initially refused to tell her if he had any children or not. But he'd given in, shared a little when he didn't have to.

There was a lot of himself he was putting on the line for her. Bryan had made every effort to help her. Lexi understood he would be disappointed if she decided to shut the door on her past.

"I'm not used to talking about myself," she told him. "But…I'll make an exception with you, Agent Atwood."

His smile made Lexi's temperature rise a few degrees. She brushed the back of her hand against the aircraft window. It felt cool to the skin. She wished she could press her face against the glass.

"When I was finishing my residency at Flagstaff Medical Center in Arizona, I started volunteering on a weekly basis at two outpatient facilities on the Navajo and Hopi reservations. Juan and his aunt were regular visitors of mine. He was a sickly toddler with a low immune system. He seemed to catch every childhood disease and take three times as much time to kick it."

Lexi thought back to that time. Juan's happy attitude, despite the constant fevers and colds and asthma and allergies and everything else, caused Lexi to step out of her shell and forget about her own bad fortune. He was such a bright spot. She truly looked forward to seeing him.

"He was so smart. He was like a little old man inside the body of a toddler," she smiled. "He understood so much. He was so sensitive. He was curious about everything around him. I'd be checking him, listening to his lungs, and he'd be trying to tell me word for word what he'd heard on the news that morning, or what the weather forecast was for the week, or he'd whisper that his aunt's smoking was why he couldn't breathe. He would say things that were totally unexpected of his age. A lot of kids can barely speak in sentences at that age."

"So you adopted him because be was a smart kid," he said, smiling.

"I adopted him because I knew he had no parents and his aunt wasn't going to keep him too much longer. She spent whole days in bed because of being sick and she was a chain smoker. She had no money and barely could take care of herself. In fact, I got a sense that there might have been some kind of financial assistance she was getting from somewhere, but that was about to end."

"That's interesting," he said.

"But what really motivated me to adopt Juan was the fact that she didn't want him. She said she couldn't afford to take care of a child. She told everyone about Juan's parents and what horrible people they were to die and leave her with this burden. She said that the toddler was only staying with her short term. She'd contacted social services to find him a home."

Thinking about it, she felt like it was yesterday. Lexi saw Juan at least twice a month. It was very sad.

"I think Juan understood it all. He knew he wasn't wanted. Still, he kept up a good attitude, kept his chin up. That child's spirit made me think so much about who I was and about what I was going through. I talked to his aunt and she agreed. You know, at the time, I adopted Juan because I thought he needed me."

Lexi thought about what she'd just said for a moment. She was actually talking. She might as well tell him the rest of it.

"The truth is, I adopted Juan because I needed *him,*" she said quietly. "During my last year of med school I lost my father. He was my only surviving parent. We were very close. And then, six months before going to Flagstaff, I was diagnosed with cervical cancer. The prognosis was good, but I had to have a couple of surgeries. And after I was done with them, I was told that I would never be able to have children."

Bryan's hand reached for hers, and he gently squeezed it. A mix of feelings rushed through her. After so many years, Lexi was at peace with her cancer. Still, there were moments like this, when she was talking about it, that emotions avalanched down on her. Good and bad, sad and indifferent, what she'd missed and everything she'd gained, they were all there, popping in from every corner of her conscious and subconscious. Each conflicting emotion was fighting to control her mood.

"I definitely needed him more than he needed me," Lexi repeated.

She couldn't bring herself to look up at him for fear of losing control. She was on the way to see Juan, she reminded herself. She had to stay focused on what was important. She kept talking.

"Juan filled my life with everything that was missing. He made me look outside of myself. He was this active little bundle of joy that I needed to focus my attention on. He got healthier and healthier, and he taught me how to be a mother, how to be a better person." She laughed. "Even how to be neat and organized."

She looked at their hands. Bryan was still holding hers.

"He made me happy," she told him. "He made me whole."

Twenty-Nine

"There will be a 6:00 p.m. flight out of Tweed–New Haven Airport," one of the FBI clerical staff members told Hank, having just finished making all the arrangements for him. "You have to stop in Philadelphia to pick up two other members of the investigating team. You arrive in San Diego at midnight. The rest of the team will be waiting in California for your arrival."

Of the three names they'd been given, Donald Gray, who became Donald Tucker after his adoption, had been the only one located immediately.

Unfortunately, the family that had adopted him had broken up. Since the divorce, the father lived in Seattle. Donald had lived with the mother in California, but she had relocated to Atlanta this past fall...

without her adopted son. Unlike each of the other cases, where the teenagers' stellar academic and behavioral performance made them outstanding citizens, Donald's early and teen years had been turbulent, to say the least. The fifteen-year-old had changed schools six times since first grade, the last stop being the Southern California Military Institute in Carlsbad, California, where he'd been dropped off in late November.

Sometimes the added structure and discipline of such a school helped, but Hank had seen this family situation many times. It fit the profile for disaster.

Geary had called Hank about it an hour ago, requesting that the psychologist fly to California and link up with the agents who would be going to the military academy. In the meantime, the local police and the guidance counsellors at the school had been warned to watch Donald until they got letters of consent from the parents to take him into protective custody. As things stood right now, there was no legal basis to pick up the fifteen-year-old. An anonymous letter with his name on a list wasn't enough to obtain a court order. They were following a trail, but it was not a verifiable trail…yet. This whole thing could be some lunatic playing games with them, sending Lexi what was already in the headlines and adding in whomever he wanted to the list.

Hank believed the list was legit. At the same time, he would await the parents' consent. Donald hadn't committed a crime. Even the school, acting in *loco parentis*, wasn't about to act arbitrarily. The problem was that Hank didn't know how long it would take to get the parents' permission. The only thing he did know was that they didn't have it yet.

So Hank was headed to California to "interview" Donald. His call on the teenager's present psychological profile would get the wheels turning for whatever action was to follow. Meanwhile, he couldn't stop wondering if tomorrow might be too late. The kids were succumbing to psychotic episodes in unnervingly rapid succession.

With regard to the others on the list, Hank couldn't understand why they still had no word on the whereabouts of Billy Ward or Roy Carter. They had the names of their adoptive families. The adoption files in the state of Arizona had them documented as Billy Ebbett and Roy Naves. But the present location of their families remained a big question mark.

Hank started gathering up the paperwork and notes he'd collected since last night, stuffing them inside his briefcase.

"We have an account name for the overnight package Dr. Bradley received today," one of the agents who'd been helping him reported from the next desk.

Good, Hank thought. Pieces of the puzzle were finally coming together.

"What do you have?"

"California State University System."

Hank stared at him. "I need something a little more specific than that."

The younger agent shrugged. "I was just on the

phone with the University Business and Finance Division. Twenty-three campuses with 44,000 faculty and staff. He couldn't immediately tell me who or even what campus that account number was assigned to. He said it would take him a hell of a long time to track it down."

"I'll bet the auditing department would love to hear that," another agent said, shaking his head. "Typical state bureaucracy."

"That's no good," Hank said, thinking out loud. "We need to get the names of all faculty and graduate students who teach biology in the university system. Then we need to pare that list down to any who are or have been involved with nanoscience or nanotechnology research."

He continued on, giving the agents other specific areas of research, too. It was a long shot, but they had to try.

"Also," he said as another thought occurred to him, "contact the shipping department at each campus. If there is a central administrator, talk to him or her. Get someone in charge, preferably the person who negotiates the rates with the freight carriers. There must be a way that they can charge the expense of each package shipped to a specific department, if not an individual."

"You don't think the business division knows what they're talking about?"

Hank shrugged. "My wife is an academic. I'm pretty familiar with how these university systems work their expenses. I'm sure there are unmonitored account numbers, but for the most part, there has to be a column for almost everything that goes out of there. For some of those administrators, bean counting is part of their existence."

Thirty

Nick Luna was one of those people who might have the potential to grow on you, but at this stage in his life he just rubbed most people the wrong way.

Looking down at him now, Bryan decided that the agent was extremely smart, but too damn young. It could go either way for Luna. He could piss off the wrong person and end up watching a monitor for potential terrorists at the Hoover Dam for the next twenty years or so. Or, he could get over the cockiness that was part of youth and learn how to deal with people.

Not that he himself had done too well in that department, but at least he'd been lucky. Luna made himself too visible to be lucky.

Bryan had no complaints with the way the long-

haired kid treated *him*. For some reason, Luna treated
Bryan with the utmost respect. Still, he managed to
tick off everyone else. And even when he was trying
to scramble after screwing something up, he just
seemed to have a penchant for messing things up more.

A perfect example of that had to do with Lexi.
Bryan didn't know what happened between these two
back at the hospital in New Haven, but she'd bristled
just seeing him as he came down to meet them at the
hospital security office. Bryan decided the young man
may have intended to make peace with her, but what
he did instead was to tell her how much time she
could have with her son and how she had to hurry
since he'd been instructed to see that she and Bryan
stayed on schedule for Reno. Basically, he'd tried
ordering her around. In the end, Lexi had stalked off
beside an FBI agent from the Buffalo field office to see
Juan and talk to Dr. Dexter, while Bryan had stayed
behind to listen to whatever urgent thing that Luna
still had to tell him.

"There was a breach in security here at the hospital
earlier this afternoon," the young agent told him as
soon as Lexi was out of earshot.

Christ. Juan was supposed to be safe here. "Did they
get to Dr. Bradley's son?"

"No. We're certain about that," Luna said unequiv-
ocally. "First, the IT department, just by chance, caught
someone trying to hack into their system for Juan's
medical files."

"Could they trace the hacker's ID?"

"No. The connection was cut before they could trace it. They were definitely pros."

"We knew that before."

"Two other incidents occurred as well."

"Busy day," Bryan said grimly.

"There was a clean break-in at the pharmacy. One of the orderlies spotted the damaged door."

"So they didn't catch anyone, I take it."

"No. The local police came in and did their thing."

"Do they know what was taken?" Bryan asked.

"They're doing an inventory check now."

Bryan shook his head. "What was the second thing?"

"Surveillance cameras picked up two unauthorized persons in one of the food-prep areas. No sign of the intruders by the time Security reached it."

"Did you send the images to headquarters in Washington?"

"Yeah, just before you got here."

"Juan *isn't* safe here," Bryan said, pissed off. "What else is being done about all this?"

"The administrator has brought in more personnel and beefed up security for the entire hospital. Only authorized persons, escorted by one of our own agents, are being allowed to step foot on that floor. No medications are being disbursed from this hospital's pharmacy to Juan. Also, there will be no food delivered from the kitchen for any of the staff for the couple of hours we have remaining here."

"What do you mean, 'the couple of hours we have remaining'?"

"Dr. Dexter is transferring Juan to the medical center at Cornell," Luna told him. "There is equipment he needs that's available there."

"Have you talked to Geary about that?"

"I have talked to him, and I was told he already knew about it. Our people are doing a security sweep of the place right now. Supposedly the only patients on one floor at that clinic will be Juan and the three other teenagers, when they're found."

Bryan nodded, considering Luna's final statement. He didn't know what legal angle Geary would use to collect the other kids that were still out there. But that was his problem. This Dexter guy seemed to be the man with the answers, as far as the U.S. government was concerned. Bryan guessed that he must have a long-standing relationship with the government, but he wondered what exactly his qualifications were. Whatever they might be, the scientist's recommendations were clearly being followed without discussion.

"Who knows about the move?" Bryan asked. "We don't want the people who are after Juan to get another shot at him."

"The SAC agrees completely. The move is being kept on the down low. There will be no briefings beyond the requisite personnel as far as the change in location and the time of Juan's transfer." Luna looked at him carefully. "And I was directed to inform you, Dr. Bradley is not to be apprised of any of the details of the move."

They'd better find something in Reno tonight to help conclude this case, Bryan thought, because he already knew Lexi wouldn't put up with not knowing where her son was. By tomorrow, when they were finished in Nevada, Bryan figured he'd fight that battle with Geary and whoever else he needed to. As far as he was concerned, Lexi *would* be taken to where Juan was being hospitalized.

"We're also going to keep the beefed-up main-floor security in place and Juan Bradley's files intact at this hospital, as if he were still here. We'll make sure the records show the room and bed are still occupied. We'll even maintain the security detail on the floor."

"That makes perfect sense," Bryan said. "What's being done about the transportation?"

"We'll take him out through the emergency room exit. An ambulance will arrive under the pretence of bringing in a patient. In reality, it'll be here to leave with Juan. There will be no fanfare when the ambulance leaves."

"How about security? Protection for the kid along the way?"

"We've planned a decoy and a convoy of unmarked vehicles to serve as escort for the ambulance."

Bryan had been in this line of business long enough to know the decoy was used with regular success. It was standard procedure for the Secret Service to use the same tactic in moving the president or the vice president or any number of visiting dignitaries from other countries from one location to another.

He asked a few more questions about the number of agents involved and the security at the medical center once Juan was taken there.

By the time Bryan left Nick downstairs and headed for the floor where Juan was, he felt very confident that the FBI had everything under control. But at the same time, he was glad that he didn't have to tell Lexi anything about it right now. She wasn't familiar with the clockwork precision with which these people worked. Knowing Juan was being moved would only add stress that she didn't need.

Bryan had to go through the same security checkpoints as anyone else when he arrived on the floor. There was only a skeleton group of medical professionals around. For every one of those, there were at least two federal agents.

He was informed that Dr. Bradley and Dr. Dexter were at Juan's bedside. Bryan was escorted to the door of the teenager's room. The nurses' station sat directly across the hall. A huge plate-glass window separated the patient's room from the hallway. There was no way anyone could walk in there without being seen.

Bryan saw Lexi and an older man whom he assumed to be Dexter talking to the left of Juan's bed. Lexi was holding her son's hand. Her gaze continuously shifted from the physician's face to Juan's.

The story she'd told him about her past wouldn't leave him. He'd been impressed and attracted to her before. But what she'd gone through and what she'd done about it made her so much more special.

In the light of tragedy and disappointment, she'd made a new life, created a family. Bryan, on the other hand, hadn't been able to dig out from under tragedy.

He'd destroyed his marriage, broken up his family. He remembered the call from Amy this morning. One of the only bright spots in his life was that his daughters still wanted to have anything to do with him.

Lexi turned around and saw him and motioned for Bryan to come inside. He walked in.

There was no life-support system, only a brain-activity monitor along with the standard monitors keeping track of the boy's vital signs. If it weren't for the IV in one arm, anyone could think that the teenager was just sleeping. Bryan realized he'd seen many pictures, but this was the first time he was seeing Juan in person.

He was tall, thin and gangly, the way so many teenagers his age were. His face was young and innocent. No facial hair, no piercings, no visible tattoos. He was just a good-looking kid with straight dark brown hair combed off his forehead.

As Bryan looked at the boy, images of another city, another hospital room, a different fifteen-year-old lying unconscious on the hospital bed flashed before his eyes.

His brother, Bobby.

Bryan had sat next to him, holding his cold hand, trying somehow to understand. He couldn't. But it was more than the inability to understand, it was the inability to forgive himself that tore at Bryan so badly. He should have seen it. This was his line of work. If he'd paid more attention...

"Agent Atwood," Lexi said, softly drawing his attention. She looked at him for the longest moment, her eyes riveted to his. Bryan felt she was reaching into his soul. She was seeing his struggle, the mourning that he'd never finished. He'd left the door to his heart open. The cuts were deep and bleeding once again. Or rather…still.

"I'm Orrin Dexter," the older man said, shaking Bryan's hand.

The reality of their surroundings shuffled everything into focus.

"How's our young patient doing?" Bryan asked.

Dexter matched the caricatured image of a scientist. Curly, uncombed blond hair, thick glasses, a beak for a nose, half a dozen pens and handheld electronic devices protruding from the sagging pocket of his somewhat ragged blue oxford shirt. Sometime in the past five or ten years, a pen had leaked ink from that pocket, leaving a blue egg-shaped stain. Bryan guessed that Dexter probably never noticed the stain, but still missed the pen. The worn boat shoes with the deteriorating stitching at the toe of his left shoe completed the picture.

"I was just telling…uh, Lexi, isn't it? Yes, Lexi…that I think Juan is progressing quite well. He's having normal pupil reaction to light. I find that very encouraging. Of course, there are a number of tests that we have to run yet. We'll start with a SPECT scan to see if there are abnormalities in cerebral blood flow. But my guess is that whatever is there, we can take care of it."

Lexi asked a couple of questions about the possible reasons for the coma. Dexter answered each one with the same tone of positive enthusiasm. Nothing was impossible.

Dexter appeared to be on top of the world. Bryan could understand it. From what he'd learned during his phone calls to Geary, this guy was the foremost expert in nanotechnology, and finding Juan presented him with the possibility of studying the radical application of what the scientific community thought had been, at that time, only theoretically possible. This was a great opportunity for him.

But Geary had told Bryan that Dexter was one of those academics who believed scientific discoveries belonged to the world, not just to a group of business-men who are willing to fund research for their own potential profit. And not just to governments who might want to use them for their own purposes. That made Dexter a bit of a renegade. Somewhere in Ithaca, Bryan supposed, there was an unkempt, practically unused apartment filled with unpacked moving boxes and a dusty stereo with a Peter Frampton album on the turntable.

Still, Dexter was not above taking the money of either American corporations or the U.S. government to fund his research. Finding Juan and being allowed to work on him meant that trucks of cash would be backing up to the loading dock of his lab at Cornell. Dexter would capitalize on the efforts—unethical as they were—of the anonymous scientists who started this disaster in motion fifteen years ago.

Thinking of screwed-up scientists made Bryan

glance at his watch. The time they'd been here at the hospital was slipping past.

Lexi saw him look at his watch and turned back to Dexter. "So is there a way that you can contact me if there are any changes in Juan over the next twenty-four hours?"

"Of course. If there are any changes, I'll have…uh, that other…busy agent get hold of you."

Bryan didn't know how honest Dexter was being about contacting Lexi, but Bryan planned to call himself and get information for her as the day went by.

"Can I have a few more minutes with him?" she asked both men.

They both nodded. Dexter started out, and Bryan watched Lexi run her fingers over Juan's brow. She leaned down and kissed him on the cheek, whispering something in his ear.

Watching them, Bryan found himself hovering once again on the dangerous edge of another earlier time. Old and painful memories were burning through to the surface.

Bryan turned and joined Dexter in the hallway. The two men stood there watching the mother and son.

"What's his real prognosis?" Bryan asked the other man.

Dexter's eyes narrowed, and he frowned at the agent.

"Will he live?" Dexter asked. "Yes." The scientist crossed his arms over his thin chest and ran the knuckles of one hand across his chin.

"For how long?" Dexter continued, almost talking

to himself. "Who knows? And if he comes out of the coma, will he have his full range of physical abilities?" He nodded hesitantly. "Maybe."

"He's come out of the coma once...."

"Yes, that's a good sign. And he is responding in very hopeful ways."

"Okay," Bryan pressed. "Assuming he comes out of the coma, what condition will he be in?"

"If you mean, what will be the condition of his intelligence or memory, there's no way to know," the doctor told him. "That's definitely uncharted territory. I don't know if the damage done is reversible or not."

"You're talking about those artificial strands that showed up in the MRI?" Bryan asked.

"Yes," Dexter replied, his face brightening. "We're moving him to Cornell to prepare for the exploratory surgery that is necessary to figure that out."

"You're not going to do any surgery until Dr. Bradley returns," Bryan said, trying to keep his tone even. In the best of situations, he couldn't imagine brain surgery was the safest of operations.

"There are a number of tests we need to do before any operation," the scientist said. He turned to Bryan with a raised eyebrow. "I didn't know Dr. Bradley was being brought back to Ithaca, though."

"Dr. Bradley is the boy's mother. She continues to be an invaluable part of an ongoing investigation. The least we can do is to respect her rights, don't you think?"

Dexter nodded. He didn't seem to have a problem with that, but that was clearly not a priority for him.

Bryan remembered what he'd promised Lexi regarding her concern about any charges that might be made against Juan. Excusing himself, he moved to the end of the hall and called Geary, laying out Lexi's request. In passing on her conditions when it came to Juan's legal situation and what she was doing tonight to help the investigation, Bryan reiterated his position that he still thought it was wrong to involve her in a potentially dangerous situation.

As he'd expected, Geary had no problem with any of her concerns. There was clearly a medical situation involved in Juan Bradley's mental state, and there was little chance of legal action as a result of the shooting. But the FBI SAC told Bryan that the decision had been made to use her in this one situation, and that it was Bryan's job to make sure that she was protected. Other agents and law enforcement personnel in Nevada would be standing by to assist him.

Geary also told him they'd located one of the three remaining teenagers on the list. Hank was flying to California to interview him. The other two were still MIA.

As Bryan hung up on Geary, Lexi came out of Juan's room. They walked together to the elevators. While they waited for the doors to open, he looked into her flushed face. Her blue eyes were shining; it was obvious she was fighting to hold back tears.

"There's still plenty of time to change your mind," he told her. "You don't have to go to Reno."

She shook her head. "What is it? You don't have faith in me, Agent Atwood?"

She stepped into the empty elevator ahead of him. They'd descended only one floor when Bryan saw her stab away at a tear on her cheek. He put a hand around her shoulder and pulled her to him.

To his surprise, she pressed her face against his chest and began to sob in earnest.

Thirty-One

Thursday, January 17, 9:20 p.m.
New York City

That arrogant sonovabitch, Bryan Atwood, had complained about problems with communication in this investigation. Even though Geary had only been telling Atwood what was essential, he had to admit that the bastard was right, to some extent.

It was defensible, though, Geary thought. This investigation involved highly sensitive information, and the damn thing was moving at rocket speed. Even now, when he wanted to meet with them, most of those involved in the case were on the move. Only nine agents were available for this meeting, either in person or via conference call. Well, the rest of them would get their briefing as soon as they reached their destination. And if that wasn't good enough for Atwood, then it was just too damn bad.

As he moved through the rabbit warren of cubicles, he forced himself to focus on what was happening. There had been no new reports of school shootings since this morning, but that didn't mean that it wasn't going to happen again.

There were too many strands that were potentially important out there, and his people had to chase every one of them down. Naturally, Geary was afraid that they might be duplicating the effort on some clues while not doing enough on the others, and that's what he was trying to avoid. Every minute counted. They couldn't afford to chase around after their tails.

Four of the agents were already in the conference room when Geary walked in. Five more of them were connected through speaker phones. Everyone was supposed to bring what they had to the table. The SAC didn't waste any time with formalities and got the meeting started.

"Johnson, you're working on Billy Ward Ebbett. What have you got?"

Johnson's voice came through the speaker phone. "I'm still in Madison, Wisconsin. The subject is presently with the adoptive father. Name, William Ebbett. The mother is deceased, four years ago. No other children. The father's employer moved his department to Frankfurt, Germany, in 2004, and the father accepted a transfer. The boy moved there with him. We've been trying to get our Frankfurt field office to locate the father and Billy, but so far they have not connected."

"You don't have a current address for them?" Geary asked.

"We thought we did. But we were wrong. The Frankfurt office has an idea that William Ebbett and his son moved in with the father's girlfriend over the Christmas holiday."

"A permanent move?"

"I...I can't really answer that. We don't know the people or what their relat—"

"I don't want their goddamn horoscope!" Geary looked up at the ceiling, exasperated. "What I meant was, did they move in just for the Christmas holiday? Did they move their furniture and clothing and everything else in with her?"

"Moved in, sir," the agent said quickly. "The apartment listed as their address has been vacated, though the company's personnel files have not been updated to show anything different."

"Have you identified the school Billy goes to out there?"

"He goes to the International School. With the difference in time zones, we haven't been able to contact them directly, but our local agents there will be in touch with the school administrators in just a few hours."

"Just because Billy Ebbett isn't in the U.S., that doesn't mean we can let down our guard," Geary barked at the phone. "He can do the same kind of damage there. We're talking lives at stake."

"I understand, sir."

Geary looked down at the next line on his notes. "How about Roy Carter…Naves? Roy Naves?"

There was absolute silence from everyone.

He looked up at the four who were in the room. "Where the hell is everyone? Are you all sleeping?"

Three agents started speaking at the same time, two on the speaker box and one of the agents in the room.

"He's nowhere," one said.

"The same thing goes for his family."

"The first search for this family is turning up nothing," the third agent in the room agreed. "For the past eight years, there is no record of employment for the parents. Nothing on their social security records. The last address we have for them—which was temporary—was Lancaster, Pennsylvania. But they don't live there anymore, and no one has heard of them."

"Whole families don't disappear," Geary exclaimed. "Have you checked the death records? The national file for unidentified dead?"

"We have," the same agent answered. "We've only been looking for them since this morning, so I can't say they've really vanished, sir, but so far we're coming up empty."

"Motor vehicle registration, driver's license applications and renewals, the last place of employment, credit card records…the references they used on the adoption papers. They had to have other family. Are you looking at this from every possible angle?"

The answer of "yes, sir" from three agents wasn't enough. This wasn't good at all, Geary thought. This constituted the most uncontrolled situation of the three teenage boys they were after. There wasn't even a specific area where they could focus their search. No school districts that they could warn.

"We're not done with the Naves family investigation. We'll continue this discussion individually," Geary told them. "Next item. I have an update on Donald Gray Tucker. We've located him, but no action will be taken to take him into custody until preliminary psychological testing of the boy takes place. As we speak, Agent Gardner is flying to San Diego to talk to him. The school officials have been notified of the possible danger. The local police have been alerted. All precautionary steps have been taken."

Geary looked at his list again. "Anything more on tracing the account number of the package sent to Dr. Bradley?"

"We have some information," an agent at the table reported.

"What have you got, Smith?" he asked.

She glanced down at her notes. "The package was sent from a self-serve UPS drop box on West Liberty Street in Reno."

"We need more specific information about the account number used on the package. Any luck tying it to one of the campuses or a specific department?" Geary asked.

"We did get a little more specific information, but still it's a very long shot."

"What did you find?"

"The account number has been used most in recent weeks by the admissions department, but that doesn't mean that they are the only ones who may have had access to it. Anyone at the university who has communicated with a potential student may have used that account," the female agent explained. "We're back to 44,000 faculty and staff."

"That's not too hopeful," another agent said aloud.

"There's something else," the young woman started again.

Geary liked "something else." He strongly encouraged "shots in the dark." He looked up at the agent. Lillian Smith had been with the bureau for only two years. She had a thin, plain face and a very unassuming manner, the type that people—men or women—generally didn't look at twice. But she had a sharp mind and had already proved herself as someone who could think outside the box.

"What you got, Lillian?" Geary encouraged.

"I checked to see if that CSU account number was used for shipping anything else on the same date," she told everyone. She looked down at her notes, dug up a page. "There were a total of thirty-one packages and envelopes. But it happens that *two* were picked up at that drop box location on West Liberty Street in Reno with the CSU account number."

"That's great work," Geary said.

Lillian nodded. "So unless it just happened that someone else working at the university happened to be in Nevada, at that box, shipping a package, the same night…"

"Not very likely. Our friend shipped two packages. Excellent," Geary continued. This could be a huge break, he thought. "Who was the second package mailed to?"

"To a Mr. Curtis Wells, president, at NanoCure Research Company, in New York City," Lillian responded, reading the address.

"Delivered?"

"This morning."

"What do we know about Wells and this NanoCure Research Company?" Geary asked.

"I just started digging into it a few minutes ago. All I have so far is that it's a privately held company, five and half years old and about to go public. They do biomolecular detection in the field of nanotechnology, nanobiotechnology and nanomedicine. Curtis Wells is the founder and president. They just so happened to hold a press conference this afternoon."

Looking at his watch, Geary considered contacting Curtis Wells tonight but decided against it. He didn't want to burn a bridge before he crossed it.

"I'll visit Mr. Wells myself, tomorrow morning," Geary said. "He could be the best lead we have."

He sat back in his chair.

"NanoCure, huh?"

Thirty-Two

There had been no time specified in the e-mail, only the name of a motel, the address, and the day she was expected to be there. There had also been no mention of whether she should come alone or not.

Lexi stared for a moment at the half-lit signboard in front of the motel. The red-neon vacancy sign beneath the name flickered in the dark. A plastic garbage can lay on its side next to the rusted metal posts holding the sign. From what she could see, the rooms in front all looked dark. Another neon sign indicated the location of the office. The motel looked positively decrepit. Not a place she'd consider staying at, never mind going into by herself. Not in a hundred years.

But she wasn't alone.

Bryan had stopped the car some fifty yards before the motel. "I don't think this is such a good idea," he told her.

"Too late," she whispered. "Let's go in and see what he's got in store for us."

"I can still call up a replacement."

"Bryan," she said sharply.

"Oh, no. The mother's voice." He shook his head, still failing to put the car in gear. "Do you know that was the first time you've called me by my first name?"

She glanced at him, surprised.

"I like it," he said, but he quickly looked back at the front of the motel. "But I definitely don't like this location. This place doesn't look safe."

"I'm here. I came all the way to find out what this guy has to say. Besides, you told me yourself that there are at least a dozen agents in the vicinity. So let's just go and meet the man."

He still didn't put the car in gear.

"I *can* walk, you know," Lexi said, unbuckling her seat belt and reaching for the door handle.

Her threat did it. He slipped the car in gear and pulled into the lot, stopping in front of the office. "Just remember that you don't get more than a foot away from me. Whatever arrangement he has made here, I'm going in with you. We're a team. You don't go anywhere or do anything alone."

"You're repeating yourself. But whatever you say, Agent Atwood...."

"I liked 'Bryan' better."

She smiled, grabbed her purse and stepped out. She

wasn't used to having protection of this kind. She wasn't accustomed to having anyone tell her what to do or lecture her on what was and wasn't safe. Still, it wasn't too bad at all. Lexi had to admit, hesitantly, that she enjoyed it.

He was out of the car and by her side by the time she reached the door.

"We'll be okay. I'll take care of you," she whispered, winking and going inside ahead of him.

A loud electric bell sounded as they entered. The musty smell of the office attacked her senses immediately. The office was no more than an eight-by-eight room, painted lime-green. A high counter divided a third of the room from the rest. A door behind the counter had been left open and they could hear a TV in the small back room. An occasional cough could be heard over the sound of the TV.

An old computer sat to the right of the door. The monitor had a flying stars screen saver. Three sheets of instructions were posted on the wall next to the computer. To the left of the door they'd entered was a rack with hundreds of tourist brochures stuffed into it. On the wall, above the brochures, was a plaque from the AAA showing a three-star motel rating. The plaque was dated 1989. Above the plaque, brown rings stained the ceiling from where the roof must have leaked. The stains on the worn wall-to-wall carpet matched the rings on the ceiling.

No one came out of the back room to greet them. Lexi hoped she wasn't late. She glanced at the computer, thinking that there might be more information about this meeting that she had missed. She saw an old-style bell on the counter and walked to it. Just as she was about to ring it, a heavyset, balding man in his seventies walked out of the back room. He coughed as he approached the counter.

"Can I help you?"

He had a dry hacking cough, like someone who had allergies.

"Yes, I...we need a room." That didn't sound right. Lexi wondered if the old man's next question would be for how many hours.

He pushed a photocopied sheet in front of them. The top part consisted of a standard registration form. The lower section contained the prices of the rooms.

She stared at it for a minute.

"You don't have to bother with all the stuff on top. But that's the rate down there. We take Visa and MasterCard. We also take cash, but it has to be paid up front."

All the "stuff on top" was personal information, like the name and address and phone number. Interesting that he didn't need that.

"Actually, now that I think of it, we might already have a reservation," she said on a whim.

"That so?" The look on his face was comical. "Let me check with the reservations department," he cracked.

The comment *was* funny, she supposed, considering they hadn't seen a single car in the first row of rooms. With the exception of other FBI agents, Lexi wondered if anyone else was staying at this motel.

He looked down at something behind the counter and coughed again. She stood on her toes and looked over the counter. He was looking through about a dozen little message slips.

"Huh!" he said with surprise, picking up one of the slips. "What's the name?"

"Bradley," she said. "Lexi Bradley."

"As a matter of fact, you do," he said, grabbing a key out of the cabinet and putting it on the counter for her. "Room 114. It's in the back."

"Don't we need to pay for it?" Bryan asked.

"No, it's all paid for. You're staying for one night. That right?"

"Only one night," Lexi repeated, looking up at Bryan before taking the key.

They walked toward the door. At the last minute Bryan turned around. "Why that room and not one of the ones in front?"

The old man shook his head. "Sheryl was working last night. I wasn't here." He picked up a yellow sticky note and waved it in the air, coughing again. "Thursday, January 17, room 114, Lexi Bradley, paid. I couldn't care less if you want to change the room. We've got about twenty others that you can have."

"No, that's okay," Lexi answered.

"Was anyone staying in that room last night?" Bryan asked.

"If you mean do we clean the room or not between guests, count on it. Jo is proud of the two girls who help out. The sheets and towels get changed every day, and we even wash the blankets regular. And they vacuum—" He had to pause to cough again.

"I wasn't worrying about cleaning," Bryan told him. "I was just curious if that room was rented last night."

"You work for the IRS?"

At the airport, Bryan had changed into jeans and a black shirt, totally shedding his federal agent image. Lexi thought he looked pretty good, in fact.

Bryan put both hands up. "No way. I was just curious if the same friend who'd paid for the room for us was staying there last night."

"I don't know. That would require keeping books. I manage the place, but Sheryl is the owner's daughter. She doesn't give a shit, if you'll pardon my French. I keep track of which rooms are rented for the sake of the housekeeping crew. When I'm not on, I still have to look in on things every morning, to count how many keys are out. That way I know how many rooms were rented that night, and then I put that number in the books. What I'm telling you is that we pay our taxes. We're not hedging on anything, so if you *are* from the IRS, you're wasting your time. But as far as keeping names…what's the point? People can use any name they want. They show up at the casinos and do some drinking and gambling and they want a place to put their head down for the night. Now, if their wives or…"

Lexi touched Bryan's hand. The old man behind the counter was definitely lacking company. They'd opened up the floodgates, and he wasn't going to stop talking unless they left.

"Thanks for your help," Bryan called, opening the door.

Lexi took a lungful of night air as they stepped out. The old man's cough had to be caused by the mold in that office.

As she waited for him to unlock the car, she watched two pickup trucks go by on the road. "I'm here, wherever you are," she whispered, looking around at the empty lot.

They both got into the car, and Bryan immediately locked the doors. He took his time driving around to the back. As he drove, he spoke with another agent who was staying at the motel through a small walkie-talkie. There were four cars parked by a row of rooms on the side. Around the back, where room 114 was, she saw two more cars.

Lexi looked at the license plates, makes and models of the cars, trying unsuccessfully to decide which of them could belong to agents.

Bryan backed the car into the parking space across from the row of rooms. The headlights of their car shone on the door of room 114. The curtain in the front window was partially open. The lights inside the room were off.

"Shall we?" Lexi asked, feeling the jitters starting to make her lose courage.

"How about if you wait here until I go and check the room?" he asked.

"Remember that 'don't get more than a foot away from me' statement?" Lexi looked around the lot. "I really don't want to sit alone in the car. If you don't mind, I'm coming with you."

He took something out from under the seat and stuffed it in the back of his belt. She figured it had to be a gun. He grabbed a windbreaker from the backseat and started to pull it on.

"Is this one of those FBI jackets with reflecting letters you can see from thirty thousand feet away?"

"I'm not in the FBI," he said, not taking his eyes off the motel room door.

Lexi was trying to lighten the mood, but he obviously wasn't game. She'd never seen him as serious as he was now. He quickly glanced around at the lot and at the other cars as he clipped the walkie-talkie onto his belt and fitted an earpiece into his ear.

"There's no reason for this guy to drag me all the way out here if he wanted to hurt me," she said reasonably.

"What if he holds a grudge because of what Juan did?" he told her. "In my line of work you see some very strange people. You can't assume anything."

Lexi thought about that. Just as she didn't appreciate anyone undervaluing her professional opinions, she decided not to disregard what Bryan was telling her. It was a possibility, she supposed.

"Tell me what to do," she told him.

"Hold on," he said, holding the earpiece in place. Someone was talking to him through it. Bryan turned to her. "We're going inside. Don't forget the one-foot rule."

"Whatever you say."

On his orders, she stayed inside the car until he got

Jan Coffey

their overnight bags from the trunk. He came around and opened the door for her, and Lexi stepped out.

"Do you think he's here now, watching us?" she asked, quietly taking her bag from him.

"No. Our people have checked everyone staying here tonight. None of them seemed to fit the profile."

They crossed the parking lot to the room. Lexi handed Bryan the key. She stood close to him as he unlocked the door, turned on the light and went in ahead of her. He asked her to give him ten seconds, but before she could count to ten, he was ushering her in. Closing the door behind them, he tried to set the latch.

"This isn't much use," he murmured.

She moved to the window and drew the shade, looking around at the room. A double bed, neatly made, an old TV. The lines on the carpet showed that the room had been recently vacuumed, possibly even today. She dropped her bag on one of the chairs. She guessed a partially open door on the far end of the room must be the bathroom.

Bryan had already shed his windbreaker. He was checking inside the cabinets, looking in the small closet back by the bathroom.

"So what do we do now?" she asked.

"Sit and wait," he told her.

Thirty-Three

Thursday, January 17, 11:30 p.m.
Manhattan, New York

Curtis had a splitting headache. His wife kept all the medication in their bathroom, but he wasn't going there. He wasn't about to leave his study and chance waking his family up. He cradled the phone against his shoulder and pulled open the drawer of his desk. There had to be a Tylenol in here somewhere.

As he rummaged through the drawers, the man at the other end of the call continued with his tale of woe, listing the myriad reasons why they hadn't been able to reach Juan Bradley. Interesting, Curtis thought, how the tone had changed. Even as he listened, though, Curtis's mind churned. Considering the overnight package he'd received from Mitch, Juan's survival might be the least of their problems.

What happened if the files they'd destroyed in Reno hadn't been everything? How much data about their research had Mitch kept? Could some of that include information about their investors? In those days, he hadn't worried about computer security. Their business and financial records were kept on the same central computer system. Mitch could have copied some of those files, as well.

They shouldn't have killed Mitch, at least not until they had some of these answers. Curtis closed the drawer and sat back. No Tylenol.

"The good news is that Juan Bradley is still in a coma," the man on the telephone said cheerfully.

Curtis had to find a way to minimize potential damage. Between the two hospitals, they must have already run diagnostic tests on the boy. They'd have to be blind not to see that something had been implanted in the kid's head. Injecting the devices into the infants' brains as a serum had been brilliant, even if it did mean that there was no hiding whatever was left of the device at this point.

And there was another problem he had to consider. One goal of the scaffolding they'd created for the developing brains had been to implant the potential for triggered early memory.

This was a step above high intelligence. The possibility of having a photographic memory from a very early age was what had drawn in a number of investors. Of course, too many of the test subjects had died to provide any results that mattered. Curtis thought about that now. They'd never had a chance to completely test the outcome, so he really didn't know if he should consider Juan a threat or not. If the triggered early memory had not developed the way Mitch had theorized, it was probable Juan would never remember anything from those early days.

But if any records Mitch had failed to destroy were found, it wouldn't matter if Juan had no memory at all.

"I don't want you to do anything stupid in Buffalo," Curtis barked into the phone. "No burning the hospital to the ground or shooting up the place. From here on, everything that is done is to be done discreetly. There are to be no traces of foul play that leave a trail. Understood?"

His contact agreed.

"Now, are you sure that Mitch's body isn't going to be discovered? That there's no way they're going to identify him?"

"We put him in a solid waste incinerator," the other man said. "There's *nothing* left."

He didn't want to know where or what they had done with the rental car.

"I might have a follow-up job in Fullerton, California." That's where Mitch lived. Curtis could have these people sweep through the house, to make sure nothing was left there. And they could also search his office at the university. But that had the potential of being too messy. If they didn't get in and out cleanly, questions would be asked. There would be too many coincidences, especially with Mitch still missing.

"Tell me when and where."

"I'll get back to you on that," Curtis said, ending the call.

He sat at his desk and buried his head in his hands. He needed to calm himself and try to think straight. His head was pounding.

An idea occurred to him. Mitch's wife Elsa had been invaluable to him before. Maybe that was the angle he should pursue again. Curtis looked at his watch. It was 11:42 p.m. here on the East Coast. They were two hours behind where she was in Arizona. She'd told him that she was staying there all week.

Curtis paged through his apartment phone's caller ID until he found Elsa's number. He dialed it. The phone rang a few times. He didn't want to leave a message. Just as he was about to hang up, a woman's sleepy voice answered. It sounded like Elsa. He immediately introduced himself and apologized for calling too late.

"You've heard from Mitch?" she asked excitedly, not allowing him to say anything else.

Curtis tried to think quick on his feet. She wouldn't be in a mood to answer any questions unless he had some good news for her.

"I haven't heard from him directly. But a couple of our mutual friends have spoken to him," he lied.

"Oh, thank God!" She let out an audible sigh, totally awake now. "I called the police in Fullerton again from here this afternoon. But they still thought I was over-reacting. And I guess they were right. So what did he say? Where is he? Why isn't he answering my calls? I'm going crazy here. This is not like him at all."

"I wish I had all the answers for you, but I don't," he said softly. "From what I can gather, it sounds like he's dealing with some academic-related issues."

"Yes," she responded. "He's been feeling down about his work for the past few months. He doesn't like to talk about it."

"I'm sure it'll work out," Curtis said. "I just thought you'd want to know that he's okay and someone has talked to him. I'll see if I can get word to him that you've been worried."

"So is he in New York?" she asked.

"I *think* he's in New York. That's the impression I got. I've been trying to call him myself since you and I talked. As you know, my schedule has been pressured these days. Things are happening with NanoCure." He figured his wife had been telling Elsa all about it during their weekly calls. "You know, Elsa, I was thinking. I could use some of the files from the early days for this presentation I have to make next week. But I wasn't sure if I have the stuff in Connecticut or if Mitch has it. Now with the snow we're dealing with, there's no way I can shoot up to Connecticut and back easily. The roads are still horrible. Everyone is trying to stay off of them. By any chance, do you know if Mitch keeps a storage place? This stuff would probably be too old and musty to keep in your house."

Curtis hoped the barrage of information might confuse her enough to just answer the damn question.

"Well, let me think. There was the storage place in Reno I told you about. But, it did strike me as strange that he had that place. He's had a storage unit in Fullerton for eons. He got it when I complained one time about the boxes in the basement ten or fifteen years ago."

He knew it. It was so much like Mitch to save every scrap of paper that might cover his ass. He never should have trusted him to destroy those materials.

"Do you know where in Fullerton that storage place is?" he asked. "If I can get hold of Mitch, I'm going to see if I can convince him to send one of his graduate students up there to check on that material for me."

"No, I really don't. I never went there with him," Elsa explained. "We always had plenty of room in the basement for our other things."

How many storage places could there be in Fullerton? Curtis thought. He quickly typed the information into a search engine. Four of them popped up right away. There could be more, those that didn't advertise or weren't Internet savvy.

Elsa was getting chatty again. She was telling him about the grandchildren and their kids and how he and his wife should come to California for a visit when she got back there. Curtis's mind was busy making a list of everything that had to be done. He had to contact his people again. Have them go through Mitch's house and search for some bill or piece of paper that might have the address of the storage places. If that failed, they could also break into each of the storage places and go through their books. Mitch wouldn't use a fake name, not in his own hometown.

Curtis searched for a polite way to end the call. His

exit came when the door to his office slowly opened and his grandson David, sleepy-eyed, walked in.

"Grandpa, I'm thirsty."

"Did you hear that?" Curtis said quickly into the phone. "I have a sleepy boy here who shouldn't be out of bed this late. I have to go."

Elsa perfectly understood and said goodbye, thanking Curtis profusely.

He hung up the phone and came around his desk. As he picked up the small child, David put his head on the old man's shoulder and wrapped his arms around his neck.

"I thought I saw a glass of water next to your bed when I came in to kiss you good-night before," he whispered to the young boy, rubbing his back.

"I know." David let out a contented sigh. "But I just missed you, Grandpa."

Business was business, Curtis thought, but in the end, family was what really mattered. Family and this little boy, in particular.

Thirty-Four

No phone calls, no one showing up at the door, not a single car driving past the room…nothing.

Bryan had talked to his team members in and around the motel a few times, and it had been the same with them. No one new had checked into the motel since they'd come in, no one had stirred from the other rooms, and very few vehicles had passed by.

He pushed himself up from the chair he'd been sitting in near the door and stretched his legs and back. He'd slept, more or less, for about an hour on the last leg of the flight out here, so he was feeling good, but he knew he needed to keep his blood flowing. He needed to stay alert.

Lexi was cuddled up on one side of the bed, her

hands tucked under her cheek. The book she'd been reading was on the floor. She was sound asleep. He'd spent most of the past hour, since she'd fallen sleep, watching her. Something about the way her lashes fluttered on her skin as she dreamed, the curve of her ear, the soft rise and fall of her breast. He'd had to look away more than once as he felt the stir of desire. It wasn't just her looks. He was attracted to everything about Lexi Bradley—her no-nonsense approach to problems, her sense of humor, her intelligence, her compassion, her independence, her intensity. The list went on and on.

It wasn't like him to be attracted to someone in this kind of situation, but she wasn't like anyone he'd known before.

And he guessed she was somewhat interested in him, too. At least, enough that she trusted him. Still, neither had done anything to jeopardize their working relationship. He admired that in her, too.

Maybe, when they were finished with this case, he'd try his luck and see if she'd consider seeing him again. He hadn't felt like this since his divorce. He wondered if this simply meant that he was finally getting back to normal. The image of Juan in the hospital bed immediately came to his mind. The helplessness she must be feeling from not being able to do anything for him recalled bad memories. He felt every inch of his body grow tense. The pain was back.

He walked to the bathroom. His throat was dry. He filled a glass with water and stared at the sediment floating in the clear water. It was so much like him, so much like what was going on inside of him. Every now and then everything settled. For that moment, he felt as if things were normal. But inside he knew that it was just that no one had stirred things up. All the old feelings were right there, ready to emerge and cloud the waters.

Bryan poured out the water and put the glass on the sink. Turning the water on to run, he leaned over the sink and stared at his face in the mirror. His brother, Bobby, had had his eyes and crazy curly hair. Everyone had always said the Atwood brothers looked so much alike.

He picked up the glass and filled it again. He didn't look at the water this time, but drank it down. As he downed the water, he looked in the mirror. The wrinkles around his eyes were getting more and more pronounced. The years were adding up. He didn't mind it, though.

Lexi made a soft noise in her sleep, and he put down the glass. He was crazy to think about all that now. He hadn't gotten enough rest on that plane. It was catching up to him, whether he admitted it or not. Still, he had a job to do…and a woman to protect.

Walking back in the bedroom, he pulled the blanket higher on Lexi's shoulder. She'd kicked off her shoes and climbed under the covers fully clothed. He picked up her book and put it on the side table, then switched off the light on her side of the bed. Before he could straighten up, though, Lexi's eyes opened.

"Anything from Buffalo?" she asked sleepily.

"No."

"How about from our mystery friend?"

He shook his head. "Go back to sleep."

"No. No. It seems like that's all I do around you. Sleep."

She stifled a yawn and then smiled at the hurt expression he faked for her amusement.

"I didn't mean it like you were boring," she said, adding with a straight face, "Well, not *exactly* boring."

"I'm glad to hear that."

She leaned over and looked at the radio-alarm clock bolted to the side table.

Bryan thought she looked stunning with her hair a mess and her eyes a little puffy with sleep. She caught him looking at her and ran a hand through her hair. He walked to the window, pulling the shade aside slightly, and looked out at the dark parking lot. He had to put some distance between them.

When he turned around again, she was sitting up in the bed, a couple of pillows stuffed behind her. Her arms were folded across her chest, and she was watching him very closely.

"Can I get you anything?" he asked her.

"Yes, room service."

"I already made that call. I ordered eggs benedict, fresh squeezed orange juice, the pastry platter and some fresh fruit."

"And what did they say? You should have your order around the year 2025?"

"Actually, the response was slightly less civil," he smiled. "There's tap water that tastes horrible. There's a coffeepot over there." He pointed to a table near the door to the bathroom. "The expiration date on the package of coffee passed about a year and a half ago, but I'm sure it's still delicious."

"Hey, I've never had a patient get sick from drinking old coffee."

"Do you want me to make some?"

Lexi shook her head. "Not yet. I have this nice warm feeling right now from sleeping, and I don't want the adrenaline rush quite yet."

Bryan sat down on the same chair he'd been sitting in before.

Rather than picking up her book again, Lexi continued to watch him. He took a minute more of her scrutiny before reaching his limit.

"Okay, what is it?"

She bit her lip, not saying anything, but she continued to look at him. Bryan didn't think she was trying to memorize his features. There was certainly nothing romantic in the look. She didn't seem to be looking at the extra head he'd grown in the past hour, either. It was more of a look of interest, as if she were trying to understand him…or maybe phrase a question, but she couldn't quite find the right words.

"Come on, ask," he said finally. "I promise not to bite your head off."

"It's a personal question," she said.

He contemplated if he should raise the barricades.

"I asked you a personal question on our way to Reno," he said instead. "So I suppose you have a right to ask. Of course, I might or might not answer it."

Lexi pulled the blanket higher on her lap. "There's one thing about you that I don't understand, Agent Atwood."

"If it's only one thing, then you're way ahead of everyone else. And that includes my family," he said lightly. "And why are we back to Agent Atwood again?"

She hesitated a moment and looked away, plucking at the blanket as she responded, "I think you know why. I'm feeling like we're on the edge of some dangerous waters."

"Then maybe you shouldn't ask the question."

Lexi shook her head. "I've been thinking about it too long. I need to know, especially after today."

"When today?"

"At the VA hospital in Buffalo," she said.

"What did I do?"

She didn't answer right away, studying him for a few moments longer.

"I saw you looking at Juan in that hospital bed. There was so much hurt there. I can't describe it, but if there had been a mirror and you could see your face in it, you would understand. You looked like a person... well, in mourning."

Bryan *was* mourning, and he didn't need a mirror to see it.

"Even before that. Back in New Haven," she continued. "You were the only one who seemed to understand what I was going through. The one person who tried to help me. I thought later that it might have had something to do with the work you and Agent Gardner did before, the work on those high school shootings a few years ago. But I'm not sure."

"You knew about the work we did before?"

"Detective Simpson told me this morning, back at my house. I think you were making a phone call."

"Then you have your answer," he said.

"I don't think so," she said gently. "I spent a little time with Hank, too. He's objective about this work. He seems untouched by it, the way you are. But you seem…I don't know…as if this all has rubbed you raw…inside."

"Hank is a psychologist. He deals with these kinds of things all the time. He definitely has a thicker skin than I do."

Lexi didn't look convinced, but she didn't say anything. She reached over and picked up her book. Switching on the bedside light, she opened the book on her lap.

Bryan watched her for a couple of minutes.

"It's hard to talk about my past," he said finally.

Her gaze shifted from the page to his face. "I know. For me, it feels sometimes like it makes me less strong if I talk about it. More vulnerable, I guess."

"But you're not more vulnerable for having had cancer. As a doctor, you know that getting the disease wasn't your choice. And you've done everything right since then, too. You have to be proud of what you've done."

"Maybe that's the way you should think of your situation, too."

He shook his head. "I can't. I was responsible for something that happened. A life was lost, and it was because of me. That is a little different from your situation."

Lexi closed the book and put it on the table. "Was it a case you were working on?"

Bryan rubbed the back of his neck. He stretched it from side to side. How do you say something like this right out?

"No. I lost my fourteen-year-old brother. He committed suicide in his bedroom. And he used my pistol to do it."

As he'd expected, she looked stunned.

Bryan got up and walked to the window again. He looked outside. Nothing had changed. As he stood there, the built-in heat-and-air-conditioning unit beneath the window groaned sickly and came to life. The smell of warm dust and mildew filled the air.

"Please, don't stop there," she told him. "You didn't give him the gun. There has to be more."

He continued to look out.

"How many years ago did it happen?" she asked.

He turned away from the window, let the curtain fall in place. Lexi had pushed the blanket away. She was sitting on the edge of the bed. Bryan figured she'd decided to ask him bite-size questions, only big enough that he wouldn't choke himself.

"Eight years ago," he told her.

"He was a lot younger than you."

Bryan nodded. "Bobby was the 'oops' baby for my parents. He was the youngest, and I was the eldest of five children. We were the only two boys, twenty-five years apart in age."

Bobby was closer in age to Bryan's daughters than

he was to any of his own siblings. The three sisters born between them had come two or three years apart after Bryan. Their parents had four children in a span of ten years. And then fifteen years later came Bobby.

"How old was your mom when Bobby was born?"

"She was in her mid-forties," he remembered. "She had me when she was only nineteen."

"And your father?" she asked.

"He was older. Let's see. He was fifty-one when Bobby was born."

"Your parents must have never needed babysitters for him. I imagine Bobby was probably spoiled by all of you."

There was a lot of truth in that. "Two of my sisters and I were already out of the house. But my father passed away only two years later, so we each spent our share of days back there trying to help our mother raise Bobby."

"That's so sad. Your father was young when he died," Lexi said.

Bryan sat back down in the chair. He and his father had had their share of arguments when he was young. Bryan was too independent, too stubborn. Too much like his father, he supposed. In those years, he didn't know how to shut up and let the older man have the last word. But, despite all the yelling matches, they loved each other, and Robert Atwood's death had been a tough blow on everyone.

"How did he die?" she asked.

"He was shot in the line of duty. He was a New York City police officer."

"I'm sorry," she whispered. "You went into the same line of work."

"Similar, but not exactly. Mine has been a lot more white-collar than his ever was. I was never in the type of danger that he put himself in day in and day out."

"You give yourself no credit for good things and you take all the blame on yourself for the bad things," she told him.

He looked at her curiously.

"You make it sound like your job at the Secret Service is a stroll in the park. But then, you say your brother's suicide was directly your fault."

"He used my gun," Bryan said again, wondering why she couldn't understand the ramifications of that.

"Yes, but if it wasn't your gun, don't you think it would have been something else?" she asked softly. "I'm no psychiatrist, but I know that suicide is a tricky thing. If he couldn't find a gun, then he would have gone looking for another way to do it. There are a hundred ways that teenagers use to take their lives when they're bent on destroying themselves. I see it in my own practice. The problem wasn't that he found that gun, but that something was not working inside him. Something was driving him to take his own life. Sometimes we see it and catch it. Sometimes we don't."

"I could have stopped it if I'd paid more attention."

"How, Bryan? Were you around him all the time?" she asked somewhat sharply. "Could you possibly know all of his friends and his moods and who was giving him a hard time at school?"

There was no holding back with her. He'd opened the gates, and she wasn't going to give up until every drop of the mess was out.

"I was working with teenagers," he replied. "I was interviewing and reviewing the files of fourteen- and fifteen-year-olds who saw no value in their lives."

"And in no one else's lives, either," she corrected quickly. "Don't mix Bobby with kids who acted out of revenge and killed innocent people. He took only his own life."

"The end result was the same," he said sharply.

"No, it wasn't. I know." She took a deep breath. "I have a son who's accused of hurting others. My pain this past week has been for those others, too."

They were both on the edge, raw with emotion. Bryan wanted her to understand. He wasn't carrying his feelings about Bobby's death because of one thing. Every way he looked at it, he was involved…or should have been and wasn't. He could have stopped it.

"The week before Bobby died, I moved back temporarily into my mother's house. She needed help and, at the time, my wife and I were separating. I was in the middle of the school-shooting cases with Hank. I was spending a lot of time on the road, so it worked out for everyone, I thought. That's how Bobby found my gun."

She shook her head. "My next-door neighbor had his guns in his basement in a locked cabinet, but Juan was able to get in there. Do you see me blaming them for what Juan did? Do you think they blame themselves for what happened?"

"I can only tell you how I feel," he said.

"I can understand that your brother was important to you. I can see that you feel you didn't do enough. But I cannot understand why you haven't forgiven yourself after eight years."

Bryan held his hand out, palm up. "You see? You admit that there's something that needs to be forgiven."

She nodded, her eyes fierce with conviction. "Of course there is. There is *always* something in us that makes us need to be forgiven. As humans, we are so big on guilt. Our neighbor's house gets broken in to, and we feel guilty that we didn't pay closer attention to who comes and goes in the neighborhood. A teenager is involved in a bad accident, and we feel guilty for not telling his parents the week before about seeing him with a six-pack of beer."

"Bobby was no stranger. He was my brother."

"And Juan is my son," she said with the same force.

They were both locked in a battle of wills. Bryan couldn't take his eyes off her flushed face. She was beautiful, passionate. This was the first time since Bobby's death that someone was challenging him to let go, to let his life move on. Those sessions he'd gone to hadn't done it, and yet...

Lexi pushed abruptly to her feet and started for the door. "I'm just going as far as the car. I need to get some fresh air."

Bryan caught her hand as she went by. She stood there, looking down at him. Her eyes shone with unshed tears.

"I know…Lexi…" He struggled for the words. "Thank you. I know what you're trying to do."

She leaned down and kissed his lips. He hadn't expected it, but he didn't try to stop it, either. Her lips were even softer than he'd imagined, and her kiss was full of tenderness. She drew back, and it took great control not to pull her on his lap and kiss her deeply. He wanted to make love to her, to lose himself in her.

She must have seen some of what he was thinking in his face. "I think we both could use some fresh air."

Bryan nodded and released her hand. "Wait a second."

He stood up and turned off the lights in the room before she opened the door. She moved out onto the cement walk that ran along the building. The air had cooled off considerably, though even in the forties, it was considerably better than Wickfield or Buffalo. The number of cars in the parking lot had not changed, which meant FBI agents were the only paying customers on this row.

She took a few steps along the walkway and then leaned her back against the window. She looked up at the sky. He stood in the doorway and studied her profile in the dark for a moment and then looked at the sky as well. The stars were glittering brightly in a way that you only see in the desert. There was a crispness to how the stars stood out in the deep, blue-black expanse.

"I can't imagine your brother would have wanted you to suffer like this, so many years later," she said softly.

"You're right. Bobby wouldn't have wanted this." Bryan had been his idol. They'd spent so much time together when Bobby was little. Later, Bryan had tried to make up for the absence of a father in a teenager's life…except that they could talk. There were no disagreements, no arguments.

"Did you ever find out what was at the root of his problem? Why he did it?"

"He would get down." As Bryan stared upward, a star cut a swath across the night sky and disappeared. "I don't know if it was clinical depression. He just had mood swings that I thought were normal for a teenager. But what made him flip finally was a problem with a girl."

"She hurt him?"

"No. She was his first real girlfriend. She was killed in a car accident six days before."

"How did it happen?"

Bryan frowned. "She was a passenger in her sister's car."

"How very hard that would be for anyone," she said, looking at him. "But one thing I've learned from being a doctor is that dying is part of life."

"I know that."

"And you surely also know that you couldn't have followed him around every minute of that week. You had a job that had to be done. There were others who relied on you. Who can tell just how many teenage lives you've saved over the past few years through the work you were doing then?"

He leaned a shoulder against the side of the doorway and looked at her. "Juan must be an amazing kid, and not because of whatever those strands are in his brain.

Because of the way you must have raised him. Because of the kind of person you are."

Even in the dark, he could see she was smiling at him. "We seem to have a little mutual admiration society going here, don't we?"

Bryan nodded slowly, his eyes taking in every inch of her face.

"We're in the back lot of a desert motel. We have a room with a queen bed…and how many agents watching us?"

He grinned.

"So maybe we shouldn't go there."

"Maybe we shouldn't…not tonight, anyway."

She laughed, looking away.

The two of them stood in silence for some time. While they were watching the stars, the climate-control unit suddenly stopped. Except for the sound of other units, it was very quiet.

"What time is it, anyway?" she asked.

Bryan checked his watch. "Quarter to twelve."

"There's only fifteen minutes before today becomes tomorrow," she said. "He asked me to meet him *today*. Do you think we came too late?"

"I think if the time mattered, he would have said it." Bryan had talked to the other agents on surveillance at the motel an hour ago. They'd set up a phone tap for the main line going out of the motel. They were monitoring cell phone use, as well. No one had come in or gone out. Nothing was going on. The night was dead.

He thought about the robbery and shooting at the

copy place near here last night. There was a strong possibility that their man was taken out of there. He could have been abducted or murdered. As time wore on, Bryan was becoming more convinced that their would-be contact might be dead.

"It doesn't look like he's coming, does it?"

"Maybe he was planning to, but something held him up," Bryan told her. "We'll wait the night."

The eyewitnesses near the scene last night hadn't offered anything tangible. The Reno police were on the watch, though, and would notify the feds in the event that any John Doe turned up.

"It still doesn't make sense for him not to have specified a time," she said.

"He could have planned to call you," Bryan suggested.

"He hasn't done that yet, either."

Bryan glanced at his watch again.

"He knew my name. Why did it matter which room I stayed in?" she mused. "If he called, they would connect him to my room, anyway."

"Good point," he responded, straightening up. "You're thinking that maybe he wanted you in this room for a reason."

"Exactly," Lexi said. There was excitement in her voice. "Maybe whatever it was he wanted me to know, he left in this room."

Bryan had searched the room quickly when they'd first arrived, but he'd been worrying more about intruders and anything that might pose a danger to Lexi.

"Let's take a look," he told her.

They went back inside the room. Bryan locked the door before turning the lights back on.

"I'll start right here by the window. You look anywhere you think is a logical place for him to hide something."

She nodded. "What do you think we should look for?"

"Your guess is as good as mine. He was trying to fax you some documents, so maybe he…or she…left you some kind of file. It may be in the form of a computer disk or a flash drive or a CD."

Bryan eyed the climate-control unit. That was a good possibility, but it would take some work to get into it. He looked at the control panel and shined his penlight into the vents and under the unit.

Lexi immediately started with the closer of the two bedside tables, pulling out the drawers, looking under them, checking the thin space between the bottom shelf and carpeted flooring. She pulled it away from the wall to see behind it.

Bryan searched the chair he'd been sitting on, then moved to the straight chair next to a small table near the door. Next, he stood on the chair and looked on top of the ceiling fan. Other than the grime of a dozen years on the blades and more than a few dead flies, there was nothing else to see.

"Hold on a minute," he warned. Climbing down, he opened his bag and took two pairs of plastic gloves out of a compartment. He gave her a pair and put the other on himself.

"Good thinking. It's gross," she said.

"It's not just the dirt," he replied. "We'll want to

preserve anything that might be used for identification later."

She nodded and pulled the cover off the bed. She took off the sheets, shaking each layer. An old crumpled tissue fell on the floor from between the sheets. She shook her head with disgust.

"Put anything that you find, anything that even stands a remote chance of being a clue, here on the floor." He pointed to a spot next to the door.

Bryan watched her pick up the tissue and put it where he was pointing. He pulled the chair over to the open armoire that housed the TV and looked on top of it. The flora and fauna he found there matched the top of the fan blades. An old TV channel directory was covered with the grime. The filth around it had not been touched in God knows how long. There was no way anyone could have planted that directory there recently. Still, he picked it up and paged through it, looking for any possible writing on it.

Bryan climbed down and put the directory on the carpet by the door.

"His e-mail mentioned molecular sensors. Maybe what he left us here is not even big enough to be seen with the naked eye."

"We won't give up the room right away. Whatever happens tonight, I'll have a group of forensics technicians go through it very carefully."

Lexi had pulled up the mattress and was looking under it.

"I can take care of heavier things like that."

"I can handle it," she said confidently. "But I can only imagine what the cleaning crew...what was her name?"

"Jo and her girls."

"Yeah. I can only imagine what Jo and her girls would think we were doing here tonight."

Bryan looked over his shoulder at her. Lexi was on all fours, checking underneath the bed.

"I can't see anything down here. Maybe you can help me tip the bed frame up later, and we can see if anything is under it."

"I'll take care of it."

Standing on top of the chair, Bryan looked down at the patterns on the rug. The lines from the vacuum cleaner were visible throughout the room, but there were also the traces of rectangular impressions in the carpet between the bed and the far wall. Whatever was there must have been fairly heavy. Possibly file boxes, he thought.

"Don't walk over there," he said to Lexi, and pointing. "I'll have some of our people check those impressions. There might be something we can use there. There may even be shoe impressions that we can't see."

"I think after medicine, forensic science would have been my second choice for a career," she told him, coming and crouching before the three drawers of the armoire beneath the television.

"You and the rest of the television-watching public," he joked.

"I mean it. It has always fascinated me."

"Well, both save lives." He stepped down from the chair and looked behind the television.

Lexi pulled a phone book and a Gideon Bible out of the top drawer. She leafed through the thick phone book. "Is this worth adding to the pile?"

"Absolutely. Anything marked in there or any pages that are ripped out could provide information."

She put it next to the TV directory near the door. "I feel sorry for whoever has to go through it. Talk about grunt work."

Bryan found a take-out menu from a local restaurant behind the television. He quickly glanced at it and added it to the pile.

"What is this?"

Bryan turned around to see what Lexi was looking at. She was holding a white plastic card with a strip of magnetic tape on the back.

"I found it right here in the middle of the Bible."

"Is there anything else with it?" He crouched down next to her.

They both looked. There was nothing. He took the card out of her hand and studied it, front and back. It appeared to be a key card for accessing something.

"It looks like someone scratched off the name," she said.

It wasn't regular wear and tear. Lexi was right. On one side of the key card, someone had used a sharp object to scratch off the name and most of the logo.

"It's not as flimsy as a hotel room key card," he said.

"It looks old, too," Lexi commented.

Bryan held the card up to the light. Two lines of text had been crossed off. The bottom portion of the second line was still partially visible.

"Storage," he said. "I'm sure this word is 'storage.' I think this must be an access key to a storage facility."

"Do you think this is it?" she asked excitedly. "I mean, what he wanted me to have?"

"I don't know. We'll find out."

"How are we going to figure out what storage place this belongs to?" Lexi asked.

Bryan tapped the card. "Someone in the FBI office in Reno will be able to track it down for us."

Thirty-Five

Friday, January 18, 6:30 a.m.
Manhattan, New York

Curtis took longer in the shower than usual. He'd barely slept a wink all night.

Nothing was going as it should. His people in California hadn't been able to get inside Mitch and Elsa's house during the night. His man had plenty of excuses, of course. They were going to try it again tonight. As far as the storage places, they'd only been able to go through the client base of one of the facilities because the others didn't have centralized computer records. Naturally, Mitch's name wasn't listed on that one.

He had time, Curtis told himself as he dressed. He needed to keep himself in a mind-set where *he* was in control. *He* was the one to set the pace in his world.

His time. *His* pace. *His* world.

As he knotted his Stefano Ricci necktie, he thought over the two phone calls he'd received around 6:00 a.m. from people that they'd worked with years ago. Naturally, they were still on the payroll, in a limited way. The timing of their calls in itself indicated the panic, though. It was clearly time to disconnect with them.

The first call came from Curtis's top insider in the social services program that they used illegally years back. She didn't mention her name, but Curtis knew who she was immediately. He could hear traffic in the background and knew that she was using a pay phone. She just wanted Curtis to know that in the past couple of days, there'd been a deluge of government agents in the state and private offices going over the welfare and adoption records.

The second caller wanted to let Curtis know that he was running for a political office in Arizona this coming fall, and while he couldn't accept any donations from citizens that might be considered illegal or unethical, he just wanted to inform him of his plans. The caller rambled on for a while, but the subtext of the message was clear: something was happening in Arizona.

He considered the phone calls carefully. Because of the news conference and all the press releases that had gone out over the past few weeks, NanoCure and Curtis's name and picture were appearing in the business pages of papers all over the country. Those people who'd helped him in the early days…for a price…were surely seeing his name. And with the activity in Arizona, he was also sure that he'd probably be fielding a few more nervous messages from others who'd been involved.

In the kitchen, Curtis found Ann waiting for waffles to pop up out of the toaster. Little David was already awake and at the breakfast table.

"Where's the rest of your family?" Curtis asked the young boy after planting a kiss on top of his head.

"Sleeping. That's all they do, sleep." He wrapped his thin arms around Curtis's neck and gave him a sloppy kiss before letting go of him.

"We'll get the rest of them up pretty soon," his wife said meaningfully. "Today is a big day for someone."

Curtis looked at her. She frowned at him, her expression saying he'd better remember. Shit, he thought. He'd almost forgotten.

"I'll say it's a big day." He gave David another hug. "A big birthday, I believe. Happy birthday, my boy."

"We're having a party here at seven o'clock." Ann emphasized the hour, reminding him not to be late.

"I'm more excited about lunch," David said. "Mommy said we're coming to pick you up at work at noon, and we're all going out for lunch."

Curtis remembered he'd promised his daughter that he'd take her and the kids out today, since they were all planning to go home on Sunday. It was on his schedule, but he'd forgotten about it.

"Well, I can't wait, either," he said.

There was a call from downstairs that his driver was here. Curtis made some quick excuses about having a breakfast meeting and poured himself coffee for the ride to the office.

His wife brushed a kiss on his cheek, whispering that she'd kill him if he was late for David's party tonight.

His grandson picked up Curtis's briefcase and carried it as far as the door. David gave him another hug and handed it to him. "Love you, Grandpa."

Going down the elevator, Curtis thought about how critical he'd always been of Mitch and his tenderness and devotion to his family. It was ironic that Curtis was only learning now the value of family…and all through one little boy's affection.

By the time the doors opened in the lobby, though, he was thinking about NanoCure and all he had to do today.

Back on track. Back in the business groove. Back in his world.

Thirty-Six

Friday, January 18, 3:50 a.m.
Reno, Nevada

Lexi had reread the same page at least a hundred times.

The words kept dancing before her eyes, but that's as far as they ever got to sinking in. Lexi realized that part of the problem could possibly have to do with falling asleep as she read. Dozing and reading really didn't produce any kind of coherent understanding, she decided.

Her dreams had been vivid enough, however. They were all about Juan. In her mind's eye, she had seen him on a stage during one of his music concerts. Then the dream would jump to seeing him in a wheelchair, incapable of operating the simplest controls to push himself forward.

She'd had more than a dozen patients over the years

who had become comatose because of a stroke or a head injury. The survival rate for those patients had been slightly better than fifty percent. And even at that, the recovery for all of them had been slow and grueling, with only one of the patients regaining the full physical capacities of her pre-injury condition.

Lexi knew that she and Juan would have a long road ahead of them. But she was prepared for it. With her son not going to prison or to some kind of government institution, she knew they would do whatever they had to do to make him better. Maybe not perfect. But as close as they could make it.

Lexi realized that she'd had a life before this, and now she had another life to live. She missed her son.

Turning the open book over on her lap, she looked at Bryan. He was sitting in the chair.

"How long do you think it'll take before they have an answer for us?" she asked quietly.

The key card had been picked up some time ago by one of the agents staying at the motel. Bryan and Lexi decided to stay where they were, in case whatever they'd found didn't amount to anything. There was still the possibility that there was a person out there trying to contact her.

"I assume we'll know something by morning," Bryan told her.

She noticed that he was on the phone.

"I'm sorry," she whispered, making a motion of zipping her lips. He'd been on his cell phone a lot during the past couple of hours. She couldn't even imagine what investigations were like prior to having this technology.

"That sounds very encouraging," Bryan said. "Now, I want you to repeat all of that one more time."

Lexi found him watching her.

"Yes, she's right here," Bryan said a moment later, getting up and coming toward her, holding out the cell phone.

She cleared her voice, having no clue who was on the phone. A second later, she was thrilled to realize Dr. Dexter was the one who'd been giving "encouraging" information to Bryan. She'd tried to reach him twice overnight, but each time had only been able to get as far as his voice mail. This was the real person.

Lexi sat up straight in bed.

"What I was telling Agent Atwood a minute ago was that Juan has started displaying a generalized response," Dexter said cheerfully. "He's a bit inconsistent, but that's expected this early in his recovery."

"How are his reflexes?" she asked, pushing the cover back and hanging her legs over the side.

"Reflexes are limited and are mostly the same, regardless of the stimuli we've been using. But once again, that's to be expected," the neurologist explained. "In a couple of hours, we'll start testing his localized response."

Lexi knew with the localized test, patients' responses were also generally inconsistent and were directly related to the type of stimulus used. Once the patient became somewhat conscious, the doctor might, for instance, create a specific sound and look for a response such as turning the head toward the sound. As they progressed, they might also present an object and look for the patient's ability to focus on it. Following simple commands, even in an inconsistent and delayed manner, was part of this stage, as well. They were obviously testing and moving up the ladder on the Rancho Los Amigos Scale.

Lexi asked the physician some specific questions about Juan's physical condition. The answers were all definitely encouraging. The episode back at the hospital in New Haven didn't appear to have caused any serious damage. By the time Lexi ended the call, she was feeling incredibly upbeat.

She stood up and handed the phone back to Bryan.

Standing by the window, he looked tired. The circles under his eyes showed his lack of sleep. He'd changed into a navy-blue T-shirt after their search of the motel room.

"Did you call him or did he call you?" she asked.

"There were so many calls. I really don't remember," he said, pocketing the phone.

"Agent Atwood, I'd like an answer," she said, not letting him drop the subject.

"Does it really matter?" he asked, starting to move past her.

"It does to me," she said softly, taking hold of his arm to keep him from walking away.

"Okay, I called him."

"I knew it." She smiled and slipped her arms around his waist, pressing her face against his chest. His arms closed around her.

"Does this mean that you'll forgive me about the other thing?"

"What other thing?" She looked up into his face.

"Dexter had Juan moved to another location."

"Was there another threat against him?" Lexi felt herself growing immediately tense. Even though she released him, Bryan held on to her, not letting go.

"Security there wasn't perfect, but no problem ever really materialized. No one got as far as Juan's floor. This move was completely covert. No one, outside of the personnel required to make the move, was told about it. His current location is also being kept under wraps. No one is to know where he is except for the lead investigators."

"So that excludes me?" she asked warily.

"Of course not," he said, smiling gently. "You're absolutely our top investigator."

Thirty-Seven

Friday, January 18, 6:55 a.m.
Carlsbad, California

Hank was in the second of three gray sedans that drove in through the gates of the Southern California Military Institute. After stopping at the security kiosk, the line of automobiles continued toward the large white administration building.

The sun was just rising above the distant hills behind them, and Hank glanced past the long shadows at the orderly clusters of dormitories and classroom buildings on the right side of the drive. Students in uniforms consisting of navy-blue shirts and royal-blue caps and pants could be seen moving alone and in groups between the buildings. A crew of maintenance men was already working around an air-conditioning unit.

Between the rows of whitewashed stucco buildings,

the Secret Service agent caught glimpses of an athletic field. Squads of teenage boys were drilling there, marching in close order. Beyond that, he could see the Pacific Ocean.

"Not a bad place to go to school," the red-haired agent beside him said.

"I went to a prep school back east," Hank replied. "It was pretty, but not like this. We definitely weren't so active this early in the morning. Different approach to discipline here, I think."

"Interesting you should say that. I have a cousin who sent his kid here. The discipline made a real difference for him. He wasn't making it in the public high school."

"Did he go on to any of the academies?" Hank asked.

"No, as a matter of fact, he went to UCLA," the agent replied as the cars pulled up to the front door. "The kid is in his second year of law school now."

Hank looked out the window at the manicured lawn and gardens. Perfectly shaped azaleas were beginning to bloom, the first of the open flowers brilliantly scarlet in the early morning sun.

A local police car was already there, and the federal agents poured out of their vehicles. As Hank got out, a tall man in uniform stalked out the front door with a Carlsbad cop on his heels. A rather worried-looking man, also in uniform, came out with them.

"Gentlemen, I'm glad you're here," the tall man said, approaching them. "I'm Commander Cobb. I'm the head of the institute."

Hank stepped up and quickly introduced himself. Something was wrong. He could see it in the man's face.

"Cadet Tucker appears to be missing," the commander said without any prompting.

"What do you mean, missing?" Hank asked. "Where could he be?"

"We don't know that, sir. Tucker wasn't feeling well this morning during muster. He went to the infirmary immediately afterward. From there, he was escorted to his dormitory. That was approximately forty-five minutes ago." He glanced back at the worried subordinate behind him. "There was a miscommunication among my staff regarding his being kept under surveillance. We've just ascertained that he left the dormitory sometime after that."

"He was supposed to be watched, Commander," Hank said.

"We understand that, sir. I take full responsibility for our failure to keep watch over him."

FBI couldn't reveal any specific details about what Donald Tucker's potential for violence might be or let the school know the tie-in to all the other recent school shootings. Hank figured the vagueness of why they had to keep Donald under surveillance was the reason for this mess up.

"Could he have gone home, Commander?" another agent asked.

"It's possible," the head of the school replied. "We're still searching the grounds of the institute, however. He may still be here."

A thought ran through Hank's mind. "I assume you have weapons and live ammunition here on campus," he asked.

"Yes, sir. We have an underground shooting facility."

"Donald Tucker has only been here since early December. Would he have access to weapons and ammunition?"

"No, sir." The commander paused with a frown. "We do have classes there this morning, however." He turned to his subordinate. "Go down there and see if Cadet Tucker is there, or has been seen there this morning."

As the man turned and ran back into the building, Hank glanced thoughtfully at the street beyond the wrought-iron fence. The morning traffic hadn't really gotten started yet. Donald could be far from the school if he'd hitched a ride out of here forty-five minutes ago.

"Commander, we need to make some decisions as to where he might have gone," he said.

"Of course," he responded, adding, "For the record, we take our responsibility for knowing where our students are very seriously."

"I'm sure you do," Hank said. "You said that Donald Tucker complained of not feeling well."

"That's correct. He was having difficulty focusing on instructions at muster, and when asked about it, he complained of incapacitating headaches."

"Do you know if he's had headaches like this before?"

"Not to my knowledge, sir. We can check with his company leader—his dorm-floor monitor—but I can tell you that we don't generally excuse students from classes or activities for minor illnesses such as headaches. We only sent him to the infirmary today because of your call during the night."

"Commander, do you have a 'lock-down' procedure?" Hank asked.

"Yes, we do."

"Then I suggest you lock down the school immediately while we bring in the Carlsbad Police Department to conduct a thorough search for the boy. In case he's left the campus, we also need to see if we can determine what he might be wearing…if he is still in uniform or if he changed into civilian clothes."

"Of course." Taking a small walkie-talkie from a hook on his belt, the commander turned away and spoke into it. "Security, this is Commander Cobb. Code white. I repeat…code white. And I need to see my emergency staff in my office now."

Hank turned to the uniformed police officer. "We need officers here immediately…and a statewide APB broadcast on Donald Tucker."

The policeman nodded and spoke into the communications device clipped to his shoulder.

It was a long shot that the boy would still be here, Hank thought. He could be heading for home…or anywhere else. And God help anyone who got in his way.

Thirty-Eight

"I hope this is a legitimate lead, and we're not going to Fullerton for nothing," Lexi said as they climbed into a small plane that was going to fly them to California.

"No one contacted you at the motel," Bryan said. "This is our best chance."

As he'd hoped, the FBI lab, with the right optical and research tools, had been able to come up with the name of a storage facility in Fullerton, California, from the key card. Bryan had been on the phone with Geary twice this morning already.

"But as I said before," he continued, "you don't have to come with me. We don't need any kind of search warrant. With this key we should be able to get inside the storage facility. You could be on your way back east."

Lexi shook her head. "I feel like we're so close. A couple of hours won't make a difference. I want to be there, just in case. This guy picked me to contact. Maybe there is still a role I'm supposed to play."

Bryan was less nervous today about having Lexi involved and accompanying him than he'd been the day before. Going through an entire night without incident definitely helped.

"Were they able to come up with a name of the person the key card had been assigned to?" she asked.

"No, not yet. The storage space was taken more than ten years ago, apparently, when the facility was new and they offered a number of the spaces for purchase…like a condo. The files were computerized since then and the name for the owner in the electronic file just says 'Purchased.'"

"Well, that's helpful."

"Exactly," he responded. "They're searching the facility's archives for the original registration and sales paperwork now. The manager of the facility says that by the time we get there, they might have the information."

"How did he pay for it?"

"Tough to tell, at this point," Bryan said. "Rental storage places apparently have fewer regulations to worry about than that motel we just left. Osama bin Laden might be renting the storage space next door, for all we know."

The plane's engines were warming up prior to takeoff. Bryan figured with the sunny West Coast weather, this would be a much smoother flight than the two they had yesterday.

"I think I know what he must have put into the storage," Lexi said.

"Really?"

"Yes. I think they're medical files. I think what we're going to find are the data for the experiments they ran on these eleven kids, including Juan. If that's what he has stored there, then it's also logical that he would contact me. I'm an MD. He figures I'll know what to do with the files and the information in them. At least I'll be aware enough to get them into the hands of the right people."

"What I don't understand is why he'd go to Reno to contact you. Why couldn't he have done it from California, where the storage facility is?"

"Maybe he's not from California. Maybe he's from here."

"He used a California State University account number for shipping. My money says he's from California. In fact," Bryan said, pulling out his cell phone, "there's a branch of CSU in Fullerton."

She thought for a moment. "Are they still on their semester break there?"

"Could be," he replied. "We can check that easily enough."

"Maybe he was vacationing here and decided to do something about all these shootings?"

They were thinking aloud, both of them.

"All the children on that list were adopted in

Nevada, Arizona and New Mexico," Bryan said. "Maybe the lab or the clinic or hospital they worked out of was located in Nevada. He came back here to his old stomping grounds for a reason."

"Is anyone looking at the listing of private clinics or hospitals around here?"

Bryan nodded. "Geary has people on it."

"Is there going to be another team of agents meeting us in California?"

"Absolutely. But don't forget, the one-foot rule still applies there, too."

"Yes, Agent Atwood." Lexi sat back in her chair as the plane taxied onto the runway for takeoff. "I can't wait to see what's in that storage facility."

"I think maybe after medicine and forensic science, becoming a detective would have been a good career choice for you."

She smiled brightly at him as he speed-dialed headquarters. "You already know me so well."

Thirty-Nine

Friday, January 18, 10:45 a.m.
Manhattan, New York

Curtis continued to stare at the message his secretary had slid onto his desk less than a minute ago. He was on a conference call with one of the largest investment groups in the Midwest.

Calendar addition—FBI Special Agent in Charge Don Geary is coming in at 11:30 this morning to speak with you.

There was nothing else on the paper. He looked up and caught his secretary's attention just as she was ready to close his office door. He wrote on the same piece of paper *About what?* and held it up.

She shrugged and shook her head, mouthing the words "Official business."

She left the room and Curtis felt like someone had dumped a bucket of cold water on him.

They couldn't have found Mitch's body. He was toast…no, powder. But the files. Had he sent the FBI their old stuff? He took a handkerchief out of his pocket and wiped his forehead and the back of his neck. The FBI wouldn't come here so casually if they had that kind of information, he reasoned. There would be a warrant for his arrest, and they'd be breaking down his door. No, if they had anything as concrete as that, they'd be pouring in here right now and hauling him away.

Just to be safe, Curtis thought, he should call his lawyer.

"Are you still there, Mr. Wells?"

Curtis looked at the phone. He'd totally forgotten about the conference call. One of the people had asked a question a second before his secretary had tiptoed in. Curtis couldn't remember what the question was.

"I'm very sorry, gentlemen," he said. "I had an unavoidable distraction. Where were we?"

One of the callers started explaining what they'd been discussing. Curtis realized it was futile to try to continue this conversation. He couldn't concentrate. He wasn't hearing anything that was being said. His mind was racing with the thought of the FBI visit. And this was no regular rookie that was visiting him. He looked down at the note again. Special Agent in Charge. Shit.

"Excuse me, gentlemen…and ladies. But there is an urgent matter in the office that requires my attention. How about if we continue this conversation at another time that is convenient for you."

"I hope you're not thinking of cutting us out of this, Curtis," one of the principals of the investment group groused. "We've put a lot of preliminary work into a potential deal with you. If you think you can just leave us out in the cold because other firms are interested—"

"No, Everett. That's not the case, at all," Curtis said. "I have no intention of leaving you out of anything. This is entirely separate."

"Well, this isn't the way we do business here at—"

"I have to ask you to trust me on this, gentlemen. I'll transfer you now to my secretary to set up the time."

Curtis didn't wait for a response. He punched the button on the speaker and picked up the receiver, transferring the call to his secretary.

"Take care of this," he said, hanging up on her.

He looked down at his watch.

"Shit. Shit. Shit."

He dialed his attorney's office. The attorney would not be back in the office until Tuesday. If it wasn't an emergency, would he like to leave a voice mail message? Curtis asked to speak with another of the partners.

Fuming, Curtis thought about how much money he paid to this firm, keeping them on retainer. They should fucking *jump* when he needed them.

Two of the other senior partners were out. Curtis ended up getting transferred to an associate in the firm. Probably two years out of fucking law school and not a care in the world. No reason to get worried about a simple FBI visit. Of course, he didn't know anything about what was at stake.

The young lawyer certainly didn't see why there was a need for someone from their office to be present for the interview, since the FBI had made no indication that Mr. Wells was the subject of any criminal investigation. However, if he'd like one of the attorneys to be present...

"Morons!" Curtis shouted into the phone before hanging up.

His private cell phone vibrated in his pocket. He looked at the display. Two missed calls from his man in California. He should be in Fullerton right now, and he was trying to call him again.

He had to remember to get rid of this phone before he met with the FBI, or at least put it somewhere that wouldn't be available to them. Available? He was too wound up to think straight. He didn't know what the hell he was doing. They couldn't confiscate anything from him.

The phone vibrated again and he answered it

"Tell me you have better news," Curtis said shortly.

"We want to know what level you'd like us to go to in getting the files."

"What the hell do you mean? Do you know where the files are?" he snapped, seething with anger.

"We're still not a hundred percent sure," his contact said. "But we've had our people watching the different places since your call last night. The storage facility on Harbor Boulevard has been getting police attention the past couple of hours."

"What do you mean, *police attention?*"

"There's a police car parked at the entrance, watching all the traffic in and out. They're not going in, but they're keeping an eye on things. It looks like they're waiting for someone to arrive."

It had to be done. Curtis couldn't take the risk of sitting idly by and having them drive him into a corner. Maybe by the time Geary arrived at eleven-thirty, they'd have in their possession whatever files Mitch had stolen years ago.

"I want you to go in. Do you hear me?" Curtis told them.

"We don't have a key, and we don't know what unit the stuff is in. The facility is too big to torch in broad daylight, especially with the cops around. If we can get the unit number and wait until tonight—"

"You have to do something. *Now,*" Curtis said angrily.

"That's why I called you. We'll get inside and wait and see if somebody shows up. If it's the police that come in, it'll make things a little more difficult, if you know what I mean. Of course, if we think we can do something, we will. But one way or another, our financial agreement has to be renegotiated."

"Nothing is to leave that facility. Do you understand me? You take it to whatever level you need to in order to get the job done. I'm doubling our financial arrangement."

"Now I hear you."

"If you have to…you know, take someone out to accomplish your job, you *do* it. Am I being clear about this?"

"We'll take care of it, boss."

Forty

Friday, January 18, 8:45 a.m.
Venice Beach, California

Hank scanned the early morning joggers and walkers on the Oceanfront Walk. It was too early for any big crowds, thank God, but once the stores started opening, it would be a nightmare trying to spot the teenager.

Stopping at the window of a T-shirt shop, he watched the reflection of the half dozen skateboarders grinding, power-sliding and doing kick-flips off the multileveled surfaces of the skate park just opposite the row of stores. He didn't like the idea of these potential teenage victims enjoying their hobby while they were so blissfully unaware of the danger they were in. There wasn't much more that he could do about it than he was already doing, though, for there was no certainty that Donald Tucker would even show up here. On top of that, this was Venice Beach. It would probably take an entire squad from LAPD to move these kids out of harm's way.

The Venice Beach skate park was right next to the Oceanfront Walk and the beach, a fact that was causing Hank added anxiety. There were so many ways for Donald Tucker to approach, if he came at all. Yes, the psychologist thought, the boy could do real damage here, especially as the day progressed.

The only good thing was that school was in session. According to the lieutenant in charge of the LAPD substation in Venice Beach, there would probably be fifty or more kids here on a weekend, with thousands more potential victims on the Walk and the beach. Hank wondered why these kids weren't in school.

With the assistance of the head of the military institute, Hank had determined that the boy was indeed armed, having stolen a .45 caliber Smith & Wesson SW99 from the shooting range, along with three nine-round clips. That made twenty-seven potential casualties. Donald had put on civilian clothes before disappearing from the school, and there had been no sign of him since.

Two female tourists meandered along the Walk, looking into the storefronts and obviously enjoying the perfect weather. Hank looked past them at the area between the Walk and the skate park.

By the old pavilion, he could see two LAPD officers in shorts and T-shirts sitting and talking. On the Walk, near the skateboarders, another pair of officers in street clothes were wandering inconspicuously through the area, pretending to be tourists. One federal agent was sitting on a concrete wall right next to the skate park, reading a paper.

One of the skaters took a vicious spill doing a three-sixty off a ramp and came up bleeding profusely. His friends just laughed, and he went right back to it.

Hank crossed the Oceanfront Walk to a locked postcard vendor's cart that sat ready for the daily lunch-time business of strollers, joggers and inline skaters. Looking up and down the Walk, Hank searched the distance for a solitary teenage boy.

This locale hadn't been the favored spot to look for the missing boy for many of the other members of the team. Other agents were covering the school in Carlsbad, his old high school in Santa Monica, the bus and train stations, even LAX and the John Wayne-Orange County airports.

Hank thought this was the most logical place for him to come. He'd learned that Donald and his mother had lived in a luxury apartment in nearby Santa Monica after the divorce. The teenager had spent a lot of time here in Venice Beach before being sent off to boarding school.

All that information had come from the fiancée of the father, who was now living in Seattle. The federal agents had yet to reach either the father or the mother.

Hank's reasoning in staking out this area had been simple. Every one of the other shooters had returned to the place where they'd been comfortable and achieved success. The others had directed their violence almost entirely at people they cared about in the schools they attended. Donald Tucker had never had that success in school. His achievements, according to the father's fiancée, had come here at the Venice Beach skate park.

Hank looked at his watch—8:58 a.m. He looked up and down and at the beach. He'd flown up here by helicopter from Carlsbad, but the kid could easily have made it here by now, he thought. As he looked around at the stakeout, he really didn't feel he was getting the full support of the local law enforcement.

If the stakeout stretched into the midday hours, there would be a lot more foot traffic on the Oceanfront Walk. With the projected seventy-degree weather and the sun shining, more people than Hank wanted to think about would be turning out to enjoy the beachfront bars and restaurants and lie in the sand for the afternoon.

Just then, three boys and two girls, all carrying book bags, appeared on the Walk to the south of the skate park. They had to be on their way to a neighborhood elementary school, but they didn't seem to be in any hurry to get there. They were coming toward him at a snail's pace, laughing and pushing one another. Hank watched the two uniformed police officers on bicycles ride to them. Smiling and obviously trying not to frighten the kids, the two cops urged them along.

As he watched them, Hank's gaze refocused on a figure coming through a crowd beyond the group of schoolchildren. As he was dressed in baggy jeans, a Tony Hawk T-shirt and a blue jacket, there was nothing to call attention to himself except for his awkward, stiff-legged manner of walking. To anyone looking closely at him, the teenager might have appeared to be stoned. As he stalked along the Ocean-front Walk, he simply stared straight ahead, occasionally pressing one fist to his temple. He kept his left hand in his jacket pocket.

Donald Tucker was left-handed.

The group of children was between the teenager and the skate park. Hank turned slightly and spoke into his communication microphone. The two cops on bikes didn't react; they didn't appear to be on the same frequency. But the agent saw the others begin to move in to cut off the boy from the skate park.

No one stood between the teenager and the school-children, though. Hank started down the Walk as quickly as he could without drawing the boy's attention. When he was about ten feet from the children Hank saw the teenager bump into a passing jogger. The boy staggered slightly, righted himself and looked over at the skate park. He was talking to himself as he walked. The teen was only about fifteen feet from the group of kids when he stopped, turned his head and looked at the officers. Walking their bikes, they were both talking to the kids and trying to keep them moving. They hadn't seen Donald yet.

The teenager's gaze moved slowly from the cops to the skaters and back to the group of children. Hank sensed that the boy had seen the adults moving toward him from the skate park. The agent was only fifteen feet from Donald when he saw his left hand start to come out of the pocket. Focusing on that hand, Hank broke into a sprint, yelling at the cops as he passed them.

The pistol went off just as Hank grabbed the boy's wrist, the bullet missing him and burying itself in the ground next to the walk. Hank's momentum drove them both to the ground, and the two bicycle cops were on them in an instant. The agent hung on to the gun and the hand as another shot fired. Donald was scratching Hank's face even as he tried to pull his hand free.

It took only a second for one of the bicycle cops to wrench the gun from the boy's hand. Then the rest of the team was swarming around them, pinning the teenager's arms and legs to the ground.

Just like that, it was over. Donald simply lay there, looking up at Hank through dilated pupils. The agent still had all of his weight on the teen's chest, and the sound of the boy's breathing could be heard above the screaming of the schoolchildren standing not ten feet away.

Donald's mouth moved, but no words came out. Hank started to ease himself off the boy.

"Be careful with him," he said to the others. "The boy is not a criminal. He has a medical cond—"

Before he could even get the words out, he saw the teenager's body go limp as his eyes rolled back into his head.

Forty-One

Two FBI agents had been waiting for Lexi and Bryan at the Fullerton Municipal airport. After meeting so many of them over the past couple of days, Lexi no longer felt like an outsider. They all greeted her as if she were on their team. No conversations appeared to be censored. There were no secret handshakes. She credited all of that to the way Bryan treated her in front of them. As a senior Secret Service agent working on the case, he had a lot of clout. And she thought he was using it to get her accepted.

As soon as they got into the car, one of the agents gave Bryan a summary of what they'd found on the storage space in Fullerton.

"This key opens a five-by-ten space that was purchased back in May 1994 by Mitch Harvey. Here's his address in Fullerton." He handed Bryan a piece of paper with the pertinent information on it.

Lexi saw the signs for Interstate 5 and Highway 91. The morning traffic was still heavy.

"What have you been able to find out about Mitch Harvey?" Bryan asked.

"Age sixty-two, resides at the address I gave you with Elsa, his wife. He's a professor of neurophysiology here at Cal State Fullerton. He also teaches courses in…" He looked at his notes. "In nanosystems and molecular machinery."

Lexi and Bryan looked at each other.

"We have our man," she said aloud.

"He has a very impressive résumé," the same agent continued. "This is what we were able to get off CSU personnel files." He handed Bryan a folder. He started thumbing through it.

"Where is Dr. Harvey now?" Bryan asked.

"He appears to be missing. Last seen two days ago," the agent answered. "There have been two phone calls from his wife to the Fullerton Police Department. She's pretty worried, I understand, but no missing persons classification has been made to date."

Bryan was still looking through the files.

"There's some digging that we still need to do here in Dr. Harvey's files. There's an employment gap for the years between 1990 and 1994. All that is listed here for those years is a research article, 'Ascent of the Mind: The Evolution of Intelligence.'

No university or research facility affiliation is listed for those years."

"That article, the time period…everything matches," Lexi whispered to no one but herself. This was amazing. They had the name of the person who had started the experiment. At least, one of the people, she corrected.

Lexi had mixed feelings about how she felt about Mitch Harvey. She wanted to hate him. He'd been one of the people responsible for all the teenage deaths and for what Juan had done. But at the same time, he'd been trying to reach her. Why had he been trying to do that?

Lexi didn't think she'd know how to feel about Dr. Harvey until she met him.

"I also need reports on his cell phone activity for this past month, credit card use, ATM withdrawal locations…"

Bryan's list of things he'd needed right away continued while Lexi's excitement grew over what they could find in the files. From her own experience, she knew it was so much easier to treat someone when you knew the cause and extent of the injuries.

She hoped her experience proved right.

Forty-Two

Friday, January 18, 11:55 a.m.
Manhattan, New York

For the past twenty-five minutes, Curtis had been unable to do anything but watch the clock.

Special Agent Geary had contacted Curtis's secretary at eleven thirty-five and told her that he was running late but he was on his way. He'd said the Midtown traffic was horrendous today, but Curtis wondered if he was doing this purposely to play mind games with him. Try to build up his anxiety. Frighten him.

Well, it wasn't going to work. With each passing minute, Curtis felt better about the appointment, because he was going to cut it short. He had a viable reason for excusing himself. He had a luncheon appointment with his grandson, and no government agent was going to mess that up.

He glanced one more time at the clock. It was late enough now that he actually no longer cared when Geary arrived. The federal agent had missed his window of opportunity.

His daughter Liz was going to call him from the lobby when they got into the building. As the seconds hand on the clock advanced, Curtis decided maybe it was best just to go downstairs to meet them. It would be even better for his secretary to make excuses about why Curtis was no longer available.

He took his winter coat out of the closet and held it over his arm. The present he'd had his secretary pick up for David the day before was all arranged in a gift bag and sitting on the coffee table. They'd have a substantial gift for the five-year-old at home tonight, but Curtis thought David would get a kick out of receiving a little care package from his grandfather for the airplane ride back home.

Liz hadn't called yet. The time was twelve noon. He'd definitely wait downstairs. Curtis pulled on his overcoat, grabbed his gloves and the gift bag. Coming out of his office, he saw two men dressed in cheap suits and trench coats. He felt something slither around inside of him. These had to be the federal agents speaking to his secretary.

Curtis wished he could go around them and totally avoid the meeting, but there was no way to do it. One of the two men looked his way.

Curtis fought the fear freezing his limbs and put on his CEO smile as he approached them. His secretary gave him a helpless look. The agent who'd spotted him came over and met him halfway.

"Mr. Wells, my sincere apologies for being so late. But after all that snow yesterday, I think everyone must have cabin fever. I don't recall seeing this many people on the streets at this time of the year."

He was smooth, well spoken, definitely a politician, but behind the "I'm your best friend look," Curtis sensed the man was smart and dangerous.

"You must be Special Agent in Charge Geary."

"Yes, sir," he said.

They shook hands and Geary introduced the other agent.

"Special agent in charge sounds important."

"Just another level of the bureaucracy, Mr. Wells. But if we could step into your office, we won't take much of—"

"I don't know if my secretary mentioned it or not, but I have a very important luncheon appointment today. With my grandson. He turned five today," Curtis explained, not giving them a chance to corner him.

"Yes. Yes, she did mention it. What we have to ask, however, really will only take a few minutes," Geary said.

Curtis glanced at his secretary. She was on the phone but motioned to him to wait. He didn't bother to acknowledge what the agent had said until the young woman hung up the phone.

"Your daughter and the kids are downstairs," she told him.

"Wow! The timing," Curtis said, shaking his head

at the federal agents. "As I said before, this is a very special luncheon for my grandson. So unless your questions can be answered on our way down in the elevator, you might want to make another appointment."

The two agents looked at each other briefly. Geary was the one who spoke. "Sure, I don't see why not. And if need be, we can always come back this afternoon."

Curtis had already decided that he was taking the afternoon off, but it would be his secretary's job to tell them that.

He led the way to the elevator, hoping that it would be crowded. He wanted to know why these agents were here, but if they were going to accuse him of anything, they wouldn't do it on a crowded elevator.

They had to wait for an elevator to arrive.

Geary didn't wait; he got right to the point. "You received an overnight document from Reno, Nevada, yesterday, Mr. Wells. We were wondering if you could share with us any information you have regarding the contents of the package or any information about the sender."

Curtis knew exactly what they were talking about, but he gave them a perplexed look. Curiously, he found himself consciously realizing that rather than getting nervous because of the FBI knowing about that package, he was becoming much more relaxed. They had nothing. They knew *nothing*.

The elevator arrived. The door opened. Three other people were already inside. He nodded to them before stepping on ahead of the two federal agents.

Not only that, Curtis reminded himself, these men were in his territory. They were on *his* turf.

"My company receives hundreds of packages a day—from scientists, would-be inventors, students looking for internships and faculty members of research universities. All of them are people who're looking for jobs or something from me. As I'm the president of NanoCure, most of the packages are addressed to me. And as a result, none of them, with the exception of those of a personal nature, reach my desk. I have a competent staff that takes care of those things. So I really can't help you unless you can be a little more specific," he told Geary.

"We suspect the package was mailed to you by Dr. Mitch Harvey," Geary said bluntly. "Contacting his wife just moments ago, we were told you are a very close friend. Wouldn't you say a package from him would have been considered personal enough to be sent through to you, and that you would have seen it yourself?"

Curtis stared at them for a moment.

"Let me tell you what I've been doing the past few days," he began as the elevator doors closed.

Forty-Three

Bryan checked his watch and went over in his head all that was about to happen.

The storage facility was near enough to the municipal airport that the end of the rush hour traffic didn't slow them down too much. During the twenty-minute drive, there'd been a message sent to them about an incident on Venice Beach. While the details were still sketchy, the last thing Bryan had heard was that Hank was on the scene with Donald Tucker, who had slipped away from the school in Carlsbad.

That still left two of the teenagers missing.

If there were indeed files in the storage facility they were about to open, they would provide a key element in the investigation. Connecting the CSU professor,

Mitch Harvey, to the case was certainly a major break-through, no matter what they found. The troubling part for Bryan remained Billy Ebbett and Roy Naves, the ticking time bombs still at large.

Based on the latest reports this morning, Roy and his family were not even on the radar. Their last official residence, dating eight years ago, had been an isolated farmhouse that was now abandoned. The local police in Lancaster County, Pennsylvania, were searching the vicinity and interviewing the Amish neighbors for possible clues, but they were not holding out much hope. Bryan was amazed that in this country, in this day and age, a family could simply go missing for so many years and no one would notice or report it to the authorities.

A lot more information existed regarding Billy Ebbett. He had the same characteristics as all the other teenagers whose files Bryan had read. Excellent student, bright, very involved in a multitude of activities. Just an all-around great kid. He thought of Juan. Billy Ebbett sounded like a carbon copy.

The problem with Billy was that he and his father and the father's girlfriend were not in Germany where they should be. Last report was that they had gone off on an extended vacation. No set itinerary. So far, following them had apparently been like playing tag. They'd gone to Italy, then Spain, then Portugal. But it was unclear where they were now. Bryan just wondered if they'd find him before he flipped. It appeared that all of these kids were reaching their expiration date about the same time.

As the car traveled down the six-lane divided highway, Bryan spotted the large blue-and-yellow sign for the self-storage facility in the distance. He turned to Lexi. "I'd like you to stay in the car until we check the place out."

"I seem to remember some threat about a one-foot rule," she replied quietly.

He could tell she was in a much better mood since talking to Dexter about Juan this morning. "I might have to ask for an exception in this particular situation."

She nodded and looked out the front window.

"How much have the people running the storage facility been told about what's going on?" Bryan asked one of the agents sitting in front.

"We've informed them that we're planning on going through a specific storage unit," the agent in the passenger seat said. "Apparently, they know about the police surveillance, since a black-and-white has been sitting in front of the place since before dawn."

"When we told them we were coming in," the agent behind the wheel added, "we told them that a bureau mobile crime lab is on its way, too. Still, since it's a 24/7 facility, the manager wants to keep the place open until we tell her otherwise."

Bryan thought about that. There couldn't be too much traffic in and out of the place on a Friday morning. Still, he planned to have the manager close the gates while they were on the premises.

As they drove up to the entrance of the facility, they pulled parallel to a patrol car parked by the white brick walls flanking the sliding gate. Two officers inside greeted them.

"We've counted a total of seven vehicles and a small U-Haul truck that have come and gone since we arrived," one of the officers told them. "There are no visitors in the facility now."

Bryan decided to keep the police officers there at the gate, and he asked them to direct the traffic away until the gates were closed by the facility's manager. When the FBI agent pulled past the squad car, Bryan noted that the black-and-white pulled up and blocked the entrance to the lot.

They stopped outside the whitewashed cinder-block office. "Why don't you two stay here and let us go in and talk to the manager?" Bryan suggested to Lexi and the agent who was driving.

Bryan looked around as he and the other agent got out of the car. A set of high gates separated the outer lot from the inner acreage, which was filled with seemingly endless rows of corrugated steel storage buildings. Next to the gate, he could see the keypad and a video camera. Even from here, Bryan could tell that the place offered a variety of sizes of storage spaces. The garage-type doors of the white steel building were a different color on each row. It looked like a place where a person could easily get lost.

He didn't know how much time the mobile crime lab would need to be here, but if it looked like it was going to be significant, then Bryan supposed they could get away with blocking off the ends of a specific row for a few hours, depending on where Mitch Harvey's storage space was located.

"Do you know what time the FBI mobile lab is supposed to get here?" he asked the other agent.

"I would guess it should be here in another ten minutes or so. They were scheduled to arrive by nine-thirty."

The two men walked to the door of the office. There was a sign taped to the window advertising for shift managers. Inside, a middle-aged woman greeted them, wearing a blue-and-yellow shirt, the same color as the company sign outside.

"Rather than blocking the street entrance the way he's doing now," she told Bryan after hearing his concern for security, "I'd much rather have you block the gate to the storage yard for a short period of time. At least you're not stopping potential customers from coming in to the office."

Bryan figured he could live with that. The manager was being very cooperative in allowing them to go through a specific unit without showing a search warrant, even if they did have a key. Bryan knew they could produce a warrant if it was required, but a delay would not be a good thing, considering the two teenagers still on the street.

The woman handed Bryan a map of the storage yard. She'd circled the storage unit that they were looking for. Outside, Bryan motioned for the FBI agent behind the wheel to pull up to the sliding gate while the other agent went to tell the police officers to move their car to the gate after they'd entered.

Lexi rolled down her window as the car went past him. "Any problems?" she asked.

"So far everything is going like clockwork," he told her, smiling. "Don't forget, you stay in the car."

She gave him a salute.

He slid the key card through the slot. A light flashed green and the tall metal door started sliding to one side. Bryan saw the other agent walking back. The police car moved into the lot, and he motioned them to back in to the area in front of the gate. The car carrying Lexi pulled through and waited for Bryan and the other agent.

"No one else comes in, with the exception of the FBI mobile lab," Bryan instructed the local officers before walking into the storage yard.

Bryan and the other agent climbed into Lexi's car. In a moment, they were rolling slowly between the long rows of units. He handed the map to the agent in front.

Some people had gone to real trouble to stop Mitch Harvey from communicating with Lexi. There had been capable personnel on the East Coast and the West Coast, and operations on the same night in New Haven, Wickfield, Buffalo and probably Reno. Whoever was behind this obviously had a solid network of thugs at their disposal.

That was what was bothering him right now. They were just cruising into this facility. This was too simple.

Bryan loosened the front of his windbreaker and checked the weapon in the holster at his side. His gaze took in the rows of doors, the keypad locks on each one, the rooftop. Each building appeared to have about fifteen units on each side. A crossing lane separated it from the next building, and the series of units started again.

"How far away is our backup, if we need it?" he asked the FBI agent in the front seat.

The young man's eyes swept the road ahead of them. "Do you think we need it?"

"It doesn't hurt," Bryan said. "I think it would be especially good to have a chopper overhead. I don't want any surprises."

The agent was immediately on the phone, passing on directions. Bryan looked over at Lexi and patted her on the knee with a reassuring smile.

Mitch Harvey's storage unit was in the last row, facing a chain-link fence. Beyond it, Bryan could see open fields of brush, dotted with mounds of rubble that had been dumped behind the facility. This unit must have offered just the privacy Dr. Harvey was looking for, but right now Bryan was feeling a little bit exposed. The car came to a stop by the blue door of the storage unit, and he got out.

"How long will it take them to get here?" he asked the other agent as they walked around to the other side of the car.

"Fifteen minutes, tops."

He touched the key card in his pocket and decided it might be worth waiting until extra help arrived. Lexi still had her window open, and she poked her head out.

"Do you think there might be someone hiding in here somewhere?" she asked.

Bryan turned to her. "Not very likely, but to play it safe—"

"Seven vehicles and a small U-Haul truck," she continued, repeating what they'd heard earlier. "Doesn't that sound like a lot of traffic for a weekday morning?"

"I don't know."

She looked at him, her eyes rounding. "They could have hidden a small army in one of these units, and the police cruiser in front would have never known."

Bryan nodded. He should have asked if there were any new unit rentals this morning.

But it was too late. Twenty yards away, something metallic flashed at the end of the row.

"Get down," he shouted, but he was not quick enough. The FBI agent standing by the hood of the car went down like a rock when the first bullet hit him in the back.

Forty-Four

"We know you're a busy man, Mr. Wells."

His heart was pounding in his chest like a bass drum. Curtis knew the longer he avoided answering the FBI agent's question, the more they might think him guilty. He tried to remember the bullshit he'd been feeding Elsa. Perhaps the same thing would work on them.

"You know, that was a trick question, Agent Geary. You knew who the package was from and yet you asked me the identity of the sender. Why is that?" Curtis felt good about that one. Answer their question with a question of his own. Keep them off balance.

"I said that we *suspect* the package was from Dr. Harvey," Geary reminded him. "Now, did you receive something from him yesterday?"

Curtis looked at the electronic panel next to the elevator door. They were stopping at every goddamn floor. There were seven more floors to go.

"Yes, as a matter of fact, I did," Curtis said. "Mitch and I were in touch almost daily, one way or another. We regularly sent each other articles or clippings of interest. Talked on the phone regularly, too. He was very interested in the company and what we were doing."

"Why didn't you tell us that right away?" Geary asked.

"Mentioning Reno threw me off. If you asked me if I received a package from Dr. Harvey, I would have been able to answer it right away. I don't check the return addresses on every piece of mail or every overnight packet I get, you know."

He realized he was sounding rattled, but he didn't care. If he just kept talking, they couldn't ask him more questions.

On the fifth floor, more people stepped in. The elevator was starting to get crowded. Curtis was sandwiched between the two agents in the corner farthest from the door. No one else was talking, but Curtis didn't care that they were all eavesdropping on this conversation.

"Now, you tell me something. What the hell makes you think he was in Reno?" Curtis asked. "I've spoken several times to his wife, Elsa, this past week, and I was under the distinct impression that Mitch was in New York."

They reached the first floor, and the doors slid open.

Curtis wanted to push everyone out of the way and make a run for it. But he maintained his composure.

"You mentioned news clippings. Is that what he sent you?"

Curtis stared at him.

"Mr. Wells, do you still have the clipping that he sent you?" Geary asked again. "Or the envelope. We're especially interested in the envelope."

"No, I don't think I have either. I don't even remember what it was he sent me."

Curtis tried to remember what the hell he'd done with the envelope. These people would search the trash if he told them he threw it out. They might find it if they looked.

It didn't matter. Curtis was certain he'd destroyed the contents. No, he kept the list. All of a sudden, he really couldn't remember. His mind stopped working.

Everyone had stepped out ahead of them. They were the last three in the elevator, and people waiting were starting to pile in. He pushed out through the crowd into the lobby and then felt Geary's hand on his arm.

Curtis turned and looked at the agents. "I might still have it. I don't really know," he said hurriedly. "So much has been going on with my company, NanoCure, this past month. This week has been especially hectic. We'll have to continue this discussion at another time, gentlemen. I told you before that I have a lunch date that I cannot miss."

He wasn't lying. They would see his family in a minute. They'd see David. That little boy brought out the best in everyone. With his obvious disabilities, he would be an ace to play in this situation. After all, only a compassionate grandfather could receive such love from this little boy.

He turned and looked out into the lobby. The place was bustling with the usual lunch-hour traffic. He walked toward the security stop point. The two agents were right on his heels.

"I'll look forward to speaking with you again," he said over his shoulder to the federal agents. "Call my secretary and make an appointment. I'll help you in whatever way I can. I'll have her look for that envelope, too."

Curtis turned around, stuck his hand out and shook each man's hand.

"Have a pleasant day, gentlemen."

He didn't give them a chance to respond, but noted the exchange of looks between them.

"My family is waiting here somewhere," he said curtly, turning away.

Curtis walked away from the agents and searched the faces of people beyond the security checkpoint and near the door. He couldn't spot his daughter, though a tall boy drew his attention for a moment. He was young, perhaps fourteen or fifteen, with a thin face and long blond curly hair. He was looking at Curtis, and at nothing else. Caught in the boy's stare, Curtis slowed his steps. He tried to look away, but the boy's gaze never wavered. He was wearing an oversize down jacket. The front was hanging open.

He looked again into the teenager's face. The boy

was pale, the eyes not quite right, but Curtis felt the intensity of the stare all the way to his gut.

"Mr. Wells," the security guard called to him.

Curtis stopped and turned to the uniformed man.

"Your daughter will be right back, sir. Bathroom call for everyone," he relayed with a chuckle.

Curtis nodded and looked back toward the door where he'd seen the teenager standing before. The boy wasn't there. He was gone. The relief washing through him lasted only a few seconds, though, as he spotted the boy striding toward him across the lobby.

Triggered early memory. The thought flashed through his brain as clearly as any he'd ever had. The portion of the experiment they'd never tested. The facts rushed back, lining up in Curtis's mind. He had been a regular visitor at the Nevada clinic where they'd seen some of the surviving subjects. They knew his name, perhaps even developed a fear of him. He never had the patience that Mitch and others displayed. These subjects had cost him a fortune, along with the trust and backing of so many investors.

That was why, he realized in this moment of utter lucidity, it had been so much easier for him when they started to burn out.

Curtis took a step back as he saw the boy's hand come out from under the jacket. He was holding a gun.

"Grandpa!" David screamed with excitement, running across the lobby toward him.

Curtis watched in horror as the teen's hand shifted, pointing the gun at the child.

Forty-Five

Bryan had disappeared from her view, but Lexi could see two men shooting at them from the end of the row.

She shoved open the back door of the car. She didn't know where the shots were coming from, but she knew Bryan was exposed out there.

The windshield shattered into a web of lines as the agent behind the wheel slammed back into his seat with a cry. As she looked into the front seat, she could see him gripping his right shoulder. She reached over and yanked him down onto his side on the seat so that he wouldn't be a target for another shot. She gasped as another shot ripped through the side window next to her, showering her with a thousand small pebbles of glass.

At least the bullet missed her, she thought. Someone was shooting at them from the field, too.

"Take the key," Bryan shouted to her, reaching inside the open window and handing it to her. "Open the unit and get inside."

Lexi heard the sound of a police siren over the popping noise of the shooting. She tumbled out onto the ground and glanced back briefly as the patrol car that had parked by the gate skidded to a stop behind them. Bullets were raining on them, too. The attackers seemed to be all around.

She crawled toward the unit door. Bryan was crouched by the car, firing back at the assailants. Glass exploded all around her. The officers from the squad car were sandwiched between the building and the car. She could see them firing over the hood and the rear of their vehicle.

The lock to the storage unit was next to the front bumper of the car. A series of bullets pierced the metal door only inches above, close to the lock. She pulled her hand back just as another pinged through the door, leaving a hole where her wrist had been a second earlier.

Lexi quickly reached up and slid the key card into the lock. The green light went on and something clicked inside the door. She tried to pull the door up, but it seemed to be stuck.

"Get inside," Bryan urged her, shielding her with his body.

She tried again, yanking the handle upward even harder. The door started inching open.

Bryan moved slightly to shoot over the roof of the car. Lexi turned and saw the agent who had gone down by the front bumper of the car. She reached over and grabbed his hand.

"Lexi," Bryan shouted.

The man's fingers tightened around hers.

"He's alive," she cried out.

She reached behind her and heaved the door higher. There was a metallic click and then the door opened halfway.

"Good enough," she muttered.

There was no way she could check the extent of the agent's wound while he was lying in front of the car. The gunshot had struck him in the back. Whoever was shooting at them from the end of the building had stopped, and she tugged at Bryan's windbreaker.

"We need to get him inside. He could get shot again out where he is."

Bryan reached for the agent and began to drag him out of the line of fire. Lexi remembered the driver of their car. She pulled the front door open. The agent was still on his side where Lexi had pushed him down. The bleeding had soaked the front and back of his shirt. He was on the phone. Calling for help.

"I want to get you out of here," she told him as soon as he took a breath. "Is there any way you can help me and come out this way?" she asked.

He nodded his head. "I'll try."

Behind her, Lexi heard the door of the storage unit open up more. She glanced over her shoulder and saw

Bryan hauling the other agent into the unlit space inside. The agent behind the wheel was dragging himself across the seat. In an instant, Bryan was behind Lexi, helping her move him carefully out of the car and into the unit, too.

Lexi sat down on the concrete floor of the unit, her back against one wall. Across from her, Bryan knelt down and slid a fresh clip of ammunition into his gun. Where they were, the bullet-riddled car offered a little protection. The sound of shooting continued outside, bullets intermittently piercing the steel walls of the building with a series of dull pings. She didn't know how the two officers with them were faring, or what would happen if they lost this gun battle.

"Don't come out, Lexi," Bryan warned before going out again.

The two wounded agents were lying on the concrete floor next to her. She moved over to them to see if there was anything she could do, wishing she had a first-aid kit. The man who'd been shot in the back appeared to have the bullet lodged somewhere in his chest. There was no exit wound. He was in much worse shape than the other, though both of them could possibly die from loss of blood, if not shock.

Somehow, she realized as she worked on the two men, she'd almost foreseen this happening as they were driving through the gates into the storage yard. So many children and adults...so many innocent people were dead because of what was stored here. For the first time, she glanced at the contents of the room. There were boxes, rows of them, from floor to ceiling.

Lexi shuddered. This couldn't simply be the information on only eleven children. The files on what must be a legion of victims surrounded her.

The roaring beat of a helicopter suddenly moved directly overhead. As it passed, she could hear police sirens getting closer.

"Please, God," she murmured. "Let this be over."

Forty-Six

Watching Curtis Wells walk away from him, Geary was certain the businessman was neck deep in something, and he would bet money it was the same shit that his friend Mitch Harvey had been involved with.

Geary's team had only scratched the surface in their investigation, but it was already clear that the two men had been tightly linked in their businesses and their research efforts for well over a decade. Geary had an excellent knack for reading people, and what he'd seen of Curtis Wells screamed that the businessman was hiding information. Any rookie could see that he was also scared shitless.

The FBI special agent in charge didn't plan to make any appointment to speak with Mr. Wells again. Next time, he'd come back with warrants and they'd be arresting the sonovabitch.

"Call Atwood," Geary told his subordinate. "I want to know about any reference to this guy in whatever they find in Fullerton, and I want to know it immediately. Also, I want you to book me a flight west. I think it's time I have a heart-to-heart with Mrs. Harvey."

Geary heard a child cry out, "Grandpa!" He looked over in time to see the little boy running with a hobbled gait toward Wells. Then someone to their right screamed. People were suddenly scattering in every direction, some dropping to the floor, others trying to find protection along the walls and behind the security booth.

He saw the teenager, and the gun pointed at the child.

Geary and the other agent reached for their guns at the same instant.

Curtis Wells stepped forward, scooping up the child just as the teenager's gun fired. The gift package hit the floor, and Wells went down next to it.

Before Geary and his agent could fire, one of the building security guards took down the shooter. The gun was ripped out of the boy's hand just as Geary reached them. The guards held the teenager down as the SAC identified himself. There was no fight left in the tall, fair-haired boy, who simply kept staring at the body of the older man, sprawled a half dozen steps away on the marble floor in a spreading pool of his own blood.

As the little boy in Wells's arms squirmed free, pandemonium broke out in the lobby. Two people Geary assumed were doctors immediately raced to Curtis's side. Geary sent his partner to assist them and call for help while he supervised the security guards as they rolled the teenage boy over and handcuffed him.

The teen's face was incredibly pale, his eyes were becoming glazed over, almost as if he couldn't see. He looked to be under the influence.

"What's your name?" he asked the shooter.

No answer. Not even an indication that he'd heard anyone talking to him.

Geary patted down the kid's pockets. Again, there was no protest, only the blank stare in the direction of the body. The SAC found a wallet in the pants pocket. Inside, a stack of euros. He looked at the school ID inside one of the slots.

He read the name and then read it again out loud. "Billy Ebbett."

He stared grimly at the boy. It was the tenth teenager.

"Sonovabitch," he whispered.

Geary looked over his shoulder at Wells. One of the people who'd been working on him was sitting back on his heels, shaking his head.

They'd given up.

A few feet away, in front of a weeping woman, a little boy stood looking silently on.

Forty-Seven

Friday, January 18, 10:35 a.m.
Fullerton, California

Two were dead and four were in police custody. An SUV carrying an unknown number of armed suspects—the ones who'd been shooting at them from the fields beyond the fence—was leading the local and state police on a high-speed chase right now down Interstate 5. The ambulances arriving on the scene had taken the two wounded FBI agents to the hospital.

Bryan knew they'd been lucky that they'd suffered no fatalities, considering the surprise attack. The mobile FBI lab was already on the scene, going through and removing the contents of the storage unit. Work on the resulting mess from the gunfire would follow.

He'd already been in contact with both Geary and Hank. There'd been a shooting in Manhattan, as well.

They had apprehended Billy Ebbett, but not before there'd been a fatality. Thank God Hank had been more successful in Venice Beach. Both teenagers were being flown to Ithaca this morning. Dr. Dexter would definitely have his hands full with patients.

Bryan found the first opportunity to look for Lexi. Last time he'd asked, she was sitting in one of the police cruisers. This time, they told him she was waiting in the storage facility's office. He went looking for her.

A large handwritten sign that read Temporarily Closed was taped to the door of the office. Not that any customers had a chance of coming within five hundred feet of the facility, with all the police cars and vans and SWAT teams and ambulances crowding the street in front of the place.

He tested the door. It was unlocked. Inside, no one could be seen behind the counter, but Lexi was sitting in a chair against the wall, phone in hand. She had dirt and blood on her face and hands and shirt, but her smile when she saw him shone through it all. Bryan couldn't remember the last time a woman had made him feel this way.

"No more worries. I'm okay, really. Hugs to Donna and the girls," Lexi said, ending the call.

"Brothers," she said, looking up at him. "They worry too much."

"With a sister like you, I can see why," he replied, walking in and taking the seat next to her.

"What do you mean, with a sister like me?" she asked. "What's wrong with me?"

"That's the problem. Nothing. You're perfect," he said, holding her hand and looking into her shining eyes. "Are you okay?"

"You said it yourself...perfect." She smiled again. "I talked to Dr. Dexter. He had more to report on Juan. He's improving. He really is. That's not my imagination. And it's possible whatever we found here will help, too. When could I get back to Ithaca?"

He frowned, feigning disappointment. "Do you mean you're not going to hang around here and finish the job? What kind of criminal investigator do you think you're going to make when you desert your partner at the drop of a hat and—"

"Okay, Mr. Pour-it-all-on," she laughed. "Spit it out."

"What do you mean?"

She motioned with her hand for him to continue. "Tell me why you really want me to stay. Communicate with me. Use your words."

"Don't tell me Hank has been trying to recruit you in his profession, too. Do you want me to lie on that couch over there?"

"Words," she told him, leaning forward until Bryan thought she was going to kiss him, but she pulled back.

Bryan didn't have to think about that too long. "I would like you to stay...because you're beautiful. And because I'm really attracted to you. And I'd like to spend time with you to get to know you better and maybe even give you a chance to see how really scary a person I am. And if I say I like you, I want you to know that would be a gross understatement. How am I doing?"

She smiled. "Not bad."

"Does that mean you'll stay an extra couple of days?"

"No." She leaned toward him again. "But you can come and see me in Ithaca. And all the words you said…back at you."

And she kissed his lips.

Epilogue

"All aspects of cognition—seeing, hearing, understanding, planning, et cetera—are carried out using only empirical precedent and confabulation, which describes the data-processing operation in the brain's cerebral cortex and thalamus."

Dr. Dexter stood by the screen as the slide show progressed, pointing to the graphics as he explained the findings. The title of the presentation was Neural Networks.

"Others have hypothesized," he continued, "that confabulation is the only information-processing operation used in cognition. Some have even tried to use the theory to explain the cognitive mechanism by which behaviors are initiated...."

Bryan and Hank sat toward the back of the small lecture hall. The purpose of this presentation was to provide the agents and personnel involved in the case with a better understanding of what Dexter's group had initially been able to deduce from the files they'd uncovered. From the looks of things, most of the audience was already becoming glassy-eyed.

As for Bryan, he was more interested in the criminal aspects of what had taken place than the technical revelations.

The investigation had exposed the workings of a private company founded by Curtis Wells and Mitch Harvey in the late 1980s. Harvey had been in charge of research. Though Curtis Wells also had a technical background, he had become the business brains behind the operation. As they'd grown, a small team of scientists had joined them in their work. After they'd looked over the financial records, it became obvious that a huge influx of funding from a variety of investors had triggered a dramatic change in the company's breathtakingly advanced work in the then-unnamed field of nanoscience. The money had somehow induced the group to stop testing their research on animals and start using humans...illegally.

"As adults, humans can possess billions of individual items of knowledge," Dexter continued. "To achieve that in twenty to twenty-five years, the rate of acquisition must necessarily exceed one item per second, which of course is totally inconsistent with our current views of intellectual development."

The files they'd found in Fullerton had provided the entire history of the company, both financial and scientific. There'd been a total of fifty-seven children that had been used as test subjects to start with. All of them were acquired through welfare services and foster programs. Basically, they had used babies with no families. The children had been brought in under the guise of free vaccinations and healthcare, which explained why they were never hospitalized. The nanoparticles that essentially organized themselves into a kind of scaffolding in the brain were initially inserted into the skull by means of a serum, leaving no marks or scars behind. The materials used in creating the microscopic substance had been classified as "top secret" by the government, much to the chagrin of Dexter, who was not done fighting that battle.

Any files having to do with the eleven teenagers who were the last survivors of the experiment, however, were missing from Fullerton. At the same time, going through Mitch Harvey's phone records, they found another storage facility in Reno that the scientist had rented in mid-December. Curiously, the storage facility had burned to the ground the same week that Dr. Harvey disappeared. Bryan guessed that during December, Harvey must have moved those specific files from Fullerton to the new storage unit in Nevada. Unlike Curtis Wells, Harvey appeared to have become remorseful over what had taken place and what was now happening across the country. That was why he'd decided to intervene and try to contact Lexi.

"One must keep in mind that maximum *a posteriori* knowledge is not a mechanism of cognition," the scientist at the lectern continued.

Bryan had gone through some of the files himself. During the first year, a large percentage of the children had died of "natural causes," though Harvey had concluded that the deaths were actually due to the nanoparticle injections. The FBI had been able to recover the documentation sent to investors, telling them about the decision to shut down the project. From that list, they knew who the involved parties were. But at the same time, Bryan knew that criminal charges against those investors would be limited, for there was substantial evidence that most of them did not know the testing was being done on live human subjects.

Dexter was discussing some experiment run two decades ago. "For language generation, confabulation is particularly useful. In this particular research project, some eight thousand books of English-language text were fed into a computer-based confabulation structure. When two consecutive sentences within a paragraph seemed topically coherent, they were marked with symbols and linked. After just a few days of 'reading,' the confabulation structure had accumulated billions of individual knowledge links. These items of knowledge, along with confabulation, were then used to carry out the continuation...."

The violent episodes of the past year had apparently been the result of an unexpected wrinkle in the experiment. There was certainly no documentation in the older files that predicted that behavior. Billy Ebbett's encounter with a name that he recalled from his early past, however, was somewhat explicable. A news article had triggered his early memory response.

The boy and his father and the girlfriend had arrived in New York a week prior to the shooting because of a conference the girlfriend had to attend. Billy had been fighting the same kind of headaches as the rest of the teenagers. After the shooting, the police had found an article about Wells in a newspaper in Billy's room at the hotel. The article had included a photograph of the successful entrepreneur. The investigators could only guess how Billy had been able to acquire a gun. Bryan assumed the kid had bought it on some street corner in New York.

"The theory could have profound implications in the areas of medicine, philosophy, social science, education, child development, et cetera. Think of the billions of usable items of knowledge the average human adult possesses. Of course, initially there were no expectations of immediate commercial application. I believe Dr. Harvey's primary goal was simply the advancement of fundamental knowledge, but something went awry...."

Bryan felt the phone vibrate in his pocket. He looked at the display. It was his daughter, Andrea. She'd sent him a text message. *Ready?*

He motioned to Hank that he had to leave. His friend whispered to him that he was ready to go, too.

The two agents quietly slipped out of the lecture hall. Bryan stretched. It felt good to stand up.

"How long do you think he's going to keep going?"

"Probably all weekend," Hank replied.

"Good, because I'll be gone the entire time."

"Did I hear something about skiing?" Hank asked.

"Yeah. Amy and Andrea have it all figured out. They have the van packed with all the equipment."

His phone vibrated again.

"I'm coming," he said, looking down at the message. This one was from Amy. "So what are you doing for the weekend?"

"Cathy and the girls are coming up."

"Hey, you all wouldn't want to go skiing, would you?"

"No," his friend said, waving him off. "That sounds too much like exercise."

"Okay, pal. Suit yourself." Bryan said goodbye to his friend and headed out. He reached the front door just in time to see Lexi, flanked by Amy and Andrea, pushing Juan's wheelchair to the van.

Amy and Andrea were talking a mile a minute. Brian got a two-second welcome before the girls refocused their attention on Juan again.

The teenager had undergone two operations at the end of January. The same treatments were going to be used on Billy Ebbett and Donald Tucker. With only minor invasion into the brain, Dexter's neurosurgeons had removed the remains of the device. The full recovery for Juan would be slow; they all knew that. Still, he was fully cognizant and had regained part of his speech. They still didn't know to what percent he'd be able to become his old self, but the mother and son had a great attitude and every little step was celebrated.

As the girls started helping the fifteen-year-old out of his chair and into the car, Lexi looked up nervously at Bryan. "I know that Dexter cleared this trip, but are you sure this is going to work out? Skiing when he still doesn't have complete use of one of his legs and one of his arms?"

"We'll go slow and try it." Bryan motioned to the special mono-skis strapped to the top of the car. "We have the right equipment and trained instructors." He motioned to his daughters. "The question is, do you trust them?"

She looked that way. The girls were already in the backseat, each sitting on either side of Juan, their voices loud and enthusiastic.

"Yes, I do." She smiled. "And he does, too."

Bryan brushed a kiss across her lips and held the door open for Lexi to get in.

As he closed the door, Bryan spotted a short teenager, dressed in an overcoat, walking slowly toward them on the same side of the street. He felt himself tense for an instant, but then another teenager came running across the street and attacked the first one. A minute later, the two were wrestling in the snow like overgrown puppies.

There hadn't been any new shootings in any schools this past month. That was a good thing, and Bryan hoped they had seen the end of it. But something inside continued to nag at him. He knew he wasn't finished with this case.

Not until a teenager named Roy Naves was found.

Author's Note

Everyone who sends their child or their spouse off to school feels, at one time or another, the fear of what might await their loved one there. An incident of violence, so often involving teenagers, can cause heartbreak. It can destroy families and communities alike.

Generations of psychologists and educators have tried to search out the reasons why violence in a school occurs. Clearly, there are no easy answers.

In our simpler, fictional world, we're happy to pin it on a technological advance gone awry. We're delighted to lay the charge against a few scientists who have lost their way, and against a few greedy businessmen. We write fiction, after all. We only wish real life could be so simple.

For many of our readers who follow our stories, we hope you enjoyed this second glimpse of the town of Wickfield, where our book *Five in a Row* was set. In reality, we live only ten minutes from the town we've modeled Wickfield after, and we love the place. The violence we depict there is truly only a product of our somewhat twisted imagination.

We'd especially like to thank our dear friend, Dr. Carla Patton, for her assistance in suggesting a variety of ways to kill off teenagers. We're very grateful that she's never suspected us of planning to kill our own loved ones. Carla, as always, you are wonderful.

As always, we finish a book with gratitude to our sons for their support and love. They are perfect young gentlemen.

We love hearing from our readers. Write to us at:

Jan Coffey
c/o Nikoo & Jim McGoldrick
P.O. Box 665
Watertown, CT 06795

or

JanCoffey@JanCoffey.com
www.JanCoffey.com

From the Mary Higgins Clark
Award-winning author of *Dark Angel*

KAREN HARPER

EVIL SPREADS LIKE WILDFIRE...

When bush pilot Lauren Taylor flies a stranger into her isolated hometown of Vermillion, Montana, her actions may be the spark that starts an inferno. Because the mysterious passenger bears an undeniable resemblance to a serial arsonist wanted by the FBI—and he's disappeared into the tinder-dry woods....

FBI agent Brad Hale doesn't have time to fly into picturesque towns based on one woman's vague suspicions, but when Lauren's young son goes missing, he realizes the little boy may hold the key to his investigation. Hot on the stranger's trail, Lauren and Brad will do anything to stop a man bent on destruction...even if that means rushing headlong into the flames.

INFERNO

"Harper has a fantastic flair for creating
and sustaining suspense."
—*Publishers Weekly*

*Available the first week of January 2007
wherever paperbacks are sold.*

MIRA®

www.MIRABooks.com

MKH2404

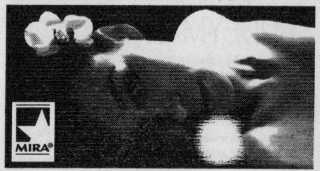

REQUEST YOUR
FREE BOOKS!

2 FREE NOVELS
FROM THE ROMANCE/SUSPENSE
COLLECTION PLUS 2 FREE GIFTS!

YES! Please send me 2 FREE novels from the Romance/Suspense Collection and my 2 FREE gifts. After receiving them, if I don't wish to receive any more books, I can return the shipping statement marked "cancel." If I don't cancel, I will receive 4 brand-new novels every month and be billed just $5.49 per book in the U.S., or $5.99 per book in Canada, plus 25¢ shipping and handling per book plus applicable taxes, if any*. That's a savings of at least 20% off the cover price! I understand that accepting the 2 free books and gifts places me under no obligation to buy anything. I can always return a shipment and cancel at any time. Even if I never buy another book from the Reader Service, the two free books and gifts are mine to keep forever.

185 MDN EF5Y   385 MDN EF6C

Name	(PLEASE PRINT)	
Address		Apt. #
City	State/Prov.	Zip/Postal Code

Signature (if under 18, a parent or guardian must sign)

Mail to The Reader Service:
IN U.S.A.: P.O. Box 1867, Buffalo, NY 14240-1867
IN CANADA: P.O. Box 609, Fort Erie, Ontario L2A 5X3

Not valid to current subscribers to the Romance Collection,
the Suspense Collection or the Romance/Suspense Collection.

Want to try two free books from another line?
Call 1-800-873-8635 or visit www.morefreebooks.com.

* Terms and prices subject to change without notice. NY residents add applicable sales tax. Canadian residents will be charged applicable provincial taxes and GST. This offer is limited to one order per household. All orders subject to approval. Credit or debit balances in a customer's account(s) may be offset by any other outstanding balance owed by or to the customer. Please allow 4 to 6 weeks for delivery.

Your Privacy: Harlequin is committed to protecting your privacy. Our Privacy Policy is available online at www.eHarlequin.com or upon request from the Reader Service. From time to time we make our lists of customers available to reputable firms who may have a product or service of interest to you. If you would prefer we not share your name and address, please check here. ☐

BOB07

Jan Coffey

32319 SILENT WATERS	___ $6.99 U.S.	___ $8.50 CAN.
32057 FOURTH VICTIM	___ $6.50 U.S.	___ $7.99 CAN.
32192 FIVE IN A ROW	___ $6.99 U.S.	___ $8.50 CAN.
66859 TRUST ME ONCE	___ $5.99 U.S.	___ $6.99 CAN.
66919 TWICE BURNED	___ $6.50 U.S.	___ $7.99 CAN.

(limited quantities available)

TOTAL AMOUNT	$ _____
POSTAGE & HANDLING	$ _____
($1.00 FOR 1 BOOK, 50¢ for each additional)	
APPLICABLE TAXES*	$ _____
TOTAL PAYABLE	$ _____

(check or money order—please do not send cash)

To order, complete this form and send it, along with a check or money order for the total above, payable to MIRA Books, to: **In the U.S.:** 3010 Walden Avenue, P.O. Box 9077, Buffalo, NY 14269-9077; **In Canada:** P.O. Box 636, Fort Erie, Ontario, L2A 5X3.

Name: _____
Address: _____ City: _____
State/Prov.: _____ Zip/Postal Code: _____
Account Number (if applicable): _____

075 CSAS

*New York residents remit applicable sales taxes.
*Canadian residents remit applicable GST and provincial taxes.

MIRA®

www.MIRABooks.com

MJC0107BL